THE GIRL
WHO HELPED
NED KELLY

By

CHARLES TAYLOR

Introduced by Gabriel Bergmoser

Illustrated by Raymond Wenban

ETT IMPRINT

Exile Bay

Published by ETT Imprint, Exile Bay in 2019

First published by United Press Pty Ltd in 1929
A version of the introduction first appeared on the website
www.aguidetoaustralianbrushranging; our thanks to editor Aidan Phelan

Originally published in serial form in *Table Talk* (Melbourne), *The
Advocate* (Burnie), *Register-News Pictorial* (Adelaide), *The Western
Mail* (Perth), *The Advocate* (Burnie) in 1929, *The Queenslander*
(Brisbane) in 1938.

ISBN 978-1-925706-92-5 (paper)
ISBN 978-1-925706-93-2 (ebook)

Cover art by Raymond Wenban
Designed by Hanna Gotlieb

INTRODUCTION

It's impossible to write this introduction without giving a bit of personal context, so please bear with me.

I went to primary school in Mansfield, about a hundred metres from where Sergeant Kennedy, Constable Scanlon and Constable Lonigan were buried after being shot by Ned Kelly at Stringybark Creek. With the Kelly Gang being a big part of local history, in 2002 my class spent a few weeks studying bushrangers and to tie in with this theme, every lunch our teacher read us a little bit of the only novel she had on the topic – a long out of print book called *The Girl Who Helped Ned Kelly* by Charles Taylor. At the time, being around ten, I was utterly transfixed.

We never finished the book, much to my consternation, and as my teacher's copy was an antique she wasn't about to lend it to me so I resolved to find my own. But it didn't matter how many places I searched over the coming years; I never saw the book.

Then, in late 2018, I was walking through Adelaide when a second-hand bookstore caught my eye. I wandered in and set about the now familiar process of trying to find a copy. No luck. But there were a couple of other gems in the bushranger section and as I took them up to the counter the lady who owned the shop commented on an evident obsession. I mentioned my ongoing search for *The Girl Who Helped Ned Kelly* and the response was immediate; "oh, it's in that cabinet over there."

Honestly, after a sixteen year long search I wasn't sure if I would even read it. Carrying it out of the store with immense reverence, the

the idea that the book wouldn't be worth it was a concern. But upon flicking through it became evident that not only would I be unable to help myself, but that the novel was a lot more significant than I'd remembered.

Originally serialised in the 1920s, a disclaimer in the front says that the names of many of the supporting characters had been changed "for obvious reasons": the book was written within the life spans of people who knew the Kellys – Taylor even interviewed Ned's brother Jim prior to writing the book, while Ellen Kelly had died only a few years before it was published. With that in mind, *The Girl Who Helped Ned Kelly* represents one of, if not the earliest romanticised fiction of Ned Kelly.

Told largely from the perspective of fictional drifter Jack Briant, *The Girl Who Helped Ned Kelly* chronicles his tangential involvement with the gang during the last year of their lives. The character of Briant, a wealthy man from Melbourne who wins Ned's trust, confounds the police and flirts with Kate Kelly seems very much like a way for an author brought up in the aftermath of the Kellys' time to play out a kind of wish fulfillment. By extension, this makes him an audience surrogate and perhaps accounts for the popularity of the book upon its initial release - there is an undeniable thrill to being given a front row seat to the Kelly story and *The Girl Who Helped Ned Kelly*'s emergence when the events were only just taking on the sheen of legend feels both opportunistic and almost prophetic.

Beyond the gang, Superintendent Hare and Aaron Sherritt, most of the supporting characters are either loose analogues for people like Wild Wright or Tom Lloyd or, like Briant, made up entirely. The titular 'girl' is neither Kate Kelly nor Maggie Skillion, but rather a fictional lover of Ned's who only appears briefly in the second half of the book. These tweaks and additions sit alongside some more egregious diversions from history; namely the Siege of Glenrowan occurring several weeks after Sherritt's murder and Dan dying well before Joe and Steve at the siege itself. You could chalk this up to ignorance, were it not for the afterward that includes many of the correct dates and details.

But accuracy is not what makes this book important and nor, realistically, is narrative. What makes it worthy of discussion is the fact that it represents a blithe fictionalisation of the Kelly story written at a time when the events were still very much within living memory. And despite Jim Kelly publicly stating his disgust towards the book, it would be far from the last. From *Our Sunshine* to *True History of the Kelly Gang*, the literary class might have evolved, but the fundamental ethos certainly hasn't. This story is our defining cultural myth, so writers and artists will always be drawn to create their own versions.

The Girl Who Helped Ned Kelly, then, signifies the moment when writers started to twist the story to suit their own ends, in the process creating new interpretations that would ensure the legend was kept alive for generations to come. Whatever your opinion on the practice, that fact alone gives this book a place in the canon. And after being so inspired by it as a kid, it's gratifying to see it finally be republished, allowing a new generation to discover a noteworthy part of the slow transition from history to legend – along with an adventure story that retains the power to set a child's imagination alight and encourage an obsession spanning nearly two decades.

Gabriel Bergmoser

"I've got you, Ned Kelly!" There was an
exultant thrill in the youngsters voice.

CONTENTS

FOREWORD

The principal people in the story are the men and women who took part in this biggest drama of the Australian bush. The Kellys are real. So are Superintendent Hare and Aaron Sherritt. For obvious reasons the names of the policemen and of the sympathisers of the gang have been altered.

The exploits of the Kellys have been faithfully recorded, facts hitherto unpublished having been obtained by the author after exhaustive personal investigation.

No attempt has been made to canonise these young criminals or to justify their outlawry, but few people will read the exploits of the gang without feeling a tinge of pity for its ringleader - a brave, though misguided, young Australian, whose superb qualities of leadership, almost unexampled endurance and uncanny bushcraft would have taken him far if Fate had willed for him a more honest career.

1

Tramp and Bushranger

"BAIL UP!"

The pleasant-faced young man in shabby but well-cut clothes who sat watching his billy boil turned sharply.

When he saw a big man who obviously was young, in spite of his beard, covering him with a formidable looking revolver, a smile chased the wonderment from his face and he laughed softly.

"Quick now- put your hands up!"

The command was peremptory, but the young fellow made no effort to obey it. Instead, he held out his hand.

"I've often wanted to meet you, Ned Kelly," he said.

"Won't you shake?"

The big man watched him for a moment. "You're game, boy." His tone mingled amusement and admiration. "Who are you, and what are you doing in these parts?"

"Jack Briant- looking for work. The billy's nearly boiling. You'll have a drop of tea with me, won't you?"

The other's eyes were very searching as he inquired, "Are you sure you're alone?"

"Yes - all alone!" Something in the boy's voice induced the outlaw to lay a sympathetic hand on his arm and ask:

"No friends?"

"None that is any good to me," he replied bitterly. Ned Kelly smiled.

"I beat you there. I'm a bushranger, with a price on my head, but I've got the truest friends in the world. If I hadn't I wouldn't be here today."

Briant poured out a pannikin of tea and handed it to his strange guest.

"You first," said Ned.

The younger man did not at once grasp the significance of the remark. When he did he took back the pannikin and laid it on the log on which they sat. Pouring some tea into the billylid, he waited for a few moments for it to cool, then with a cheery "Good luck!" drank it in a few gulps.

Ned reached for the pannikin. "One can't be too careful," he said, as he raised it to his lips. "Better luck, boy!"

A twig snapped, and the outlaw was on his feet in an instant, his hand going instinctively to his revolver holster. Briant, too, had risen, and with eager eyes searched the bush.

For many tense moments they stood thus. A faint click came from the scrub in front of them, and was thrice repeated, each time more faintly. "A 'roo," remarked the bushranger, as he resumed his seat.

"My God, what a life!" The young man said it half to himself, but the quick ears of his companion did not miss it.

"Yes- it keeps a fellow on the jump. Hunted like an animal, eh? Because of that dirty cur Fitzpatrick. By God, if ever- "

The fierce light quickly died out of his eyes, but there was little mirth in the smile that parted his lips.

Jack Briant gazed at him in frank admiration:

"You're not a bad chap, after all, Ned Kelly," he said.

"I didn't believe half the things they said about you."

"What did they say about me?"

There was obvious eagerness in the inquiry. Ned Kelly had his weaker side. There was a strong streak of vanity in his make-up. The best brains of the police force had been pitted against his own and he was still a free man. There was a substantial reward for his capture, dead or alive, yet none of his confidants had betrayed his trust. Small wonder, then, that his egoism was flattered.

"I've worked my way up from Melbourne," replied Briant, "and everyone is talking about you. Some say you're the biggest blackguard Australia has ever seen; that you murder people in cold blood, and that when you're caught hanging'll be too good for you."

Briant noticed the outlaw's just perceptible shudder at the mention of the gallows.

"Others say you've been driven to it, and that after all they don't blame you. You've got the sympathy of most of the women, I've noticed. There's a girl down at Seymour who says she'd give five years of her life to be able to help you."

That recalled to Briant the stories he had heard of Ned's sweetheart- a mysterious girl who was supposed to have performed prodigies of valor on the outlaw's behalf in the way of keeping him advised of police move-ments and supplying the gang with food.

"God bless her for that! Have you ever talked to the police about me?"

"To a few of them. They're not bad chaps, either."

"B-- loafers!" The bush ranger spat the words out.

"You're wrong there," persisted Briant. "You can't run a country without police, and the fellows who're after you are only doing their duty. They're not all Fitzpatricks, you know."

Little pin points of hate shone in Kelly's eyes, and he bit his lips to stifle the words that rose unbidden to them. Twice his hand caressed the butt of his revolver, but he did not speak.

"Why don't you get out of the country, Ned?"

The suggestion seemed to surprise him, but it elicited no reply.

"They must get you in the end," Briant went on. "Perhaps," answered Kelly in a voice that indicated that his thoughts were far away.

"They've got you now!"

The sudden change of tone caused the outlaw to look up quickly. The muzzle of a big revolver was within a few feet of his head. Instinctively his glance fell on his own empty holster.

"I've got you, Ned Kelly!" There was an exultant thrill in the young ster's voice, and the clear blue eyes behind the weapon glowed fearlessly.

"Up with your hands before I put a bullet through you!"

Kelly hesitated, but Briant's "Quick now!" brought his arms above his head.

"You damned police pimp!" shouted the trapped bushranger. Briant jumped to the other side of the log.

"1 ought to shoot you now," he said. "You're just as valu- able dead as alive."

"Then shoot, and be damned to you!"   There was no trace of fear in Ned's voice.

For fully a minute they stood facing one another, the silence broken only by the wind soughing through the trees.

"Anything you want to say? Any message to your friends?"

Kelly ignored the question.

"Surely you've got some confession to make," the young man persisted.

"I'll promise to record it faithfully."

Ned's brain was working fast; but there seemed to be no escape from the trap into which, unwittingly, he had fallen. The hand that held his revolver was as steady as a rock. Suddenly the outlaw's eyes gleamed, and, looking intently into the bush, he shouted excitedly. "Quick, Dan, shoot him!"

Briant laughed. "Try again," he said. "Those old tricks are worked out.

Trapped as he was, the bush ranger could not help admiring the callous bravery of the youth who had him at his mercy. Admiration changed to astonishment as he saw Briant lower the revolver and come forward with a smile on his lips.

"I couldn't resist the temptation, Ned," he said quietly.

"I'm no more a police pimp than you are. I just wondered what it would feel like to hold up a real 'ranger, so I sneaked your revolver when you turned your head. There isn't a policeman ill Australia who wouldn't have given half a lifetime to have had a chance like that. Sorry if I scared you. You must admit I did it rather well."

Anger surged in the outlaw's heart, but the smiling boyish face of the man who had tricked him, and wounded his pride, dispelled it. His Irish sense of humor also helped him, and before he knew it he was smiling, too.

"You young devil, I ought to shoot you for that," he said, as he returned his revolver to its holster. "You had a fortune in your hands, and you let it slip. What do you mean by it?"

"I'm on my uppers," Briant admitted with a rueful grimace, "but I'm not as hard up as that. I say, is there any chance of joining you?"

The bushranger shook his head.

"Why not?"

"This isn't your affair."

"Couldn't trust me, eh?"

Kelly paused for a moment before answering. "After what you showed me just now I'd trust you anywhere. Who are you, boy?"

"Just a down-and-outer tramping the country, heading for God knows where. Why not let me come along? I'm sure I could be useful."

The bushranger's "No" was so definite that Briant knew that further argument was merely a waste of breath.

Ned held out his hand:

"You deserve better than this. Got any money?" Briant turned out his pockets and showed him a few shillings and a penny or two.

"Take this." He thrust several notes and a handful of silver into the young man's hand. "Never mind where it came from," he added, as he noticed his hesitancy to accept it. "You could do with a fresh rig-out."

"You're right there," Briant agreed. "I hate these rags. They're - they're not quite what I've been used *to*, you know."

"I guessed that. A fellow who keeps his chin clean like you do has seen better days."

Briant ran his hand over his smooth cheeks. "That's one thing I can't seem to do without. I say, why don't you get rid of that scrub?"

Ned fingered his silky brown beard caressingly, and shook his head.

"You'll trip on it someday, and then they'll cop you," Jack laughed.

"I'll chance that. Well, I must be going. It's a good job you didn't play that trick on Dan. You mightn't be alive now. I may see you again- who knows? Good luck to you, sonny!"

"And good luck to you, Ned!"

Their hands met in a lingering grip.

Then the man with a price on his head stepped silently into the bush- so softly that the young fellow, noting his bulk, wondered at his lightness of foot.

As he watched him go, a wave of pity surged through Briant's heart. For the bushrangers there could be but one end, but the thought that their inevitable fate meant a broken heart for at least one brave girl depressed him.

2

A Strange Old Couple

JACK BRIANT stood watching the retreating figure of the notorious criminal with whom Fate so strangely had brought him into contact. When the bush had swallowed him up he took from his pocket the money the outlaw had given him, and counted it.

Four pounds nine and sixpence! Compared with his miserable earnings since he had become a tramp, it represented real wealth. He removed his well-worn boots, carefully placed the notes inside them, and put them back on his feet, smiling to himself as he did so.

Gathering up his few scanty belongings, and scattering the embers of the fire, he noted the height of the sun, and, with his bluey slung over his shoulder and his billycan in his hand, he swung along the track that joined the Benalla road.

An old man who had stopped his dray to adjust the harness of his horse eyed him suspiciously.

Briant flung him a cheery "Good day!"

As there was no response, he repeated the salutation.

Again it was ignored.

"Are you deaf?" Jack demanded. "I bade you good day."

The old man's beetling brows contracted into a frown. "I can choose the likes of them I speak to," he growled. "Meaning?"

"I ain't got time for no police pimps!"

Briant laughed.

"So that's it, is it? That's the second time today someone's made that mistake. Ned did ten minutes ago."

The old man stiffened. "Ned 'oo?" he snapped. "Ned Kelly, of course."

"Reckon you're a smarty, I s'pose?"

The smile which revealed a set of irregular tobacco-stained teeth was half a sneer.

"Look here, you're old enough to know better than that," Briant laughed back at him. "Anyway, I'm looking for a job. Anything at your place?"

"Not for the likes o' you!"

"So you still think I'm a police pimp?" "I bid you good-day!"

The old man jumped up into his dray with an agility that belied his appearance. Jack seized the horse's head.

"Hold on, you needn't be in such a hurry." "Let go of them reins, or I'll brain you!"

The threat was accompanied by the flourish of a stout stick which had lain on the floor of the dray.

"Ned wouldn't like you' to treat a friend like that," the boy told him.

The old man dropped his stick and got down.

"Who are you to say you know Ned?" he demanded, eagerly scanning the smiling face that confronted him.

"Give me a job and I'll tell you all about it."

The veteran countryman did not reply. Instead, he rapidly ran his hands over Briant's soiled clothes.

"Looking for a pistol?" asked Jack.

"Git up in the cart," snapped the old fellow.

As the vehicle lumbered over the rough bush track, Briant told him of his meeting with the bush ranger.

Apparently his story sounded convincing, for the old man thawed to the extent of talking once every half mile or so.

"Me name's Jackson, and me place is over the rise," he said. "Might be able to find something for you for a coupla days leastways."

"I shall be very grateful, Mr Jackson," Briant assured him. "It isn't all beer and skittles tramping the country."

"No more is it farmin' in these parts," the old man cut in- "what with them interferin'--"

He stopped in the middle of the sentence, and, although his companion looked inquiringly at him, he showed no inclination to complete it.

Long shadows were creeping across the track, and the air was becoming cooler as the dray drew up before a wretched little bark humpy set in a clearing of a few hungry-looking acres. Two big dogs bounded to meet it, both of them eyeing the stranger and voicing in vicious yaps what obviously was a protest at his intrusion.

"Better mind them dogs," Jackson warned him.

Briant jumped down from the dray and snapped his fingers at the unfriendly animals. "Come here, you rascals!" he cried. The bigger of the pair looked at him doubtfully for a second or two, and then wagged his tail. The other was less conciliatory; but, taking the cue from his mate, he advanced gingerly and sniffed the travel-stained trousers of the stranger.

"Bark at me, would you?" said Jack, taking the shaggy head between his hands, and looking intently into the animal's still distrustful eyes.

"Best be careful," Jackson warned him again.

"Dogs never bite a good man," laughed Briant. "Come here, you!" The bigger dog gave vent to a delighted yap, and fawned on his new-found friend. The other expressed confidence by his vigorous tail-wagging.

"Them dogs have never took to strangers before," remarked the old man, wonderingly.

"All dogs are friendly with me," rejoined Briant.

"Recognise me as one of themselves-one of the underdogs, I suppose."

A wizened little woman came out of the hut, wiping her hands on her apron. "Who you got there?" she demanded.

"A young feller lookin' for work, Mum," her husband answered, a little sheepishly, as though uncertain as to the reception that would greet an addition to the struggling household.

Mrs Jackson was about to make some remark when she noticed the fuss the dogs were making of the newcomer. The old man followed her gaze.

"They seemed to have took a fancy to him, don't they?" he commented.

She nodded her acquiescence, and, without a word, re-entered the hut.

"You go along inside. I'll take the horse out," Briant said to Jackson. "You must have had a long day, and can do with a spell."

"Spell! There's no, spell for folks as come to this district. Well, you can put the harness in the shed there, and turn Roney loose."

Having someone to do any sort of work for him was a new experience for Jackson, and it pleased him.

A few, minutes later the new "hand," with the two dogs at his heels, appeared in the doorway and asked if he might come in. He was motioned to the end of the rough stool on which Jackson sat.

"It's rough," remarked the old man, as he noticed Jack's survey of his squalid surroundings. "People as come to the bush don't have many fal-lals. We ain't got any place for you to doss in but the shed out there, but there's plenty o' bags to keep you warm."

Briant assured him that that would be luxury compared with some of the quarters to which he had been used.

At that moment Mrs Jackson, who had gone outside, came in quickly, eager interest in her faded eyes. She looked significantly at her husband, who hastily followed her through the door.

There was something in their attitude that aroused the watching young man's curiosity, and he walked across the room. The old couple stood with their backs to the house, intently gazing at the far-distant purpling hills.

Breaking a couple of boughs from a nearby sapling, Jackson brought them inside and threw them on the fire. Dense volumes of smoke arose from the green leaves.

"You might run acrost to the shed and get me that box outer the dray," said Jackson; and Briant, knowing at once that something was about to take place that was not intended for his eyes, instantly obeyed.

It was not the contents of the dray that claimed most of his attention, however. From the rough stone chimney which he noticed was unusually high, and had the appearance of recently having been added to-a cloud of blue smoke ascended, followed at regular intervals by two more clouds. When he returned to the hut with a small box from the dray the place was full of smoke, through which he noticed Mrs Jackson carrying a big piece of hessian into the other room.

"These here boughs smoke somethin' terrible," the old man remarked.

"They certainly do," Briant agreed, rubbing his eyes.

"Soon clear away, though."

"Yes, I suppose so."

That was all that was said, but for a long time Jack felt that the glances which the old couple cast in his direction were prompted by a desire to discover how much he had seen.

For the first time for five days Briant sat down to a hot meal. A huge plateful of steaming meat, a junk of coarse damper, and a mug of milkless tea were set before him on the bare boards of the improvised table. The meat had an unfamiliar flavor, but was by no means displeasing. He was ravenously hungry, and his helping disappeared with astonishing rapidity.

"Ever taste that before?" asked Jackson quizzically.

"Not that I know of. What was it - kangaroo?"

The old man bared his discolored teeth. "That's a good guess, anyway. Some as says they can't touch it, but it's fillin'- and when you get it young I reckon there's some goodness in it. We don't have roast beef or turkey regular, you know."

"High living isn't good for you, anyway - it gives you gout," laughed Briant.

After the meal, which was consumed almost in silence, Jackson drew a stool up nearer the fire and filled his pipe. "Smoke?" he asked.

"Rather; but I'll have a whiff later."

Then, to the old lady's astonishment, she felt two strong hands on her shoulders, and was gently pushed into the rickety rocking chair that claimed pride of place among the rude appointments of her home.

"This is your off night," Jack told her. "I'm the maid-of-all-work for once. You just watch me clear up those dishes."

A ghost of a smile hovered round the old woman's colorless lips as she beheld the unusual sight of a man discharging one of the duties that formed part of her ceaseless round of toil. It was good to sit by while someone did even a small portion of the work from which there seemed no possible chance of escape.

"There now, how's that?" Briant asked, as he pointed to the dishes, which carefully, if clumsily washed, he had piled in a neat heap on the box near the end of the table.

"You're a good boy," remarked Mrs. Jackson, with a little quaver in her voice.

They talked on various subjects for an hour or more.

Neither Jackson nor his wife was disposed to discuss the Kellys and their exploits or the girl whom Ned was supposed to love, although several times. Briant adroitly turned the conversation into that well-worn channel. Every time he mentioned the outlaws they cut him short and introduced more congenial, if less enthralling, topics.

By the aid of a lantern Briant sought his sleeping quarters. The shed was cold and draughty; but, as the old man had said, there were plenty of bags, and with these he made his bed. Because of the notes concealed in them, he did not remove his boots. In strange country it always paid to be cautious. Next day he would find a safe plant for his money...

For a long time he lay thinking of the events of the day, and particularly of the smoke signals by which the old folks had sent some mysterious message to friends whose identity he felt sure he could guess.

His meeting with Ned Kelly thrilled him. Somehow he felt he would see much more of the outlaw leader in the near future- that, indeed, the bush ranger would play some considerable part in shaping his career.

Then sleep overtook him. How long he slept he did not know, but when the barking of the dogs awakened him he heard the sound of horses' hoofs. His first impulse was to get up to see whom these nocturnal visitors might be, but prudence dictated another course, so he lay still.

After what seemed to be hours of waiting he was just dozing again when he heard stealthy footsteps approaching. A man with a lantern entered the hut, and by its fitful rays he could see that he was younger than the stubbly growth on his chin indicated. When the stranger came closer and subjected him to close scrutiny, he feigned sleep. Evidently the examination satisfied the man, for after a few seconds he left the shed.

Jack saw out of the corner of his eye that the stranger walked backwards and kept the lantern well in front of him. He noted, too, that a heavy revolver hung from his belt.

A little later again he heard the sound of horses' hoofs, but this time fainter and fainter until eventually they died away.

3

The Police Call

WHAT were the dogs barking at last night?" Briant asked Jackson next morning.

The old man regarded him intently for a moment, then replied with a nonchalance that obviously was assumed:

"They woke me, too. You never know what they see in the bush o' nights."

"Perhaps it was the police on the lookout for the Kellys."

"Not likely," returned the old chap. "They know the gang don't come this way. I got nothing they would want to take. You won't see a police-man round these parts."

Jackson was wrong there, for early that afternoon two well-mounted horsemen pulled up at his hut. Although in civilian clothes, they were easily recognisable as troopers. One, a big fellow, heavily bearded, apparently was no stranger to the old couple,

"What tricks have you been up to lately, Jackson?" he demanded.

"Just the same old tricks, constable," was the ready reply- "tryin' to make a livin' by hard work."

The younger trooper laughed.

"Haven't had any help lately, I s'pose?"

"No, worse luck - I got no one to help me 'cept the missus, and God knows she does her best."

"You lying old hound!" cried the bearded man. "We'll get you yet, Jackson, just as sure as we'll get Ned and his gang."

"There's nothing you can get me for, you know that." "We've told you before what it means to harbor criminals," the younger man said, as he dismounted.

Jackson pointed to his miserable habitation. "Fine place to harbor anyone, I'm thinkin'."

"You're a cunning old devil, and your old woman isn't any better."

Jackson's eyes blazed.

"You wouldn't dare say that if I was a younger man. I'd flay the skin off your dirty carcase! You hunt for Ned Kelly! And what would you do if you found him? Run like hell, I'll warrant. I know your sort. Bullyin' old men and women's more in your line. You --" Want of breath cut short the angry tirade.

"Don't you talk any more like that, or we'll take you along with us," the bearded trooper warned him.

"And what would you charge me with? Assaultin' the police, maybe. You've made fools enough of yourselves already. If you want to make yourselves the laughin' stock of the country you'd better take me now. But don't forget what happened to O'Donellan when he handled old Sam Thompson rough. He ain't in the police force now. P'r'aps you'd like to know where he is. Down in Melbourne without a friend. There's things people won't put up with, even from a policeman. Now, get off my land!"

"That tongue of yours'll get you into trouble yet."

It was noticeable that the young constable's attitude was less aggressive.

His companion, who had gone to the shed in which Briant had slept, came back excitedly.

"So you had a visitor last night," he exclaimed. "Look here, Costello. You come along, too, Jackson. Who slept there?" he demanded, pointing to the heap of bags which had formed Jack Briant's bed.

"The young feller that works for me." Both troopers laughed.

"So we're an employer of labor now, are we?" jeered one of them. "What's the name of your farm assistant?"

"Jack Briant."

"Where is he now?"

"Down the gully, splittin' posts."

"Then you'd better call him."

"Call him yourself, if you want him."

The young policeman's eyes glinted dangerously.

"Look here, Jackson, we've had about enough of this from you!"

"And I've had enough of you. If you want my man you'd better go and get him. I shan't."

"You go, Costello."

Costello was back in a little while with Briant beside him.

"Is your name Briant?" Jack was asked.

"It is."

"What are you doing here?"

"Working for Mr Jackson."

"When did you come?"

"Yesterday afternoon."

"Where from?"

"Melbourne - worked my way here."

"What made you come to this district?"

"I don't know - luck, fate, or whatever you like to call it."

"Where are you making for?"

"Anywhere. I'm not particular. A fellow's got to live, and one place suits me as well as another."

"Ever been in trouble?"

"Many a time. Oh, I see what you mean - trouble with the police. Not yet."

"You're not used to this sort of work. What's your game?"

"Oh, it isn't a game, I assure you. It's damned hard."

"Supposing we arrested you on suspicion?"

"Well, that would be a new experience. But on suspicion of what - being Ned Kelly?"

"None of that cheek," cut in Costello, "or we'll deal with you!"

Briant laughed.

"And don't you laugh at me!"

There was something in the young officer's tone that annoyed Jack, and for a moment he lost his head. "Look here, if you weren't a trooper, I'd--"

Jackson, now thoroughly alarmed, seized his arm. "Don't be a fool, boy! Interferin' with the police is dangerous. They'd tell no end o' lies about it, and send you up for years."

"Don't worry about that," Briant returned. "I might know more about the law than both of them put together. I don't want to run foul of the police, who have quite a number of privileges, but many obligations as well. This youthful representative of law and order evidently forgets that."

The troopers looked at one another as though not quite certain of themselves. It was evident that this strange farm hand was a man of education, and that put them at a disadvantage. They felt the handicap which so many men feel when opposed to those of superior upbringing and keener mental equipment.

Meanwhile, Costello was taking stock of the impudent youth who had had the hardihood to insult him. He was as tall as himself, though not as broad, and he looked as hard as nails.

"I'll get him yet!" he muttered to himself.

The other trooper had been keenly interested in some hoof-prints near the hut.

"Who came here on horseback last night?" he asked Jackson.

"No one that I know of."

"Come on now, no lies. Who was he?"

The old man glared defiantly. If I didn't see anyone, how can I say who he was, if there was anyone? Them tracks look pretty old to me."

"And they look pretty new to me. Which of the gang was it?"

"Gang! gang! gang! That's all you think about.

What would any of the gang want here, I'd like to know?"

"That's what we would like to know. We do know that you've been helping the Kellys, and that means gaol."

Jackson snorted. "The Kellys can look after themselves without coming to a poor old man like me for help."

The bearded man turned to Briant. "You'd better get away from here. This company isn't good for you. This old scoundrel is a known Kelly sympathiser and is dangerous to mix up with."

Jack smiled.

"Is it a crime to be a Kelly sympathiser? If it is, there aren't enough gaols in Victoria to house that kind of criminal."

"How do you know that?"

"I've worked my way up from Melbourne, as I told you, and I've kept my ears open."

The policeman beckoned him to one side.

"What did you hear?" he whispered. "You know there's a big reward for the Kellys and anyone who gives useful information is entitled to a share of it."

"But I couldn't give you information that would help."

"You said you heard people sympathising with the Kellys."

"No, I didn't."

"Well, what did you say?"

"I said, or I meant to say, that the talk I had heard on my way here gave me the impression that half the countryside was sympathetic."

"Tell me the names of some of the men."

"I couldn't do that. They told me at Seymour that a few of the police were known to be friendly - or at least, they weren't anxious for the gang to be caught."

"Who told you that?" eagerly.

"I think it was one of the storekeepers. I'm not sure, though it might have been the butcher."

"Don't lie to me. Get out of this, you mongrel!"

One of the dogs who had been sniffing round the policeman received a vicious kick that sent him off howling.

Briant's eyes blazed.

"What did you kick that dog for, you damned coward!"

"You – you talk to me like that!" the trooper spluttered. "By God, I'll --" He made a vicious blow at Briant, who easily dodged it. Again he rushed at him, but Jack was much too quick for him. Whipping out his revolver he covered the young man. "We'll take you back with us! You'll smart for this! Get over there!"

Briant did not move.

"Get over there, I said!" roared the irate representative of the law.

Costello now took a hand. He seized Jack from behind and threw him heavily. With an angry snarl, one of the dogs buried its teeth in his leg. Between howls of pain and oaths Costello drew his revolver, but before he could use it Jackson had jumped in front of the dog.

"Get out of the way!" commanded the trooper.

"Keep back there, Spot," shouted the old man, and the dog, still snarling, obeyed, it was impossible to fire at it without endangering its owner. The other policeman walked a few yards to the right, and Briant, who had risen, realised why he had moved and stepped in front of him. The dog was thus protected from two angles.

"Step back or you'll get shot!"

Before Jack could hurl a defiant reply there was a sharp report of a firearm from the bush at the back of the hut, and a bullet pinged past them.

"My God, the Kellys!"

Both troopers said it simultaneously, and both reached their horses at the same moment. Without looking back, they dashed for the track, and in a few seconds had disappeared from sight.

When the sound of their galloping horses had died away there emerged from the scrub the wizened figure of Mrs Jackson, a big revolver in her hand.

Her husband ran to meet her.

"I guessed it was you, Mum. It did the trick to rights!"

Wonderingly, Briant watched her walk quietly into the hut, as unconcerned as though circumventing the police by clever strategy was part of her daily duty. He followed his employer inside.

"By Jove, Mrs Jackson, that was wonderful of you!" he cried. "Things were getting awkward, and you saved the situation."

The old woman bared her almost toothless gums.

"I was watchin' you two for quite a while. I didn't like the look of things, so I just sneaked off into the bush, keepin' the house between me and them. My! But didn't it just scare 'em!" She laughed silently at the recollection of the policemen's undignified exit.

"They'll be back again tomorrow," remarked Jackson, "p'r'aps with a couple more with 'em."

Briant looked alarmed. "I say, that'll be awkward for you. They're sure to be nasty. What are you going to do? How about clearing out for the day?"

"And have the place burnt down?" No fear! We'll stay here."

"But-but-"

"We'll find a way of beatin' 'em somehow."

Jackson said it with an easy confidence that Briant did not share. To the young man the outlook was alarming. What could this fearless old man do against two vindictive troopers, who had the advantage of the law on their side if extreme measures were considered necessary?

He felt, too, that in some degree he was responsible.

He shouldn't have cheeked Costello. For the sake of the old couple he should have kept a civil tongue in his head. Yet the insolent bearing of the younger trooper had made him lose his temper.

It was with an uneasy mind that he sought his shakedown in the shed that night. For hours he lay awake, starting at every sound that came from the bush around him. Then sleep overtook him, and when he awoke the sun was high and Mrs Jackson was standing beside him.

4

Another Police Visit

"STAYING there all day?" she asked.

"I'm sorry if I'm late. What time is it?"

"Gone past six."

When Jack dressed and went over to breakfast he noticed there were only two plates and two cups on the table.

"Where's Mr Jackson?" he inquired.

"Went away on a message a good two hour ago."

"He needn't have done that. He could have sent me."

The old woman shook her head.

"That wouldn't have been no good. Only him as can do what he wants to do."

Briant felt decidedly uneasy. Suppose the police - who had a habit of turning up at all hours - arrived, what would happen? His misgivings did not seem to be shared by the brave little woman of the bush who sat before him. She appeared as unconcerned as though both the police and bushrangers had combined forces to protect her.

"Do you think the troopers will come again today?" Jack asked her.

"Maybe - maybe not."

He might have asked her whether she thought it would rain for all the emotion her voice betrayed.

"What would you do, Mrs. Jackson, if they cut up rough?"

"They won't," she replied, quietly. "I wish I thought like that."

She noted the anxiety in his voice, and a flicker of a smile played round the corners of her wrinkled mouth.

"They've been com in' round these parts for months, and nothin' ain't happened worth mentionin'."

"After their scare yesterday they mightn't show up again for a while," Jack suggested.

"One never knows."

He looked at her searchingly.

"Mrs Jackson, I don't want you to think I'm prying into your affairs. Don't tell me if you' think I shouldn't know. Who was the man who came here the night before last on horseback, and had a look at me?"

"Did someone come here?" she inquired, with a slight tilt of her wispy eyebrows.

Briant laughed.

"Did you ever play poker; Mrs Jackson?"

She shook her head.

"You'd make a fortune if you took up the game." Whether or not she understood the allusion he did not know, but she made no comment.

A hoofbeat sounded outside, and Briant hurriedly went to the door. It was Jackson astride his ancient carthorse. Jack went outside to meet him.

"You're early astir this morning," he remarked.

The old fellow slid out of the saddle.

"We don't call this early in these parts. Ain't had visitors since I been away, by any chance?"

"No. Were you expecting any?"

"You never can tell."

Briant detained the grizzled countryman as, having slipped the saddle and bridle off Roney, he was about to walk over to the hut.

"Mr Jackson, I'm afraid I acted very foolishly with the police yesterday. I don't want you to suffer through it. If they come again today it'll be me they'll be after. Would it help you at all if I cleared out?"

Jackson's brows contracted in a frown, and he turned, almost savagely.

"Scared of 'em?" he snapped.

"I'm' not. Let them come, and be damned to them!"

A faint glimmer of pride lighted the old man's eyes.

"I didn't think you was the sort to run from a couple of crawlin' troopers."

"The police don't seem to scare you, either?"

Jackson snorted.

"Why should they?"

"Well" – hesitatingly -"you're-you're not as young as you used to be, you know-and they don't seem to be too' friendly towards you."

"The b--- loafers!" snarled Jackson, as he strode into the hut.

That was the term which Ned Kelly had applied to them, Briant noted. What was the relationship between the gang and this fearless old man and his equally courageous wife? The police had accused them of being Kelly sympathisers. What service could they render the outlaws? Then he remembered the smoke signals on the day of his arrival, and the mysterious midnight visitor. What were the secrets hidden within the walls of that rough bush humpy?

Jack's ruminations were cut short by the sudden appearance on' foot of Constables Martin and Costello. So quietly had they approached that they were almost at his side before he was aware of their presence. Smothering his surprise, he bade them "Good morning."

Martin nodded, but Costello did not return his greeting. "We've come to give you another chance," Martin said.

"We warned you yesterday you were in bad company, and people who keep bad company often get into trouble. Still sometimes they're useful. I suppose you could do with a slice of the Kelly reward?"

Briant's first impulse was to tell him to go to hell, but he checked it, and replied with a smile:

"I suppose there are quite a lot of people who could do with it, too. But I'm not likely to be one of the lucky ones. I'm afraid if Ned Kelly turned up I'd break a running record."

Costello, interpreting the remark as an allusion to their hurried departure on the previous day, adopted a menacing attitude, but his companion pushed him back.

"What happened after that shot was fired yesterday?" asked Martin. "Did anyone come here - any of the gang?"

"I didn't wait to see," Briant replied with a chuckle.

"I went back to the gully. I didn't want to risk an ounce of lead."

The big trooper took a step forward. "Is that the truth you're telling me? We have a way of dealing with liars that isn't good for 'em."

"Then I shall be careful not to lie."

"Didn't you see anyone about except the old man any woman?"

"Not a soul."

"How long did you stay down the gully?"

"Till tea-time."

"And there was no one about when you came back?"

"Only Mr and Mrs Jackson."

"There's something in the shed I want you to look at," said Martin. "You'd better stay here and keep an eye on the hut"- as Costello was about to follow him.

"Now, look here, my boy," said the big policeman, as they stood beside Briant's rough bunk, "you and I can help each other to get a bit of that reward. You stay on here and keep your eyes and ears open. I'll come to the burnt bridge every day, and you can meet me there."

Jack shook his head.

"I couldn't do it - it'd be too dangerous."

"How do you mean?"

"You never know who might be watching. The old folks might get suspicious. You'd better come along here like you did today, and I'll find some means of telling you anything of importance."

"Good boy! We'll get that money yet."

Briant pretended not to see the policeman's hand as he proffered it, and led the way out of the shed.

"Mum's the word to Costello," Martin whispered, and Jack winked knowingly in response.

They found Jackson, who had come outside at the sound of the trooper's voices, exchanging angry words with the young policeman.

"And I tell you I don't want you dirty loafers round my place!" he was saying.

"You'll find us here when you least expect us!" Costello retorted. "We'll get you red-handed yet, Jackson."

From the other side of the clearing a stranger emerged from the bush. At almost the same moment a second man approached from the opposite direction. Jackson waited until they were close enough to recognise, and then turned on the two policemen, his face distorted with rage.

"Two of you wasn't enough to interfere with a harmless old man, so you brought two more dirty sneakin' hounds. Get off me land before I shoot the lot o' you!"

He rushed towards the hut-into the arms of one of the newcomers.

"Phwat's the hurry, ould Spyglass?" quizzed the man, a burly fellow with a short sandy beard.

"It's you, Macguire, is it?" sneered Jackson, wrenching himself free. "Another of the lyin' mob. What d'ye mean be comin' here?"

Macguire laughed.

"Just to pay a friendly visit loike," he replied in a rich Irish brogue. "Sure, you wouldn't afther wantin' not to see yer ould friends. And how's the bhoys? They tell me Dan was here the noight before last. 'Tis a pity we missed him!"

The old man's whiskers bristled again.

"If Dan ever came here he wouldn't find any of you crawlers about. He's a better man than any half-dozen of you."

"Oi loike to hear a mahn sthick up for his friends," jeered Macguire.

"We've come to have a pape at yer foine mansion there - to look at yer trisures an' all that."

"You won't set foot inside my doors without a warrant," cried the old man, his voice rising almost to a shriek.

Macguire made a deprecatory gesture.

"Oh, come now, Mishter Jackson, that's unkoind av ye! What'd we be wanting wid a warrant? Friendly visit we're payin', that's all."

He pushed the wildly gesticulating bushman out of his way and strode into' the hut. At the door he paused.

"Come on, bhoys. Ye'll surely be wantin' to see the soights."

The other three policemen followed him, and Briant, with fear gripping his heart, went in, too.

"Oh! ho! we didn't know you had visitors," cried a man referred to as Kenny.

Two middle-aged men in rough bush clothes were seated at the table, one of them cleaning a double-barrelled gun.

"It's you, Red Regan, is it -- and our old friend McCullagh?" said Kenny. "What's the gun for?"

"'Roos," answered Regan, without looking up.

Briant gasped. How did those two men get there?

They couldn't have arrived with Jackson, or he would have seen them. Could they have been there all night? Whatever were the means employed, he was grateful for their presence. There was a world of comfort in the knowledge that whatever happened there were four on each side, not counting the little old woman who went about her work unconcernedly, except that her beady eyes glinted and the lines at the corners of her mouth appeared to deepen. The constables examined the room in detail, Regan and McCullagh looking 'on without a word.

"Oi'll trouble yez to sthand asoide, Mrs. Jackson," commanded Macguire, as the old woman took up her position in front of the strip of sacking that screened one room from the other.

"There's nothin' in there as concerns you," she snapped. "Far from it that Oi should disbelieve a lady, but Oi'm afther lookin' for moiself." And pushing the frail figure aside, he entered the room.

Regan and McCullagh jumped to their feet. Instinctively Jack ranged himself alongside them.

"You two stay where you are," barked Costello, "and you, too, Townie."

"And if we don't?" said Regan.

"It'll be the worse for you!"

Costello looked round.

"Where's Jackson?"

It was only then that Briant noticed that his employer had not followed the others into the hut.

"One of you had better see what that old scoundrel's up to," Kenny suggested.

"I'll go," volunteered Costello.

There was no sign of him anywhere. The trooper searched the shed, and scoured the bush round it without success.

"Damn him!" he muttered.

"Damn yourself!" cried a voice behind him. To his amazement he saw Jackson standing within a few feet of him, a sneer on his grizzled face.

29

"Where did you spring from?" gasped Costello. Without troubling to reply, the old man walked into the hut, the policeman following.

"Where did you find him?" asked Kenny.

"Over in the shed," lied Costello.

"Phwat were ye doin' in the shed, moight Oi ask, Misther Jackson?" asked Macguire.

The only reply was an angry snort.

"Did ye hear phwat Oi asked ye?" The policeman's grip on the old man's arm made him wince. Before the, others realised what had happened Regan had pulled his hand off and pushed him away. Tripping over a box, Macguire fell on his back. He regained his feet in an instant, revolver in hand. "You'll pay for that, Regan!" he shouted.

McCullagh quietly slipped a cartridge into his gun. "Oi arrist yez for interferin' wid the police in the execution of duty!" cried Macguire, advancing towards Regan.

At that moment Mrs. Jackson, carrying a log of wood for the fire, thrust herself between them.

"Out of the way, ye ould hag!" shouted Macguire.

A second later he stepped back with a howl of pain.

The old woman had dropped the log on his foot!

"Oi'll take ye, too!"

Macguire was mad with rage, and he flourished his revolver in a way that so alarmed Briant that he jumped forward and wrested it from him.

Misinterpreting his motive, the other three policemen drew their weapons.

"Drop that!" commanded Costello.

Jack threw the pistol into the corner of the room. With a bound Macguire recovered it, and levelled it at the young man's head. McCullagh, shotgun in hand, walked up to the enraged trooper until his face was within a few inches of the revolver muzzle.

"Macguire," he said, in a cold, hard voice, "there's things the police ain't allowed to do. If you want to save your skin put that pistol away."

"Ye'd threaten me, would ye? By God, Oi'll--"

He did not complete the sentence. McCullagh wrenched the revolver from him, and gave him a push that sent him staggering against the wall.

As one man the other three troopers sprang forward. Costello was the first to reach McCullagh, but he was flung aside. Numbers prevailed, however, and in a little while the big bushman, still fighting desperately, was borne to the floor. A pair of handcuffs flashed, but before they were clasped on his wrists two figures darkened the door, and a big voice boomed, "Here, what's the shindy?"

The intruders were in striking contrast. One was a giant, 6ft. 3in. or 6ft. 4in., with a body built in proportion. His clean-shaven face accentuated the long black beard worn by his companion, a little fellow who did not reach to his armpit. Each man carried a shotgun.

The troopers had jumped to their feet at the sound of the big man's voice, and McCullagh was free to rise. Ignoring the policemen altogether, the giant spoke to Jackson.

"Well, we're ready for those 'roos that's been eatin' your bit of a crop. We didn't know ye had company. We thought ten miles from here was the police limit."

"What do you mean by that, Big Manton?" demanded Kenny.

Manton's gaze conveyed a world of meaning.

"There's no one within ten miles of here that needs the police," he said.

"Is that a threat?" snapped Costello.

"This isn't a healthy district for any trooper-not further than Luske's on one side and Sheoak Creek on the other. We've come to help Jackson get rid of those kangaroos, and we're anxious to get on with the job, so-" He pointed to the door.

To Jack's amazement the four policemen, scowling angrily, left the hut. At the door Costello said, as a parting shot: "You'll hear more of this, Manton!"

"Not this side of Luske's," replied the giant meaningly.

"I'm sorry we're late, Sam," boomed the big voice again. "But we got here in time. Who's the youngster?"

Jackson led him outside, so that Briant did not hear how his presence was accounted for, or what sort of character he was given by his strange employer. Apparently it was satisfactory, for when they returned Manton gripped his hand with a fervor that threatened to reduce it to pulp.

5

Kate Kelly

BRIANT saw little more of either Regan, McCullagh, Manton, or the little bearded man. Apparently they had some private business with Jackson, for they remained inside for a long time, and when he returned from his work in the gully they had gone. Then he realised why his employer had been so unperturbed by the possibility of the policemen's return, and why he had ridden away so early in the morning.

The honors had been with the bushmen, but would the troopers let it go at that? If he had any knowledge of human nature, they would not. Still, they seemed to fear the giant who had been responsible for their sudden departure. But would they heed his warning not to come near the place again? It had been an exciting morning, but he did not like the way things had shaped. McCullagh's attack on Macguire obviously was an assault, and the fact that the policeman had been exceeding his duty might not weigh greatly with the authorities if the incident were brought under their notice.

He voiced his fears to Jackson during the midday meal. "They won't come back here for a long time," Jackson said, confidently.

"I hope you're right. All the same, it's a serious business. They might get McCullagh for what he did."

The old man shook his head.

"Who was the little fellow?" Jack asked.

"Tom Stevens - lives down by Manton's. Ain't much to look at, but there's nothin' on two or four legs as has ever scared him yet."

"And I should say that nothing in heaven or earth could scare Manton."

Jackson chuckled.

"Strongest fellow I've ever seen, but as gentle as a baby till you rouse him. He could make mincemeat of any two of them troopers without turnin' a hair."

"And they seem to have a wholesome respect for him, too."

The old man chuckled again.

'He was run in once for havin' a horse that didn't belong to him. Was silly with booze or they'd never have handled him. He sobered up in the night, tore down the wall of the cell, woke up the two troopers at the station, and told 'em he was goin' and it wouldn't be well for 'em if they interfered."

"They let him go?"

"Only too glad to."

"And was nothing said about it?"

"Police said they made a mistake or somethin'," Jack laughed.

"The friendship of a man like that's worth preserving. Your friends are very loyal to you, Mr. Jackson."

Jackson did not reply, but his wife, who had been a silent listener, turned to Briant.

"Did you ever see a bush fire, boy?" she asked. "People mightn't be on the best of terms in ordinary times, but when the fire's on they fight like one man. They dares'n't do anything else."

Next morning Jackson handed Briant a letter.

"Do you think you could take that up to Jacobson's near the Big Bend?" he asked. "I can't let you have Roney, 'cos I'm doin' a bit o' ploughin', but it's only a matter of five mile or so."

"Of course, I can take it," Jack responded. "I'm used to walking."

"Don't let this get into no one else's hands," the old man warned him, as he gave him an envelope bearing a name in an almost indecipherable scrawl. "It's terrible important."

"You can trust me for that," Jack replied, as, having received explicit instructions how to find Jacobson's, he left the hut.

It was a glorious morning, and, used to the bush as he had been for some time, he could not help being struck by its beauty. The early light accentuated the varying shades of green of tree and shrub, upon the leaves of which the dew glistened like diamonds.

With the precious missive concealed inside his shirt, he left the track and pushed through the scrub to make the short cut of which Jackson had spoken.

He wondered what he would do if a policeman met him. If he searched him would the loss of the letter mean much to Jacobson - or to his employer? Once or twice the snapping of a twig ahead of him caused his heart to miss a beat. Once he saw the cause in a wallaby that leapt through the undergrowth at his approach. The events of the last few days had set his nerves on edge, and he jumped at sounds which a week previously he would have ignored.

Suddenly through the scrub he thought he discerned the figure of a man. He dodged behind a tree. A loose stone upon which he stepped rolled from under him, and he fell heavily. When he regained his feet the pain of his right ankle was so great that he had to sit down.

Crawling on his hands and knees a few yards to where a stick lay, by its aid he struggled to his feet. By relieving the weight on his injured foot he managed to walk a short distance, but his progress was painfully slow.

How was he to cover the four or five miles that lay between him and Jacobson's? He didn't like to call for help for fear of attracting the kind of assistance he least desired at the moment. Whatever was in the letter he was carrying, it seemed certain from Jackson's anxiety that it should be delivered to the addressee that it was not intended for other eyes.

The more he reflected on his position, the more depressed he became. The only people likely to pass his way were the police. If they did find him he would have to be ready for them. He removed the boot from his uninjured foot, and placed the letter along the sole- as he had previously done with Ned Kelly's gift banknotes.

The movements caused him intense pain, and when eventually he tried to walk he found that the paper in his boot added to his discomfort. He struggled along for a little while and then sank down exhausted. After a rest he tried again. In these painful stages he covered a few hundred yards, but as his ankle was becoming more painful he was forced to give in. Crawling to a stunted gum, he sat with his back against its butt, and, wet with perspiration though the afternoon was cool, he again reviewed his desperate position.

He would have to call for help and chance who came to his assistance. No, he would wait another hour or so in the hope that someone might come his way.

He was glad of that decision the moment he made it, for the sound of a horse coming through the bush reached his ears. It was heading his way, too. After what seemed an eternity of suspense he saw its nose appear from behind a big tree, then its forelegs, and then the rider - a woman!

"Hey!" he called.

She pulled up dead and looked around her. Even from that distance Briant could read the anxiety in her face.

"This way!" he called again.

Then she saw him and cantered over to him. Although he had never before seen her, instinctively he knew whom she was. Her features were pleasing and her coloring attractive, but it was the strength of character revealed in that well-poised head that he observed most of all. She cut a fine figure as she rode over to him and with airy grace dismounted.

She looked at him keenly before asking:

"Aren't you young Briant, from Jackson's?"

How well-informed these people seemed to be of everything that went on around them!

"You're a good guesser, Miss Kelly," he replied.

It was her turn to look surprised. "How did you know my name?"

"I knew you from descriptions given me all the way from Melbourne."

She bent over him. "Are you hurt?"

"Twisted my ankle on a stone about a quarter of a mile back. I was taking a letter to Jacobson's."

There was a note of anxiety in her voice as she asked,

"Did you give it to him?"

"No, I was on my way." "Why did you go on foot?"

"Jackson was using the horse. It's only about five or six miles, you know."

"The letter--"

"It's safe - in my boot!" "Good!"

She knelt beside him and examined his injured ankle. "You poor boy!" she said tenderly. "It must be very painful. I'll get you home. You take my horse, and I'll walk."

"You won't do anything of the sort," he said, the color mounting his cheeks. "I'll be all right after I rest a bit."

She knew he was lying.

"Well, then, if you can get up behind me, we'll go that way.' Do you think you can manage it?"

"It's very good of you. I'll try."

With her help. he struggled up, and she bounded lightly into the saddle.

"Steady there, Kathleen," she said, as she patted her horse's neck! "Watch your step, old lady. Are you all right?"

"Quite all right" She laughed.

"Just hang on to me if you feel you want to."

They rode in silence for some distance. Every little while she turned to see how he was faring, and each time he met her with a smile.

"How long are you going to stay at Sam's?" she asked. "I don't know. Just as long as he needs me, I suppose." "He needs you very much, but he's as poor as a hunted dingo."

"I know that, but I'll try not to be a burden on him.

I might even help him a bit. You didn't know I was rich, did you?"

She laughed again - a merry little chuckle. "No, I didn't know that."

"Didn't Ned tell you?"

She paused before replying.

"You mean the few notes he gave you?"

Once more he wondered at the speed at which news travelled in those lonely hills.

"I'll be able to get something for the old couple with that," he said.

"But Ned gave it to you."

"To do as I like with. What do you think I'd better buy for them?"

She did not reply.

"Can't you think of anything they need?"

"I can think of lots of things, but-is that foot still painful?" It was evident that she did not wish to pursue the discussion.

"A bit jumpy at times, but it'll soon be all right thanks to you. I'm afraid I'm taking you out of your way."

"Not a bit. I wanted to see Sam. I can take that letter to Jacobson's for him."

"You're a wonderful girl!"

He noticed the color rise to her cheeks as she replied, "Many people think different to that."

"Then they don't know you."

They lapsed into silence again, and neither spoke until the smoke from Jackson's chimney was seen.

"We're nearly there," said Kate. "You'll be glad to finish this ride."

"No, sorry."

Jackson saw them as they reached the edge of the clearing, and came running towards them.

"Why, Kate, what's the matter?" he said, in alarm. "This young fellow sprained his ankle, and I was lucky enough to come along and find him."

"But the letter - the letter!"

"It's all right, Mr Jackson," said Briant. "It's quite safe, but Jacobson hasn't got it yet."

The old man's relief was plainly visible.

Between them they helped Briant off the horse, and led him, limping painfully, into the hut.

For once, Mrs Jackson's hard, wrinkled face softened, and pity shone in her faded eyes as she helped to make him comfortable on the bags she had spread on the floor in front of the fireplace.

Kate Kelly took off his boots and handed the letter to Jackson, who almost snatched it from her, and put it in his pocket. Jack's foot was badly swollen, but when it was bathed in hot water and bandaged, he felt some relief.

From the inner room, Jackson produced a bottle of brandy, and the fiery liquid put new life into Briant.

Then Kate and the old couple left him. He could hear their voices outside the hut, but was unable to detect what they were saying. Occasionally he heard Ned's name mentioned, and several times his own. When they returned, Kate bent over him and offered him her hand, which he eagerly seized.

"Good-bye and good luck!"

"Good-bye, and thank you again. I sha'n't forget your kindness."

She flashed a smile at him as she went through the door.

6

A Pleasant Interlude

"DID Kate take the letter?"

The old man nodded.

"Is it safe for her to ride through the bush alone?"

Jackson's laugh had a note of defiance in it. "Safe! Who's goin' to interfere with her? She can take care of herself sure enough."

"Supposing the police- "

"They wouldn't dare!"

Briant remained in the hut all night. Mrs. Jackson wouldn't hear of his going to the shed. For hours he thought of the girl who so strangely had come to his assistance. What a damned topsy-turvy world it was, to be sure! Nature had intended her for something very different from this, he was certain. He was certain, too, that Fate had played Ned a scurvy trick when it had sent him to roam the bush a fugitive with a price upon his head.

His injury revealed to him a side to Mrs. Jackson's nature he had hardly expected to find. Cold and relentless she had appeared to him - a woman from whom hardship had sapped all feminine instincts. Instead he found a kindly old soul to whom nothing seemed a trouble if it could help him to early recovery.

"You are very good to me," he said, giving her withered hand a grateful squeeze.

To his surprise she walked away, but he noticed, as she went through the door, she held her apron to her eyes.

Jackson, too, had been most solicitous as to his comfort, while Spot, the dog, kept him close company all the time, every now and then placing his paw on his arm as if expressing sympathy and affection.

For a whole day he lay there. Jackson appeared only at meal times, and Mrs Jackson had much to occupy her time, so that he was left pretty well to himself.

Kate did not come that day, but the day after when he was sitting on a box by the fire she arrived.

"I'm glad to see you so much better," she said, with a pleased smile. "I've brought you something I hope you'll like."

From a basket which she carried she produced a jar of what looked like meat, and half a dozen appetising-looking cakes.

"When Mrs. Jackson, warms up this rabbit I'm sure you'll like it. We cook it in a different way to most people."

"Did you cook it?" he asked. She nodded her head.

"Then I'm certain I'll like it."

Kate laughed merrily. "I'm going to be sure of it. I'm going to stay and watch you eat it."

"Please do," he begged.

Apparently the meal was satisfactory to both of them.

Jack swore he had never tasted anything better, and the girl's pleasure was expressed in her glowing eyes.

"You're a fine cook," he said, giving her hand a grateful squeeze.

"When do you expect to get about again?' she asked.

"Probably tomorrow. I hope so, at any rate."

"I thought a lot about you last night," she told him. He turned eagerly to her. "What did you think?"

"I was wondering why you were here, what brought you to the bush. You're not one of us, I know that."

"One of you - how-"

"You belong to a different class."

"Oh, nonsense!"

"But you do. Fellows like you don't hump their bluey just for fun. What made you do it?"

He smiled a little wanly.

"I'm sorry, but that's something I can't tell you."

"You can't trust me?"

"There are some things that are sacred. I wish could tell you, but, believe me, I can't,"

"I shouldn't have asked you, I know."

"Can't I help you?" he asked her after a pause.

"In what way?"

"When you go to Ned. I'd like to save you some of those lonely night rides. Do you know, you're the bravest girl in all the world!"

"Brave? Who wouldn't be to help her own flesh and blood? That's only natural. Oh, I wonder how long it can last? ... I wonder!"

A look of despair had crept into her eyes.

"I can help," urged Jack. "Won't you let me help you - and Ned?"

"They wouldn't let you."

"I think Ned would trust me."

"I know, I know, but - "

"I'm sorry for you. I'm sorry for all of you. Still, there might be a way out."

"Oh, if there only could be!" she cried, with a pathetic gesture of utter hopelessness.

"I wish I could talk to Ned," he said wistfully.

She hesitated for a moment. Then she said in a half-whisper, "You might have a chance tonight."

He looked at her in surprise. "Is he coming here?"

She nodded her head.

Jack's heart leapt. He longed for another meeting with the notorious outlaw. He wanted to know more of the man with whose deeds the whole country rang.

"Are you staying till he comes?" he asked with obvious eagerness.

"I've stayed too long now. Good-bye!"

As she left, Briant's thoughts again flew to the other girl - Ned's girl, whom he was so anxious to meet. Was she as attractive as Kate, he wondered.

7

A Close Call

NED KELLY coming tonight! The thought thrilled Briant as much as the presence of the outlaw's sister had pleased him.

"What's the matter with you, boy?" Jackson asked when he came in for his midday meal. "Can't you sit still ?"

Try as he might, Jack could not conceal his excitement. At last he blurted out, "I can't help it, Mr. Jackson, I'm too excited!"

"Ain't much to get excited about, sittin' still nursin' a bad foot, is there?"

"You know why it is. I know who's coming tonight!"

The old man started as though shot, and Mrs Jackson dropped a knife on her plate with a clatter.

"Did Kate tell you?" Jackson demanded.

"Yes."

The grizzled bushman and his wife exchanged glances.

The announcement seemed to stagger them.

"Oh, don't look so serious," Jack pleaded. "You ought to know by this time I'm to be trusted. If I wasn't, surely there wouldn't be much danger, with this foot of mine. If I were as anxious to capture Ned as you are to save him, I couldn't do very much in my condition, could I?"

That seemed to reassure them, and they went on with their meal. Jack noticed, however, that the old man was quieter and more thoughtful even than usual. He noted too, that the glances which Mrs. Jackson cast at him every now and then seemed to convey that there was still a doubt in her mind.

The day was interminably long to Briant, whose mind constantly was occupied by thoughts of the anticipated visitor.

Neither Jackson nor his wife appeared at all concerned.

Evidently Ned was no stranger to that humble home. They shared none of the young fellow's imaginative flights. The possibility of a police raid and a fight did not seem to occur to them. If it did their self-control was magnificent.

The hours went slowly by. As daylight gave place to dusk and dusk to darkness Jack eagerly listened for hoof-beats. Jackson sat by the fire, meditatively, puffing his blackened clay pipe, and his wife's knitting needles clicked industriously. If their expected visitor had been a farm neighbor instead of the man for whom the whole Victorian police force was searching they could not have betrayed less emotion. It was all part of the desperate game which they had learned to play so well.

A gust of cold night air smote Jack, and he looked round to see Ned Kelly quietly closing the door behind him! So silently had he entered that no one was aware of his presence until he was inside the hut.

The old couple greeted him quite casually, and Jackson moved up and made room for him on the stool on which he sat.

"It's a cold night," remarked the bushranger as he took his seat. Then he turned to Briant. "How's the ankle?"

"Getting on quite all right now, thanks," Jack replied, still wondering at the means by which even trivial news reached the gang. He noticed that Ned was less sprightly than on the occasion of their first meeting. He appeared to be tired and depressed.

A pot of stew had been simmering by the fire, and from it Mrs Jackson served a huge plateful, which the bushranger ate ravenously.

"It's good to get something hot after days of tinned stuff," he said, smacking his lips. "They've been giving us such a run lately we haven't been able to do much cooking."

Briant could not help feeling pity for this fine upstanding young Australian who was playing a losing game with Fate, and playing it bravely. He hobbled over to where the outlaw sat.

"I wish you'd let me help you, Ned," he said. "I believe I could."

"It wouldn't be good for you," Ned replied in a tired voice. "They'd get you in the end, and I wouldn't like that."

"But I could help you to get out of the country," Jack persisted.

A spark of hope lighted the bushranger's face, but it lingered just for a moment.

"That's the only way out, Ned. You can't go on like this for ever."

"No, I suppose not," he said, with a sigh.

"You're tired, Ned, you'd better put up here for the night," Mrs Jackson suggested.

"Let him have my bunk," said Jack.

"The shed is the only place he could sleep in," the old man cut in.

Briant did not appreciate the significance of that remark, but later on he understood it. He learned many things during the next few days, every-one an object lesson in the sacrifices men and women were prepared to make on behalf of a criminal hiding from justice.

"Better have a drop of brandy - you look as how you could do with it." Jackson went to the inner room for the bottle, and poured out a stiff drink.

"Not too much," Ned said, indicating his limit with his fingers. They sat silently for a while. It occurred to Jack that the bushranger and his friends had much to say, but were doubtful of the wisdom of saying it before him. So he hobbled to the door.

"I'm going over to my bunk for a while, I shan't be long."

"Better take this stick and be careful of that foot of yours," the old man said.

Jack found that his ankle gave him less trouble than he had expected. It was bitterly cold in the shed, and even the bags which he piled on him failed to keep him, warm. His improvised bed in front of the fire was preferable to this.

But what about Ned? Wasn't he as much entitled to comfort as himself? He would go across and tell them he would stick to the shed and let Ned have his place inside. He threw the bags off, and rose as quickly as his injured foot would allow.

At the door he met the outlaw and the old man. How silently these bushmen walked! He had not heard a sound of their approach.

"I was just coming over to say Ned had better stay near the fire - it's warmer than here," he told them.

"Ned can't sleep nowhere but here," Jackson replied, enigmatically.

"Why must he sleep in the shed?" he asked, as they walked back to the hut.

"'Cos it's the best place," was the reply, in a tone that made it clear that further argument was useless."

"I don't like the idea of Ned being out there, and me here," Jack said, when they had gone inside.

"Mind your own damned business!" snapped Jackson.

His wife looked significantly at Briant, who, understanding, let the matter drop.

Neither of them seemed to be in the mood to talk, so for half an hour or more, silence reigned.

"Aren't you folk going to bed?" Jack asked, at last.

"No," was Jackson's monosyllabic reply.

It was clear that, outwardly calm as the old couple appeared, they felt pretty keenly the responsibility of housing their much-pursued visitor. It looked as though they were prepared for an all-night vigil. Neither of them was inclined to talk. Occasionally the old man got up to put a fresh log on the fire. At times, Mrs Jackson permitted herself to doze.

"Listen!" Jackson jumped to his feet.

Briant's untrained ear could detect nothing for a while.

Then the sound of distant hoof-beats reached him. The dogs sat up, but made no attempt to bark. Evidently they sensed a friend in the approaching rider.

"Sound like Jennie," Mrs. Jackson remarked.

A girl rushed into the hut -- a girl with red-brown hair and blue eyes dilated by horror.

"Quick!" she cried. "The troopers are coming!"

"By God!" exclaimed Briant, trembling with excitement. "Let me tell Ned!"

The old man pushed him back into his seat, and hurried from the hut.

"Where is he?" asked the girl in anguish.

"It's all right, dear." Mrs Jackson's voice was calm and soothing. "You'd better take his horse away, though. It's at the big bluegum in the hollow. Ride to Manton's, and he'll do the rest."

In a moment she was gone.

"What about Ned, Mrs Jackson? What can we do? I can't stay here like a crippled thing and see him taken. Give me a pistol!" Jack forgot his injured ankle as he ran to where he knew a revolver was kept.

"No, no!" she cried. "Just leave it to Sam."

Jackson came back at the moment.

"The cards, Mum. Come on, boy."

A greasy pack of cards was produced from a box in, the corner, and they bade Jack draw a stool up to the table.

"Play euchre, I s'pose?" the old man said.

Briant nodded.

"Keep cool, then. They'll listen for a while before they come in."

Jackson's calmness gave Jack fresh hope, and while the old woman dealt the hands he took a stump of pencil from his pocket and scribbled three sets of figures on the table.

"Here they come now," whispered the old woman.

"You just go on playin' and it'll be all right."

The hoof-beats grew louder and suddenly stopped. "Down, dogs!" commanded Mrs Jackson, as Spot started to grow!

Jackson listened for a while, and then laughed.

"Thought you had me, did you?" he cried, as he slapped a card on the table. "You'll order me up with a hand like that, will you?"

"Well, I thought I had you well beaten," Briant responded.

"You've got to get up early to beat Dad," smiled Mrs Jackson.

"Looks like it, doesn't it?"

Another hand was dealt.

"Diamonds, is it? Pass!" said the old man.

"She's up!" cried Briant.

They played the hand, which Jack won. "Looked like a march, and I got a measly point," he grumbled. "That's two bob I owe you."

"And don't forget - one and three to me," piped Mrs Jackson's shrill treble.

The door was cautiously opened, but none of the players pretended to notice it.

"I'll get it back before long," Jack told them.

"Ha! They all say that," commented the old man.

Another hand was dealt. As Mrs Jackson picked up her cards she shivered. "The room's gettin' cold Sam. Put another - Oh!"

She dropped her cards and jumped up.

Four men came into the room - Macguire, Costello, Kenny and another trooper who was a stranger to them.

"Oi'm sorry to disturb yer plisant little game," jeered Macguire.

"Damn you!" shouted Jackson. "What d'ye mean? Look at me hand!" And he held up ace, king, queen of diamonds, ace of spades, and jack of hearts.

"Very pretty!" sneered Costello.

"What d'ye want, anyway?" the old man demanded.

"That ought to be an easy guess," laughed Kenny.

"Well, you might shut the door," Mrs Jackson complained.

The strange policeman closed it.

"Ned Kelly's here!" said Macguire.

"You'd better go and take him then!"

Briant marvelled at the coolness of this weather-beaten old bushman. He wondered what had become of Ned. Could he still be in the shed? Jackson's confidence certainly did not suggest danger to their outlawed friend, yet where could he hide? The troopers were certain to search every hole and corner.

This they proceeded to do, Jackson following in their wake. Every possible place that could conceal a man was examined, as well as many impossible places.

"Come a long way for nothin', ain't you?" quizzed the old man. None of them, apparently, could think of a suitable reply, so they remained silent. Macguire, taking Kenny with him, left the hut, remarking to the others as he went:

"Sthay here, bhoys. We'll have a look round the shid out yonder."

The shed! Jack checked the exclamation that rose to his lips and glanced at his employer, upon whom the announcement had no apparent effect, however.

Jackson picked up the cards and turned to Costello and the other trooper.

"Care for a game while you're waitin'?"

Costello merely scowled, but his companion said politely, "No, thank you."

"We don't play for big stakes," added the old man ingratiatingly.

Costello turned savagely.

"You've playing for damned high stakes, Jackson, and you're bound to lose."

Jackson pluckered his brows.

"Why, we been playin' all the even in', and none of us ain't lost more'n a bob or two."

Costello turned away disgustedly.

"What's the matter with your foot, son?" the other policeman asked Jack.

"Sprained my ankle as I was going down the gully to split posts," he replied.

"Don't you believe him, Leane!" snapped Costello.

Leane laughed.

"You don't seem inclined to believe anyone these days, Costello."

"Not this scum, anyway!"

Briant expected Jackson to flare up, but he kept his temper under wonderful control. He even smiled as he told Costello not to lose his head.

Leane turned to Jack again. "You'd better be careful of that foot. A sprain's a nasty thing if you don't look after it. When did you do it?"

"Two days ago."

"Ought to be all right tomorrow or next day, but you'd better go slow for a while."

A little later Macguire and Kenny returned, disappointment written on their faces.

"Well, did you find him?" asked Jackson.

"Not yet, but we will," declared the big Irishman.

Briant could not help noticing that, with the exception of Costello, who was still bitterly belligerent, the police had abandoned the hectoring, bullying attitude which characterised their last visit. Whatever was the reason, the change was most marked. He contrasted Macguire's hotheadedness with his present tolerant, almost genial, conduct.

He wondered what had become of Ned. Was there some specially constructed hiding place where he could secrete himself until danger had passed? And the girl they called Jennie? Had she got the horses safely to Manton's? Who was she? he wondered.

He cursed the injury which had made him so helpless at a time when he could have rendered her some real service.

The troopers did not wait much longer. As they left the old man bared his tobacco-stained teeth.

"It'll be lonely ridin' back tonight, specially without Ned," he jeered. "P'r'aps by and by you'll learn sense and leave me be."

"Oh, go to hell!" cried Costello, as he slammed the door.

Before the old couple went to bed Jack asked them who the girl was.

"Jennie O'Donnell," replied Jackson shortly. "Is she - is she the girl they say Ned – "

"Mind your own damned business!" snapped the old man, as he knocked the ashes out of his pipe.

8

A Traitor

BRIANT slept badly that night. The terror in the girl's eyes seemed to haunt him. He could not get her out of his mind. He hoped that she was not Ned's mysterious helper, because she appeared to be too young and attractive to be associated with impending tragedy. When eventually he fell asleep he dreamt that the police had captured Ned, and from another dream he awoke to find himself wrestling with the bags that covered him in the belief that they were Macguire.

He awoke again with a light-shining in his eyes, and sat up. Ned Kelly was at the table eating with evident relish the food which Mrs Jackson piled on to his plate.

"It's good to see you're all right, Ned," Jack remarked, getting up. "It was a close shave last night. When the troopers came, I thought it was all up with you. It scared hell out of me. Look here, Ned, why don't you let me go with you? You said you were tired of eating tinned stuff. I used to be pretty good at making snares when I was a youngster, and I could easily catch wallabies and birds. I'm sure I could find a way of cooking them without showing the smoke."

Ned hesitated, and for a moment it seemed to Briant that his offer would be accepted. But the bushranger shook his head.

"We'd like to have you, but it's better not."

Jack pleaded with him, but he could not be shaken.

"All right, you'll find me there one of these days, whether you want me or not."

"Why are you so anxious to help us?" the outlaw asked.

"Because I don't think you've had a fair deal. You've got to get away, Ned. You'll have to leave the country. My people used to be interested in shipping, and I know a skipper who'd take you I could go to Melbourne and fix it up."

It was evident that the bushranger was impressed by the scheme. For a while he sat in deep thought, chin on hand. Then he rose from the table.

"What about it?" asked Jack, eagerly.

"No, not yet!"

There was something discouraging in his tone, and Briant inwardly cursed him for his obstinacy.

Dawn was breaking when the bushranger left the hut. At the slip-rails Jackson was holding a magnificent brown gelding, which whinnied at Ned's approach. Who had brought it there? Had Jennie taken it to Manton's, stayed there all night, and led it over in the early hours of the morning? After exchanging a few words with Jackson, Kelly mounted and rode away through the bush.

The old couple had another visitor that day. Tom Stevens, the little bearded man who accompanied Manton on the night of the rumpus with the police. He came astride a huge piebald mare, and cut such a comical figure that Jack could not help laughing.

"'Day, Sam; 'day, Mum; 'day, boy," he greeted them. When he had dismounted he took Jackson aside and talked earnestly with him for several minutes. What he said evidently impressed the old man, who beckoned to his wife. Jack heard only a few scraps of the conversation between the trio, but one sentence amazed him - "Jacobson ain't square!"

If that meant that he was working with the police while professing friendship for the gang, the news certainly was alarming. An idea came to Briant's mind.

"I couldn't help hearing what you said about Jacobson," he told them. "I think I can see how we can beat him. If I could get a job with him I could keep my ears open, and perhaps upset his little game. What do you think?"

"Good idea!" exclaimed Stevens.

"You'd have to be mighty careful," Jackson said.

"Jacobson's as cunnin' as a dingo! By gum! I believe he'd take you. Alec Anderson, his man, broke his leg last week, and 'as gone away to the hospital. It's worth tryin'. If he don't take you, you could come back here."

And so it was arranged. Jack hated parting with the strange old couple with whom he had spent such an exciting time, especially as Mrs Jackson's lip quivered when she gave him her thin, calloused hand at the sliprails.

"I ain't got much money to pay you for what you've done," Jackson said.

"Don't worry about that," Briant laughed, showing him the notes which he had taken from his hiding place in the shed. "I'm quite a man of means. By the way, Mr. Jackson, I'd like you to mind three or four pounds for me."

Before the old man quite realised what had happened he had thrust four notes into his hand, swung his swag across his shoulder, and with a cheery "Good-bye and good luck!" passed through the fence.

Once more on the wallaby! What tricks would Fortune play on him now? he wondered.

He was gratified to find that his ankle no longer troubled him. All the same, he helped it as much as possible by the aid of a stick. Two miles along the road he overtook another tramp, a young man whose chin carried a week's stubble, and whose swag seemed awkwardly placed.

"Good day, mate," he said. "Where you bound?"

"Anywhere there's a bit of work," Jack responded.

"Where've you come from?"

"Beechworth. Things dead here. What with these Kellys about, everybody's got the jumps, and they don't give you no chance."

As they walked along, Briant carefully studied the stranger, whose hands were not those of the usual swagman. Neither had he the easy gait of a man used to footing it long distances.

The tramp plied him with questions. Where had he come from? What sort of people were the Jackson's? Why had he left them?

"I got full of them," Briant confessed. "Nearly every day there was some fuss with the police."

"The police? Why?"

"Oh, they think they're Kelly sympathisers, and lay all kinds of traps for 'em."

"Are they Kelly sympathisers?"

Jack laughed.

"Hell of a lot o' good they'd be to the gang. Why, they don't have enough to eat themselves, let alone- "

"But they might help other ways, givin' information and tellin' the gang when the police is about."

"They're too stupid for that. Darned if I know how they live in that God-forsaken place."

"I s'p'ose you never seen any of the gang while you was there?"

"Me? Huh! If Ned or Dan or any of 'em showed up you wouldn't see me for dust! I don't want to stop a bullet."

They trudged on in silence for a while. Then Jack asked, "Any chance of a job round these parts, I wonder? P'r'aps we could strike some thin' together."

"Not me!" said the tramp. "I'm beatin' it for Melbourne-got a sister down there what keeps a pub. Reckon it's up to her to do somethin' for me."

"You're lucky. I've got no relatives, least I don't know of any. I'm glad to get a crust and a shake-down where I can."

"Poor devil!" muttered his companion.

"Who lives over there?" asked Jack, pointing to a house surrounded by fruit trees that stood back some distance from the track.

"Ja - I don't know," answered the tramp.

"I'm goin' to try him out," Briant announced.

"You might as well try, you never know your luck. Say, when did you 'ave a shave last?"

Jack's hand went to his smooth chin. "This morning. Always carry a razor and a bit o' soap. Habit I got into."

"Funny. Well, so long mate! Hope they fix you up."

"So long," returned Briant as he climbed through the fence.

A dog sprang at him as he approached the house, but a youthful voice shouted, "Come here, Ding!" and immediately it left him, turning once or twice to show its teeth.

Jacobson's house was much more pretentious than Jackson's, in fact, it had quite an air of comfort about it. In one of the windows a miscellaneous collection of goods was displayed, and Briant then realised that its owner was a storekeeper as well as a farmer - though heaven only knew where customers came from in that sparsely settled district.

The front of the house was of weatherboard, and the back portion .of slabs, pierced together with arresting accuracy. A few flowers grew along the path and a vivid creeper trailed itself about the verandah.

As Jack went to walk round the side of the house a girl came out on the front verandah and smiled at him.

"Are you looking for Father?" she asked. "He's gone over to the scrub paddock. He shouldn't be long."

She was a pretty youngster of about 17 or 18, with blue eyes and fair hair. Her rough clothes were neater than those of most of the country girls he had met.

"I did want to see your 'father. Mr Jacobson, isn't he? I heard that your man had broken his leg, and I thought that possibly I could take his place. I'm looking for a job, you know."

"Father does want a man, but I don't know whether you could do the rough work."

Jack laughed.

"Oh, I'm used to rough work. Hadn't you better go inside? Your father wouldn't like to see you talking to a swaggie."

"I don't think you're a swaggie," she smiled at him.

"I assure you that I am. Don't I look like one?" indicating his tattered clothes.

The girl hesitated. "Well, I'm - I'm afraid, you do!"

"I shouldn't like you to get a dressing down on my account."

She showed her glistening teeth again.

"Oh, Father isn't such a bear as all that."

"Julie!" came a voice from inside the house.

"Oh, bother! That's my sister Nita."

Another girl appeared in the doorway, and jack thought her the most attractively capable girl he had ever seen, for he invariably associated feminine cleverness with a homely exterior. It was not so much her regular features, fine skin and abundant hair that impressed him as the frankness of her deep grey eyes and the confident poise of her head.

Without knowing why, Jack contrasted her with Jennie O'Donnell, whose appearance at Jackson's had been so dramatic. This girl seemed to be of a more heroic type.

The girl studied jack appraisingly before asking:

"Who's this man, and what does he want?"

Briant tried her with an ingratiating smile.

"I'm looking for work, Miss. I hear your man has left you."

"My father ought to be' back soon. Julie, run' and look at that cake."

Reluctantly the younger girl obeyed.

"Are you from Sam Jackson's?" The question astonished Briant.

Little that went on in those parts seemed to be unknown to the neighbors or was she merely guessing?

"What makes you think that?"

The ghost of a smile hovered round her lips.

"We don't often have your kind of tramp. I heard Jackson had a city fellow working for him, and it doesn't take two looks at you to see this isn't your regular game."

"I'm sorry if I'm a misfit," he laughed.

"There's Father coming now," she said, as she hurried inside.

Jack walked to 'the gate to meet him.

Jacobson was a man on the sunny side of fifty, a type which was difficult to classify, whether German, Scandinavian, or partly Jew. His eyes were blue, his cheekbones high, and his hair and whiskers' black and streaked with grey.

Jack lost no time in telling him why he was there.

"So you got tired of Sam Jackson's, did you? I don't wonder at that, either. Get any money out of him?"

"Not a penny."

"More fool you to work for his sort. I don't know if you're the kind of man I want, but I don't mind giving you a trial. Eight bob and keep. That's more than you'd get from Jackson if you stayed with him for twenty years" - as he noticed Briant's hesitancy. "Take it or leave it."

"I suppose beggars can't be choosers. I'll take it."

"Right. Go round to the kitchen, and the girls'll get you a bite to eat."

"Are you going to work for us?" asked Julie, with heightened color, as he appeared at the kitchen door.

"Your father has given me a job, and says I may have something to eat."

"I do hope you will stay," remarked the elder girl.

"It will be a pleasant change to hear the Queen's English again."

During the meal he learned from Nita something of the family history. They had lived in Melbourne until five years ago, when, shortly after her mother's death, they had come here. There was something more than the loss of his wife that had sent her father outback, but he would never speak of it. She did not know that it concerned some transaction in which he had lost most of his money.

"And you don't appreciate the change?" Jack ventured.

Nita shrugged her shoulders significantly.

"Father's trying to get back," Julie told him, "but it isn't so easy. He can't sell, except at a big loss. No one seems to want to buy anything."

"On account of the Kellys, I suppose?" Briant suggested.

"I suppose so," said Julie.

"Do you ever see anything of them?"

Nita hesitated. "Kate comes here occasionally to buy things. Joe Byrne and Steve Hart rode by one day last week.

"That was pretty daring, wasn't it, with the police scouring the country?"

"Perhaps it was. What do you think of the whole business?"

"What do you mean?"

"About the Kellys. Are you a sympathiser, like most of the people about here?"

"I'm not sure." His reply was hesitating, and she looked sharply at him. "There are so many things to consider," he added. "I'm a stranger, but you people who are familiar with everything can form a better idea. I don't think Miss Julie here, for instance, would like to see any harm come to them."

Julie did not reply, but she flushed and turned her head away, and Jack knew that his chance shot had not missed.

Nita would be a much more difficult proposition, he knew that. She was more sophisticated. He tried a feeler.

"What a life those poor devils must lead!"

"It must be terrible!" she agreed.

"And there can only be one end."

With a sigh that was half a sob, Julie left the room.

Nita's face was still Sphinxlike. "You mean that the police will get them?"

"There's nothing surer, unless they clear out of the country. That's their only chance."

"Yes, I suppose so."

Obviously, Nita was a very clever girl who had no intention of betraying her feelings to this pleasant young stranger.

"It must be a hard job to keep them in food," Jack hazarded.

"They seem to have lots of friends, and the police can't be everywhere at the same time."

"That's true, but it's a risky business, all the same. It's a pretty serious offence to harbor outlaws - it means 15 years' gaol."

He thought she started slightly, but there was no change in her voice as she replied:

"And yet there are plenty who .are willing to take the risk."

"One can't help admiring their loyalty even if it might be misplaced."

"Do you think it misplaced?"

"As I said before, I don't know. I don't know all the facts like you people do."

A broad-shouldered young fellow of about 20 came in and flung himself wearily into a chair.

"Hell! I'm tired!" he said.

"Poor old chap!" Nita ran her fingers through his long, thick hair.

"This is my brother, Frank," turning to Jack. "Your name's Jack Briant, isn't it?"

Jack nodded.

Frank shot a quick glance at him. "Come from Sam Jackson's, don't you?"

"I was there for a day or two."

"Tough old cove!"

'Yes but I suppose you can't wonder at it. The police have been leading him a merry dance lately."

Frank frowned, but made no comment.

9

A Kiss in the Dark

JACK found life at Jacobson's pleasant. His job - stacking wood, preparatory to carting it into Benalla was hard, and his back ached badly after the first day of it, but his sleeping quarters, just away from the house, were comfortable, the food good, and he enjoyed the company of the two girls. Frank was inclined to be morose.

His new employer let him know that he was the first hired hand he had ever permitted to meal with the family, and Jack expressed his gratitude. During the first two day's Jacobson had hardly mentioned the Kellys. If old Tom Stevens's suspicions were justified, it was evident that he intended to make absolutely certain of his employe's feeling before acting.

One day, when Briant came home for the midday meal Julie was playing the tinkly piano that constituted the proudest possession of the Jacobson homestead. When she came into the kitchen he complimented her upon her performance.

"I would have taken that cantabile passage just a trifle slower," he said.

Big-eyed, she exclaimed, "Oh, do you play?"

"Well, I used to."

"Then do play something."

"Your father mightn't like it."

"If he catches you, he'll never let you stop. He's music mad, isn't he, Nita?"

"Just about."

Julie took Jack's hand and pulled him from his chair.

"You must play."

He laughed.

"You'll be sorry. I haven't touched a piano for months, and my fingers are as stiff as crowbars."

His first attempt was marred by many blunders. "There you are," he laughed, getting up from the instrument. "I told you what it'd be like."

Julie smilingly pushed him back.

"You'll soon get into the swing of it."

"All right, if you can stand it I can."

Gradually Briant's fingers loosened up, and in a little while the house was filled with the melodic wonders of Bach, Beethoven, Mozart and Liszt. Julie sat enraptured, and Nita gave up her cooking to listen.

Jacobson came in, looked inquiringly at his two daughters, and then slipped into a seat. His hard, set expression gradually softened, and his glowing eyes and parted lips bespoke the enjoyment he was deriving. At the end of a crashing crescendo Jack turned round. As he saw his employer he rose from the stool, but Jacobson waved him back.

"More!" he commanded.

Briant played on and on, until his fingers ached. Then he begged to be allowed to stop.

His employer thumped him on the back.

"You are a fine musician, boy Briant. You must play for us tonight."

Thus Jack was accepted as one of the family. Jacobson provided him with a new outfit, which gave him the much appreciated luxury of a change of clothes when his work was done.

He was being treated so well that the thought that he had come there as a spy hurt him. So far he had not discovered anything suspicious in Jacobson's movements, although his employer was absent most of the day. Once, returning unexpectedly, Jack saw leaving the house a man who looked very much like the tramp he had encountered on the road. On another occasion a horseman, obviously a trooper, rode away as he came home in the evening.

Briant tried several times to ascertain Nita's feelings, but she refused to commit herself. He fancied her eyes softened at the mention of Ned Kelly's name. When he told her what had occurred when Jennie O'Donnell had burst into Jackson's hut, her lips trembled.

"Who is Jennie O'Donnell?" he asked.

"A girl who lives over near Sheoak Creek," she answered.

"Is she anything to Ned Kelly?"

'Nita remained silent, but her eyes showed that she resented the question. He did not pursue the topic.

The simple heart of Julie, he knew, was full of admiration for the outlaws. Frank was an enigma. At times he seemed to be quite dull, but at other times there was a craftiness about his expression that warned Jack to be on his guard.

One evening a young man on a horse that appeared to be nearly knocked up pulled up at Jacobson's gate. "That's Steve Hart!" Julie told Briant, her voice vibrant with excitement.

As Hart went into the little shop Jack followed him.

The bushranger turned sharply to Jacobson, "Who's this?"

"He's all right - working for me," Jacobson assured him.

The two young men took careful stock of each other.

Jack saw a thin-faced boy a few years younger than himself. His chin had not seen a razor for some days, and his stubbly cheeks served to accentuate the deep lines under his piercing dark eyes. He leaned heavily against the rough counter of the shop.

Julie looked through the window. Hart's eyes met hers and her head inclined, ever so slightly. Then she disappeared.

"You've been riding hard," Jack remarked."

''Pretty hard."

"Your nag looks a bit done up."

"Yes."

It was clear that the young bushranger was disinclined to talk. He bought some tobacco and matches, and a few other trifles from Jacobson, and left the shop without a word.

"He doesn't look too fit, does he?" Jack commented. Jacobson watched him mount before replying, "Can't expect anything else."

"I say, Mr. Jacobson, isn't it an offence to serve an outlaw?"

"What's that?"

"There's a pretty heavy penalty for helping the gang."

"And there's a pretty heavy penalty if you don't!" retorted Jacobson, with a trace of bitterness in his tone.

"You mean they might cut up rough if you refused to serve them?"

"That's it."

Steve Hart rode along the track to where a giant gum, struck by lightning, had crashed to earth, smashing several lesser trees in its descent. There he halted, and looked carefully round him. Going over to the fallen monarch, he lifted a parcel, carefully wrapped in brown paper, from the heart of the splintered trunk. Quickly remounting, he half turned in the saddle. Several hundred yards away from the edge of the clearing, a white handkerchief fluttered. He waved his hat in reply, then spurred his horse into a gallop.

After tea that evening Jack asked his employer if he would mind if he took one of the horses, as Jackson had promised him some of his wages if he came back in a week.

"You can have the horse, but you won't get any money," Jacobson told him.

"Could I come, too?" asked Nita; "I'd love a ride through the bush tonight."

"I'd be delighted to have you," returned Jack, biting back the refusal that rose to his lips. He would be glad of her company, but her presence might prove awkward. He was anxious to know how the old couple were faring, and, more important still, he was eager for news of Ned and Kate.

"You don't seem very keen on having me," remarked the girl, with a pretty pout, as they rode between the trees.

"Don't say that, Nita, you know it isn't true."

"Well, you didn't jump at my offer."

Briant paused.

"It was so, so unexpected, you know. It isn't often that the daughter of the house suggests riding with the hired man - and a tramp at that."

"Don't be silly, Jack. You know you're not a tramp, and as for being a hired man, you're miles above us. I do wish you'd tell me why you ran away."

"Who said I ran away?"

"Well, why you came to the bush, if you like it better that way"

"Well, if you must know, and you'll promise to keep it a deadly secret - I murdered my wife and seven children!"

She laughed merrily. "Try again."

"I drowned my mother-in-law in her bath water!"

"And again."

"I stole the babies' rattles from an orphanage!"

Nita did not laugh this time. Instead, she said a little bitterly, "I suppose it was trouble over some girl."

He reached over and put his hand on hers.

"Do I look the sort of fellow who'd bother very much about girls?"

She pulled her hand away. "I don't know."

They rode in silence for a while. Then he said:

"You're a plucky girl, Nita, risking a ride with a stranger like me. Supposing I was a bold, bad man and ran away with you!"

"No one is ever likely to do that," she replied, a little wistfully.

"Hundreds of fellows would like the chance!"

She lapsed into silence again, and as they approached Jackson's he thought of the last ride he had had over that track, when he had sat behind Kate Kelly, a helpless cripple. He contrasted her with the girl who now rode by his side, and wondered what prompted him to do so.

Jackson's dogs ran out barking to meet them, then gave vent to joyful yelps of recognition as Briant dismounted.

"Good doggies!" he cried as they fawned on him.

"I like you all the better for that," Nita said.

He smiled.

"Dogs make mistakes sometimes."

"Hardly ever."

Jack was curious to see what sort of reception Jacobson's daughter would get from the Jacksons. To his surprise they greeted her most cordially.

"I'm going to make a cup of tea, dearie," said the old woman. "You're just in time."

"But we've not long had a big meal," the girl protested. "Never mind-a cup o' tea's always welcome after a ride."

Jack took a long time tying up the horses, long enough to enable him to get the recent news from Sam Jackson.

"Steve Hart called for a few minutes this afternoon, and Kate was here again. She was asking about you."

"What did she say?"

"She said she'd rather you wasn't at Jacobson's."

"I wonder why?"

"You never know, just a woman's fad, maybe."

"I'm supposed to come over here for my wages," Jack told him with a laugh. It was the only excuse I could think of for coming."

"Then I'll give you them notes you told me to mind - in front of Nita."

"No, I want you to have that money, Mr. Jackson, I really don't need it."

The old man shook his head. A sudden idea came to Jack.

"Then get something that will help Ned."

"Well, I might do that," Jackson agreed with some reluctance. "Has Jacobson showed his hand yet?"

"Not yet, I'm beginning to think Tom Stevens was mistaken. They're a queer family. Julie's a whole-souled sympathiser, but I can't place Frank and Nita."

"That gal's as deep as the sea."

"Have the police' troubled you since?"

"Not since the night Ned was here."

"Mr. Jackson," said Briant earnestly, "I'd give something to know where Ned hid that night."

"Maybe I'll tell you sometime, maybe not," answered the old man as he led the way inside.

Mrs Jackson and Nita were chatting gaily; the old woman's face lighted with pleasure, for with the exception of Kate Kelly and her sister, female visitors came rarely to the little bark humpy by Sheoak Creek.

Jack led the conversation into the usual channel.

"You'd better be very careful, Mr Jackson," Nita said. "The police have sworn to get you."

"Police can't get me for nothin'!" he retorted, "no more than they can get your own father!"

She caught her breath sharply, and Jackson looked meaningly at his wife.

They talked about Ned Kelly and his gang, ventured opinions as to how they were provisioned, how they were warned of danger, and whether it was possible to hold out much longer. Mr and Mrs Jackson talked quite dispassionately, as though the outlaws had merely a passing interest for them, Nita was convincingly impersonal, and Jack, enjoying the battle of wits, made only a chance remark now and then. Whenever he mentioned Jennie O'Donnell, however, they always changed the subject.

The old man produced a pound note from his pocket.

"I'm sorry I had to keep you waitin' for your wages, boy, but here's somethin' to go on with."

Jack hesitated; but, remembering the announced object of his visit, and noting the look in Jackson's eyes, took it.

"Thanks very much, Mr Jackson," he said, as he put it in his pocket.

When they were riding home Nita remarked:

"Old Sam's pretty generous with his wages, isn't he?"

You were there only about a week, and he gave you a pound and apologised because it wasn't more."

Remembering her father's offer, and his acceptance of less than half of that, Jack could think of no suitable reply.

"Queer old stick, Sam," she continued.

"Yes," he agreed, without looking at her.

When the moon rose above the hills and filled the tree-lined track with glowing lanes of silver, Nita halted her horse. "What a night!" she exclaimed. "What a night to ride on, and on, to adventure, to hope, to peril, to love, to riches - to death - to everything that lies beyond!"

This was a new Nita, and Jack gazed wonderingly at her.

"God! If it were only possible!" She said it half to herself as she urged her horse forward.

A bit farther on she warned him to mind the hole into which her horse had nearly stumbled on the way out. The veil of romance had dropped from her, and she was herself again, subtle and baffling.

Few words passed between them for the rest of the journey. Both seemed to be absorbed in their own thoughts.

When they stood near the door, she looked up at him. There was an irresistible challenge in those shining eyes and parted lips. He crushed her to him and kissed her.

10

A Joke on the Police

WHATEVER Nita's feeling were, she was coldly unemotional when she greeted him at breakfast next morning. When Julie referred to the ride she quickly changed the subject, as though it was insufficiently important for discussion.

Macguire, Costello and Leane came to Jacobson's that day, and Jacobson rode away with them into the bush. At Eleven Mile Creek, within a mile of the Kelly homestead, they halted. From the hill there was a clear view of the shack rendered famous by the Fitzpatrick incident - the episode which made outlaws of Ned and Dan Kelly and opened up a chapter in Australian criminology which for dramatic interest had no parallel.

There were two versions of that incident. Fitzpatrick's was that when he went to arrest Dan on a charge of horse-stealing he was shot in the wrist by Ned and hit over the head with a shovel by Mrs. Kelly. The Kellys' story was that the mother of the outlaws advised her son not to go unless the policeman could produce a warrant, that Fitzpatrick then became abusive, that Dan tricked him into looking in another direction, took his revolver from him; emptied it and returned it. They declared that the trooper's slight wound was self-inflicted.

In spite of Fitzpatrick's reputation for drunkenness and unreliability, his story was believed, and Mrs. Kelly and two men who were present were sent to gaol. Ned and Dan disappeared, and the Government offered a reward of £200 for their arrest. After the shooting of the police at Stringybark Creek, it was increased to £2000.

Macguire scraped away the leaves and mould, and with a stick drew a plan, pausing every now and then to give emphasis to some strategic point.

The others studied it closely, all except Costello, who through a pair of powerful glasses had been watching the Kelly home.

"By God, there's one of them there now - it looks like Dan!" he exclaimed, hastily mounting.

A man had come out of the hut, and, shading his eyes with his hand, scanned the horizon from every point of the compass. A chestnut horse was tethered to a post nearby.

"We'll get him this time, for sure!" gloated Macguire.

"Jacobson, roide like the divil to beyant Quinn's, where ye'll foind Kenny and Martin. Till them to come in from the north."

Jacobson set spurs to his horse and galloped away through the trees. The three troopers separated.

"Shoot if ye've a moind to," was the big Irishman's parting injunction.

Heedless of the approaching danger, the man made no effort to conceal himself. He rubbed down his horse and tightened its girth-straps. Then he drew a bucket of water from the well and carried it inside. He reappeared as the thunder of horses' hoofs, approaching from four sides, reached his ears. A moment later he was confronted by four men with levelled revolvers.

"Hands up, Dan Kelly!" shouted Macguire. "We've got you now!"

'Dan' threw off 'his' hat, and a mass of dark hair fell on 'his' shoulders. The smiling face of Mrs Skillion greeted them!

"What's your hurry?" she asked.

For a while the baffled troopers were dumb with rage. "We've got visitors again, Kate," Mrs Skillion called, and Kate, laughing merrily, came to the door.

"What are yer doin' in Dan's clothes?" Macguire demanded.

"Just what Oi loike, Misther Macguire," she replied, imitating his brogue.

"Oi can arrist yez for thatI"

"Oh, don't be a fool!" said Leane. "They've tricked us, and there's nothing more to be said."

"There's much more to be said!" shouted Macguire.

"Yes, but not here. Come on!"

As they rode away, Kate called after them.

"Next time, don't let the sun shine on your stirrup irons. We can see it a mile away."

The discomfited police rode straight to Jacobson's.

He had taken a short cut home and arrived a few minutes before them.

"I don't want you to be seen too much round here," Jacobson told them. "You never know who's spying."

After some further talk Kenny went inside, and the others rode away.

"How's the boy shaping?" asked the trooper, when they were seated.

"I can't quite make him out - yet. He went to Jackson's last night."

"Ah!"

"But only for the money the old man owed him. And Nita went with him."

"What did she go for?"

"Don't know - said she would like the ride."

"Queer."

"I can't see anything queer about it," retorted Jacobson hotly.

"Well, well, perhaps not. Bill Ellis says he saw the gang ride into the ranges back of Cleggett's yesterday, and they looked pretty done up."

"I don't know about Bill," said Jacobson, doubtfully.

"He's all right," Kenny assured him. "What's that?"

"Only the wind," replied Jacobson, pointing to the window. It was not the wind, but his daughter, Nita, who had listened to the whole of the conversation. As Kenny rose to look out she tiptoed round the house.

"You're getting jumpy, Kenny," Jacobson remarked.

"It's no wonder," admitted the trooper, as he resumed his seat. "Old Josh Herman was stuck up near his place last night, and robbed of £4. He was coming back from Greta after selling a horse. Young fellow, he said."

"Mightn't have been any of the Kellys."

"Who else could it have been?"

"Why ask me? There's been a good deal of sticking up lately, and the Kellys can't be everywhere at once."

"If young Briant could only get out of Jackson when Ned's coming again we'd be right," mused the trooper. "The rest of the gang'd soon give in once we got Ned."

"Why don't you suggest it to him?"

Jacobson paced the floor irritably. "I tell you I'm not sure of him yet. You leave that to me. It'd be a damn sight better if your mob used their heads a bit more, instead of leaving it to other people."

"Oh, you needn't get shirty!" Kenny complained, "we're doing our best. I thought we could rely on you to fix things with Briant, but you don't seem- "

"I tell you I'll do that in my own good time," snapped Jacobson. "Now I'm going to do a bit of work for myself. Wasted enough of the day as it is."

Jacobson had an ugly temper and, as Kenny wished to avoid an open rupture with him, he said, as he was leaving:

"We appreciate all you're doing and we believe we're going to get them through your help. At times one gets… impatient, though."

Over the rise Jack and Frank were stacking wood. As usual, Frank was disinclined to talk. "Briant, what's on your mind?"

His companion wheeled round. "What d'you mean?"

"You seem to be brooding over something. Not worrying about the Kellys are you?"

"Damn the Kellys! I'm sick of the sound of their name. Kelly! Kelly! Kelly! It's Kelly from morning till night."

"Well, that's not surprising, is it?"

Frank did not reply.

A little later Jack asked him: "What would you do if you could lift the two-thousand reward, Frank?"

His eyes gleamed greedily as he replied: "Get out o' here tomorrow I"

"You don't like the bush, then?"

"Like it? Who does? I'm getting out, too, Won't be long before I break away."

"What about your father and sisters?"

"The old man may stays – if he wants to; and, and - you can look after Nita."

Resentfully Jack asked: "What do you mean by that?"

"Well, you're sweet on her, ain't you?"

"You're imagining things, Frank. Look here; if you're so keen on getting away, why don't you try for that reward?"

The other laughed bitterly.

"Nice chance I'd have, wouldn't I? I've got a better way than that."

"Is that what made you so late last night?"

It was a chance remark, but it had an extraordinary effect. Frank, with wide-staring eyes, jumped at Jack and seized him by the throat.

"I'll kill you for that," he hissed.

Briant had difficulty in releasing his vice-like grip, and flinging him from him.

"You fool!" he cried. "I've a damned good mind- "

To his surprise, Frank, with bowed head and hands hanging limply at his sides, turned on his heel, and walked slowly into the bush.

"Well, I'm jiggered!" exclaimed Jack, as he returned to his work.

Briant reviewed that incident many times during the day. At the midday meal, for which Frank was late, he remarked to Nita that her brother did not seem to be himself.

"He's himself all right, only more so," she answered.

"Frank's a queer fish, and no one can get very close to him."

"A girl?" Briant ventured.

"I'm not sure. Julie says he's infatuated with Kate Kelly."

"Is that so?" remarked Briant wryly.

"Kate's a fine girl in many ways, don't you think so?"

"Well, how can I tell? I've never--"

"You needn't lie," she said, with a trace of annoyance in her voice. "Everyone knows that Kate helped you back to Jackson's when you sprained your ankle."

"Isn't it possible for anything to happen in these parts without the whole countryside knowing it?" he queried.

"It isn't, when it concerns anybody even remotely connected with the Kellys. You didn't answer me. What is your opinion of Kate Kelly?"

"A brave girl - one of the bravest."

"Is that all?"

"Well, she's very attractive."

"Did you find her so?"

He looked at her wonderingly.

"Just what are you driving at, Nita?"

"Oh, er - nothing!" she replied with averted face, as she left the room.

When he returned from work in the evening Nita greeted him with smiles: At the table she outdid Julie's gaiety, and even induced Frank to laugh. Jack recalled old Jackson's words, "That gal's as deep as the sea!"

As Nita ran forward, Frank pulled the trigger.

11

Treachery

CURIOUSLY, Briant was wondering whether Jacobson was as crooked as Tom Stevens declared, when his employer asked him into the front room, Nita and Julie were clearing the table, and Frank had gone over to the horses.

"Supposing you had a chance to earn the Kelly reward, would you take it?"

Jack was rather nonplussed by the directness of the question. He had expected Jacobson to spar around a bit.

"Two thousand's a big lump of money, yet- "

"Yet what?"

"It's blood money."

Jacobson's face twitched.

"It is in a way, but someone's going to get it."

Jack laughed. "Are you suggesting that I might be able to capture the Kellys?"

"No, but you could help to trap them."

"I'm not sure that I want to trap them."

"Why not? They're outlaws and murderers."

"Not murderers."

"Didn't they kill Kennedy, Scanlon and Lonergan at Stringybark Creek?"

"Yes, but they wouldn't have shot them if the police had surrendered. They only wanted their horses, food and ammunition."

"Who told you that yarn?" Jacobson demanded.

"I heard it all the way up from Seymour."

"Well, they'll swing for it, anyway."

"I hope not!"

Jacobson gasped. "You don't mean- "

"I mean that Ned Kelly's too good a man for the gallows."

"Lots of people think that way," mused Jacobson, "but after what he's done he can't dodge it. You must admit that."

"I'm afraid so - unless he can get out of the country."

"How is he going to do that?" "I don't know."

Twice Jacobson was about to speak, but each time something stopped him. Then, bending over and grasping Jack's shoulder in a grip that hurt, he said tensely:

"I want part of that reward, boy, and you can help me to get it!"

Briant remained silent.

"I want the money to get away from this damned hole. I want my girls to have something better than this. They're young and need life. I want it, too. This is eating my heart out. Won't you help me, boy?"

Briant shuddered at the proposition and at the callousness of the man who made it. Jacobson and his family were tired of the bush, and this was the desperate way out!

Jack's first impulse was to ram the traitorous words back in his employer's throat, but he realised he would gain nothing by that, except self-satisfaction. If Jacobson was a Judas, obviously the best way to serve Ned was to watch him. If he continued to appear friendly he might learn a lot. If he broke with him and went back to Jackson's he would have little opportunity of knowing what was going on here.

"You'll help me, won't you?" pleaded Jacobson, mistaking the reason for Jack's silence.

"How can I help?"

"Play up to Kate Kelly. You stand pretty well with her, I know."

How he hated his employer for that suggestion! His fingers itched to get at him. But he controlled himself and replied: "I don't know that I do. But in any case Kate is too clever a girl to be tricked by me. What's your scheme?"

"We know Ned visits the old home, but of course we –"

"We?"

A guilty flush mounted Jacobson's cheek.

"I mean the police, of course. Well, as I was saying, no one knows when he's coming. Naturally, the police can't watch one spot every night."

"No, I suppose not."

"Kate must have a good idea when he's coming - he lets her know in some way. If you could find out, the rest'd be easy."

Briant's brain was working fast.

"But I can't go to Kate without some excuse."

"A good-looking young fellow doesn't need much excuse for calling on an attractive girl like Kate. You could fix that."

The idea was so repulsive that Jack found it hard to conceal his disgust. There was one aspect that appealed to him, however, and he asked Jacobson for further detaiis.

"Suppose you ride across tomorrow afternoon, and see what you can find out?"

To this Jack agreed.

"Leaving 'work pretty' early, ain't 'you?" remarked Frank next day, as Jack picked up his coat.

"Yes; got to go a message." Young Jacobson scowled.

"Why the hell didn't they ask me to take it?"

"I don't know," Briant lied, as he left him.

Jack's brain was in a whirl as he rode towards Eleven Mile Creek.

As luck would have it, Kate was alone. She greeted him cordially and asked him inside.

"You look worried?" she remarked.

"I am worried," he confessed. "Any decent fellow would be worried if he lived under the same roof as a traitor."

Wide-eyed, she gripped his wrist. "Jacobson?"

He nodded.

"We've been suspicious of him for some time. Tell me how you found out."

He told her the whole wretched story, "For God's sake," he added, "don't tell Ned. I don't want anything to happen."

She faced him with blazing eyes.

"Nothing to happen to a dog like that?"

"I know he deserves it, but it wouldn't do any good. Can't you see, Kate, it wouldn't help Ned if he revenged himself on Jacobson."

"It'd be one skunk out of the way, at any rate," she cried between her clenched teeth.

Neither spoke for some time. Then she said: "You're right, it wouldn't help."

"Couldn't the boys take advantage of the police being here?" Briant suggested. "They could go somewhere else that night."

The idea pleased her. "They could. There's lots of things they want at – at somewhere else. It'd be a fine chance to get them. What are you smiling at?"

"Only at the 'somewhere else.' Still a bit distrustful of me, are you, Kate?"

"Of course, I'm not. What's that?" she asked, going to the door. "I thought I heard a horse."

She came back to him.

"Tell Jacobson the boys are coming Friday night. Oh!"

"What's the matter?"

"How do you stand? What'll they do when they don't find them? They'll blame you."

He laughed her fears away.

"Don't worry your pretty head about that. I'll find a way between this and then: I wish I could help more than this," he continued, with a grave face. "There's only one way - they've got to leave the country. And Ned says he can't just yet."

"Ned knows best," she said, with simple faith.

She made tea, and as they drank it, she inquired how Jacobson's suited him.

"Apart from this miserable business, very well."

"What do you think of Nita?"

The question surprised him. It was the same as Nita had put to him concerning herself.

"Nita's a very nice girl, but hard to understand. Don't you think so?"

"Perhaps a little, but you'll get to know her better later on."

"I don't think so."

She started at his vehemence.

"You don't imagine I'm going to stay there after what has happened?"

"I think you should," she added, as she, noticed the rebellious gleam in his eyes. "It would help Ned."

"Then I'll stay, though it'll hurt like hell!"

"You are very good. My sister'll be coming back soon. She'd better not see you here," she reminded him, as she rose.

"Then I'll be going."

He rode slowly back to Jacobson's. His employer met him at the gate.

"Well?" he eagerly asked.

"Everything fixed," Briant replied, with as good grace as he could muster.

Jacobson followed him to the stable, looking round to see that they were alone.

"When?" he inquired.

"Friday night."

"Good! That gives us two days to fix things. You won't be sorry for what you've done, boy."

"I wonder!" he replied, turning his head away.

"Did Kate suspect anything?"

"I don't think so. Of course, I'll have to clear out."

"I don't see that. When we get Ned there'll be no one to give any trouble. Without him, the gang'll crack up in a week.

"But supposing you don't get him?"

"We'll get him all right - dead or alive! Cheer up!

"You look as though you'd committed a crime instead of helping to rid the country of a dangerous criminal."

Jack hung his head.

"I'm ashamed of myself. Still, there's something in what you say. I don't see, all the same, how it's going to be worth very much to you. All the police will share in the reward."

"But I'll get the lion's share. I can prove that I arranged the whole thing - that is, with your help. I'm not likely to forget you."

"You needn't consider me. I wouldn't touch a penny of it. It's blood money, and, beside that, I'm young and can get on well enough without it."

Jacobson could hardly believe his ears. Here was magnanimity, if you like. And it was magnanimity that was going to be very profitable to him. He slapped his open-hearted employe on the back.

"I sha'n't forget you, never fear!"

"I'm sure you won't!" Jack replied, his mouth assuming a curious smirk.

Young Jacobson was in a nasty mood when he slouched into his seat at the table that evening.

"I hope you took your message all right," he said, glaring balefully at Briant.

Jacobson sat bolt upright and looked inquiringly at Jack, who felt that something was expected of him.

"Frank seemed to resent my knocking off early to take your letter to Barker's," he explained.

"Barker's- bah!" Frank spat out the words.

Jacobson brought his hand down on the table with a bang that made the dishes rattle.

"You keep your nose out of this! It's my affair who I send on messages."

His son was in no way perturbed.

"If you sent him to Barker's, what the hell was he doin' at Kelly's?"

"At Kelly's?" Nita and Julie said in a breath.

"Yes, at Kelly's. I saw him ride over there!"

"So you neglected your work to watch him?" his father insinuated.

Frank threw down his knife and fork and rushed to the door.

"Damn the work!" he shouted. "I'm full of the lot of you, and I'm clearin' out."

"Don't bother about him," said Jacobson, as Nita got up. "It'll soon blow over, and he'll come back for his food."

Nita resumed her seat. "I don't know what's the matter with Frank lately. There's something on his mind."

"There'll be something on his body, too, if there's much more of that nonsense!" said his father significantly.

Frank was still sulking when Jack went into the yard after tea. "Don't be a fool, Frank," Briant said.

"Go to hell! Go back to the Kelly's, where you belong. Go back to Kate!"

Nita caught the words as she came to the door. "What did you say?" she asked.

"I told him to go back to Kate Kelly. He's in with the gang! He's been in with 'em all along! He ought to be shot with the rest of 'em!"

"It's foolish to talk like that," she said.

"Foolish, is it? Well, you'll see. You'll see the kind o' snake you're harborin'!"

With black rage in his heart, he strode across the yard.

"I'd like to know what's wrong with that boy," Nita said, looking after him.

"Didn't you say he was infatuated with Kate Kelly?" Jack reminded her.

She eyed him closely as she answered, "Yes, and perhaps he sees in you a possible rival."

"Oh, don't be silly, Nita," he said, a little awkwardly.

"You did go to Kelly's, didn't you?" she enquired after a pause.

"I had to take a message somewhere for your father."

"And you called in at Kellys on the way?"

He did not answer her.

With a look such as he had only once before seen in the eyes of a woman, she went back into the house.

12

A Narrow Escape

JACK Briant slept very little that night. He hated himself for what he had done. He was frank and open by nature, and deceit had no part in his make-up. The idea of betraying even a man like Jacobson was repugnant to him.

What if his plans miscarry, and they caught Ned after all? The very thought caused him to sit up in alarm. It was a disturbing position from whatever angle it was viewed. Something would have to be done to cover up his warning to Kate, otherwise the police would be suspicious.

Tomorrow would be Friday. As the hours went by the more nervous he became. He had helped the man and woman he had wanted to, but any elation that thought might have brought him was blotted out by the fear of failure, of some hitch which might lead the gang into the troopers' clutches.

He was so preoccupied at breakfast that he did not answer the simple questions put to him till they were repeated. Nita greeted him more cordially than he expected after her curious behavior the night previously. But he had no thoughts for anyone or anything except the dangerous game into which Jacobson's cupidity had forced him.

Frank had recovered from his tantrums, and turned up at breakfast as usual. It was evident, however, that he was still nursing a grievance against Jack, for he scowled at him across the table, but otherwise ignored him.

"You'd better keep your eye on him today," was Julie's warning, as he left for work.

"Thanks, I will."

That the warning was necessary was shown by the fact that they had not been working long when Frank dropped a heavy log which would have crushed Briant's foot had he not seen it coming and jumped back.

Without a word he threw down the wood he was carrying, and dealt his work-mate a vicious punch on the jaw. Frank fell like a log, but he was soon on his feet again, his breast heaving and his eyes blazing. Jack met his rush with a straight left, but it was guarded, and a smashing blow to the body left him gasping.

Young Jacobson followed up his advantage with a left and right to the head, and Briant saved himself by hanging on to his opponent and pinioning his arms.

"Let go, blast you!" Frank shouted.

Still Jack clung to him.

"Take that, then!" A vicious kick on the shin caused Jack to reel with pain. Also it made him see red. His anger put new vigor into him, and he rained blows on his adversary. Frank tried to fight back, but was forced on the defensive. Briant's fists seemed everywhere. Every time they found a mark they caused a groan of pain.

Half-blinded by the blood that flowed from a cut above his eye, young Jacobson reeled under the battery of blows. Twice he tried to grip his opponent's arms, but he was fought off.

It was clear that Briant had no intention of sparing the son of his employer. He must be taught a lesson for that kick. As Frank lurched forward Jack smashed a right to his mouth, laughing softly to himself as he saw the red trickle over the boy's rapidly swelling lips. A backhand jab ripped his cheek, and a powerful punch to the body sent him to the ground doubled up in agony.

Briant bent over him. "Kick me, would you?" he hissed.

"I'll - get - you - for - this!" cried Frank, between gasps of pain.

"Don't you threaten me, or, by God! I'll skin you alive!"

The fallen man put up his hands to ward off a blow.

Jack regarded him with a sneer on his lips. "Expected me to hit you while you were down, did you? That and kicking is the way you fight here, is it?"

"I'll kill you for this, you-you - tramp!" Frank shrieked, as he struggled to his feet, still holding his arms up to guard his head.

Briant's reply was a contemptuous push, which hastened him on his way towards home.

"Whew!" Jack sat on a log and nursed his aching head. He was sorry for the fight, but it couldn't have been avoided. If he hadn't punched Frank for trying to maim him something else would have started the row. That boy had an ugly temper, and he wouldn't let it rest at that, he was sure. He would have to watch him. Damn him! Hadn't he troubles enough without adding a revengeful opponent to them?

He worked on till midday. Neither Frank nor Julie was at the table. Jacobson, who was already seated, obviously was annoyed. "You should not have fought", he said.

"He asked for it, the cowardly swine! He tried to smash my foot with a log of wood, and kicked me."

Jacobson jumped up, his face red with rage. "That's my son youre calling a cowardly swine."

"You've nothing to be proud of!"

Jacobson appeared as though the words were choking him. Then he managed to blurt out: "You take that back!"

"Take it back, be damned! He's a cur, a low-down cur, and I'm sorry I dirtied my hands on him!" Jack also was on his feet.

Jacobson threw down his chair and strode over to him, purple and panting. "You'll suffer for this, you – you - "

Without troubling to reply, Briant walked to the door.

Jacobson's expression suddenly changed. Rage gave place to doubt, and doubt to abject fear. "Where-where you going?" he gasped.

"To Kelly's."

"No! No! You can't - you musn't!" Jacobson implored, hands outstretched and eyes dilated.

Amazedly Nita looked from one to the other. Her wonder grew as she saw her father seize Jack's hand and grovel on his knees before him. "You wouldn't ruin me! You can't do that! I didn't mean what I said! I was mad! I am sorry!"

As Briant pulled his hand away there came a piercing shriek and a flurry of footsteps outside the kitchen door. Frank burst into the room, with Julie clinging desperately to him. His bruised and battered face added horror to the blood lust in his eyes, and the contorted twistings of of his gibbering mouth.

In his right hand he carried a heavy revolver. The sight of his father on his knees seemed to puzzle him, and he opened his mouth to speak. The next moment, with a snarl that sound beast-like he levelled the revolver at Briant's head and pulled the trigger.

Jack and Nita moved together, he stepping backward and she forward. When they recovered from the shock of the detonation Nita lay on the floor, a red weal across her forehead.

Simultaneously Jacobson and Jack knelt beside her, but Frank flung them aside, and, lifting his sister's head, cried in an agony of apprehension. "Speak to me, Nita! I didn't mean it! Look at me, Nita! Oh God, open your eyes! Nita! Nita! Nita!" He let her head fall back, and throwing himself across her prostrate form, sobbed convulsively.

"Don't touch me!" he screamed, as his father tried to lift him. "Let me die, too!"

With Jack's help, Jacobson forced him into a chair, where he sat like one in a trance. With fear gripping his heart, Jacobson bent over his daughter. Scarcely daring to look, he examined the mark on her forehead. Then, stretching his hands above his head, he cried deliriously, "Thank God! Oh, thank God!"

The bullet had merely grazed her forehead, stunning her with the shock, and leaving a red scar on her fair skin.

They lifted her on to the sofa, and she opened her eyes.

She shut them again quickly, and Jacobson bent closer, his face contorted by fear.

"She's all right," Jack assured him. "She was only stunned. There's nothing to worry about. Feeling all right now, Nita?" he asked as she looked about her, and put her hand to her head.

"Where's Frank?" she asked, bewilderedly. "Oh!" Her relief as she saw that everyone was there uninjured was pathetic. Her fingers closed on Jack's hand, and she shut her eyes again.

"Nita!" cried Jacobson in alarm.

"Hush!" whispered Briant. "You and Julie take Frank away. Sit with him for a while."

When they had gone, Jack bent down and reverently kissed her forehead.

She looked at him with a smile on her lips. "Nita," he said, "you saved my life!"

For reply she drew his head down until their lips met.

He kissed her tenderly, and almost savagely she returned his caress.

"How can I thank you, Nita? What can I say?'"

"Say 'I –'"

"Yes?" he queried.

She laughed a little hysterically.

"I'm- I'm afraid I'm still a bit silly in the head. "Where's Frank?"- sitting up.

Gently he forced her back.

"Frank's all right. Your father and Julie are with him."

"Oh, he might have killed you, Jack!"

"But for you."

She smiled happily.

"I tried to knock his hand up, but I wasn't quick enough. Stay with me for a little while. I'll soon be all right."

With his hand in hers, and her eyelids closed, she lay back peacefully. Jacobson tip-toed through the door, but Briant waved him away. "She's all right," he whispered.

After a little while Nita sat up.

"Don't!" Briant cried. "Rest a while longer."

"I'm as right as rain now." And before he realised what had happened she was on her feet. "Where did they take Frank?" she asked.

Jack was amazed at the sudden change in her. The softness had died out of her eyes, and in its place was that fathomless something which had so often baffled him. He held out his hand, but she declined his assistance. With firm step she passed into her brother's sleeping quarters, Jack following.

"Nita!" Frank's hands went out to her, and she fell on her knees at his bedside. He kissed her lips, her cheeks, her hair. "Nita! Oh, Nita!" He buried his face in his arms and cried like a child. "I didn't mean it!" he said in sob-shaken accents. "O Christ, forgive me!"

"There, there!" she soothed him. "Everything's all right. Just lie quietly for a while."

He crushed her fiercely to him. Julie, with tears streaming down her cheeks, stepped silently from the room. Jacobson, beckoning Jack, followed her.

"I didn't mean what I said just now," Jacobson said, shamefacedly, "Don't think any more about it."

"That's all right," Briant returned. "We all lose our heads at times."

"He's my son, you know," Jacobson continued. "I went mad for a while."

"Yes, yes, I understand."

When Briant moved away his employer made to follow him, then changed his mind, and left the house.

Jack waited for a while, and' then went in to Frank again. Nita was still at his bedside. Young Jacobson avoided his eyes. Briant smilingly gripped his hand, but it was pulled away, and a choking voice gasped, "I- I tried to kill you!"

"But you didn't succeed, thanks to your sister, whom I shall never forget for that."

"I wonder!" murmured Nita under her breath.

Frank's remorse was pitiful, but at last Jack succeeded in comforting him.

"You were mad for the moment, and didn't know what you were doing," he said, "but everything's all right again, so cheer up. I'm sorry too, sorry for our little dust up," he added, surveying the marks of his handiwork on the boy's battered face.

"It was as that that made me mad," young Jacobson confessed, "no one round these parts has ever been able to beat me yet, and- and -"

"I can' well believe you," smiled Briant. "You're a great puncher, and nearly had me."

Frank turned his head away, and a flush of shame reddened his cheeks. "That kick - I shouldn't have done it. I can't forget that. It was dirty!"

"Never mind, I've forgotten it, and so must you."

"I wish I could!" he returned with a sigh. "You'll keep it to yourself, won't you?"- eagerly.

"I'll keep it all right," laughed Jack, rubbing his shin. "We're going to be good pals now, and I don't think we'll ever quarrel again."

Nita brought their hands together, and to Jack's earnest grip Frank responded with a generous pressure.

Briant moved away. "I've loafed long enough. I'm going back to work," he announced.

"Oh, you needn't do that," said Nita. "After all that's happened surely you won't feel very fit."

"There's a bit of clearing up I'd like to do to get ready for tomorrow," he replied, as he left them.

He wished to be alone, to think. Everything had happened with a rush, and he longed to sort things out. In a few hours the police would be creeping up to Eleven Mile Creek on their fool's errand.

What was he to do to show that he hadn't given away the secret? These thoughts were chased away by reflections upon Frank's murderous attack. Nita's anxiety to save him, her impassioned kiss - memory of that cloying embrace set his pulses tingling, and yet he felt he would rather forget it. Damn it! Could he be quite right in his head? Frank's punches must have rattled him.

When it came to the police raid, though, he could think quite clearly, too clearly, it seemed, but a solution of the tricky problem with which he was faced still baffled him. That something would have to be done was certain, but what that something was he hadn't the faintest idea of it before!

Jacobson was visibly excited at tea that evening. Twice he dropped his knife on the floor, and several times he ignored the questions that his daughters put to him.

"What's the matter with you, Father?" Julie inquired.

"You're as nervous as a half-broken colt."

"Am I?" he asked sheepishly. "Well, there's been enough today to upset a man, hasn't there?"

"You'd better get to bed early tonight and rest your nerves."

A look of alarm crept into Jacobson's eyes, but he made no remark. "How does Frank seem now?" Jack cut in.

"When I looked in just now he was sleeping," Nita answered. "I didn't disturb him."

"That's a good idea of yours about tucking in early, Julie," said Jacobson suddenly. "We've all had a trying day, and sleep'll do us good."

Jack shot a quick glance at him, but said 'nothing. "Where are you going?" Nita asked some time later, as her father got up hurriedly.

"Just remembered that stone in Prince's hoof. I can't let it stay there all night," he replied as he went out.

Jack followed him. "I'll give you a hand." In the stable he said to his employer: "Take him alive if you can, Mr Jacobson. I'd hate to think he was shot down like a dog."

"We might be able to, but if he gets half a chance he'll make a fight of it!"

"I suppose he will. You'd better not let him see you, in case he gets away."

"I'll look after that," returned Jacobson, a nervous tremor in his voice,

"I can't go to bed," Jack told him. "I couldn't sleep. I'll hang round till you get back. You'd better cross the creek or the girls might hear you," he added, as Jacobson saddled up the big black gelding.

He watched horse' and rider slip into the night. Then he acted quickly. Running over to the shed where two guns were kept, by the aid of matches he counted the number of cartridges in a box on the shelf. Ten! If he took two they would be easily missed, so he, reached for the old double-barrelled muzzle loader. It took some manoeuvring to load it with the aid of occasional match flares, but at last he succeeded, and carefully replaced the powder flask and box of caps where he had found them.

A minute later, with his heart thumping his ribs, he was picking his way through the bush in the direction of Eleven Mile Creek. He walked warily, stopping every minute or two to listen. He heard nothing but the strange night noises of the bush to which, he had become accustomed.

Suddenly he crouched behind a tree. The sound of horses' hoofs smote his ears. Creeping forward on his hands and knees, he reached a rise from which the light of Kelly's house was visible. Four ghostly mounted figures emerged from the bush to his right.

Good God! Were they the Kellys? Had his scheme miscarried after all? Trembling in every limb, he raised the gun to his shoulder. Two shots thundered on the night air, and reverberated from the hills.

He had just time to see the horsemen stop dead before he commenced to run. Crashing through the scrub, heedless of the noise he made, he reached Jacobson's back fence. Carefully he made his way to the shed and replaced the gun. Halfway across the yard, he halted, sick with doubt.

Hurriedly re-entering the shed, he searched with matches until he found an old rag. With it he wiped out both barrels, and carefully cleaned the nipples. Then he threw the rag in a corner and piled a number of bags over it.

Like a man in a dream he stumbled to his bunk and threw himself upon it. If they were the Kellys would his shots have warned them? If they were police, would the firing explain the non-arrival of the gang where Kate and her sister were supposed to be waiting for them?

He lay there for a long time, and then crept round the house and down the path to the gate. After what seemed an eternity a horseman appeared, and he recognised him as Jacobson. He ran out to meet him.

"Did you get him?" he asked, in a voice husky with mingled hope and fear.

"No, damn it!" Jacobson cried. "Someone fired two shots, and. they didn't turn up. Didn't you hear them?"

'I'm afraid I was too excited to hear anything," he replied. "Didn't you see them at all?"

"Not a sight of them!"

"What did the police do when they heard, the shots?"

"What could they do?" asked Jacobson bitterly. "They didn't want to run into an ambush."

"You certainly had bad luck."

"Damn bad luck!" echoed Jacobson, as he led his horse towards the stable.

When he had unsaddled it, he did not enter the house right away. Instead, he lit a lantern, and went to the shed where the guns were kept. He counted the cartridges in the box and examined the breech-loader. Next he picked up the muzzle-loader, and smelt the barrels and the nipples. Then, with a snarl like a wild beast deprived of its prey, he blew out the lantern and went inside.

13

Friends Forgather

KELLY'S house was quiet that night. One of the troopers who had crept up to the window and looked in saw the two sisters sewing. Kate's keen ears caught the sound of his soft footsteps.

"The boys can't be coming," she said, in a voice loud enough for the listening man to hear.

"Well, Ned said they were all tired, and might stay up in the ranges to rest. They've a long ride ahead of them tomorrow, you know," her sister responded.

The eavesdropper pricked up his ears.

"I don't know why they want to go to New South Wales at all," said Kate. "They're safer here."

"Ah!" The policeman could not help the ejaculation.

"Ned knows best," returned Mrs Skillion.

They lapsed into silence, and the trooper crept away.

Over the hill he rode, to where five other horsemen awaited him.

"Hear anything, Costello?" Macguire asked.

"Yes. The gang's crossing the Murray tomorrow. Kate said so."

This was news indeed, and the troopers galloped back with it to Benalla.

The telegraph wires were busy that night, and there was great activity in all the police stations further north. At last they' had something definite to go upon. If the bushrangers adhered to their programme their capture seemed certain:

While Macguire and his companions were speeding towards Benalla with what they believed to be information of first importance, four men and a girl rode leisurely towards Manton's hut in another direction. One of them halted his horse and jumped from the saddle. The girl who had ridden by his side, also alighted.

"You'll be careful, won't you, dear?" she said.

He put his arms about her.

"Don't worry. We're safe tonight. Nothing can happen." He bent down and kissed her.

"Oh, don't take any risks, Ned," she said, as she raised her face to his again.

He held her tightly for a moment. When he released her, she remounted and galloped away in the direction from which she had come.

A mile or two along the track, where it junctioned with another bush road, she drew rein. Some noise she had heard caused her to jump from her horse and lead it behind a thick clump of bushes, through which she peered anxiously. For a long time she waited, rein in hand and horse's head turned in Manton's direction, ready for instant flight if occasion demanded it. But nothing happened, and with a sigh of relief she remounted arid turned into the track that led over the hill to Jacobson's.

Manton came to meet the men as they neared his dwelling.

"So you've given 'em the slip tonight, Ned?" his big voice boomed.

"Yes, I think so," the first horseman replied. "Did all the boys turn up?"

"Every man Jack of 'em. The shanty's bulgin' with 'em."

Which was not far from the truth. Through the haze of tobacco smoke faces loomed up in every corner. Every man rose as the four newcomers and Manton came in.

"Take this seat, Ned."

"Here you are, Dan."

"There's room here, Steve."

"This box'll hold you, Joe."

Ned Kelly and his companions accepted the seats that were offered them, while Manton busied himself with the bottles on the table.

Ned looked round him. He·knew them all - Tom Stevens, with his long 'beard and short cutty pipe'; Red Regan, his shirt open, revealing his great hairy chest; Angus McCullagh, saying little, but thinking a lot; Mephan Robertson, the storekeeper, who had brought with him a generous supply of provisions; Paddy O'Rourke, of the bush shanty over the rise, who also had not come ernpty-handed; John Cavendish, the sedate, aquiline-featured schoolmaster; Harry Young, a stripling, whose heroworshipping eyes rarely left Ned Kelly's face; Guido Spirelli, whose tangled hair and piercing black orbs contrasted strangely with the flaxen locks and blue eyes of Gottlieb Jaensch, the young German farmer from Big Hill; Jim Kerry, the burly blacksmith; who had ridden twenty miles to be present; Charlie Wicks, the stationmaster from down the line; and old Sam Jackson.

"It's a treat for sore eyes to see you all again," said Ned, his face lighting up with pleasure.

A chorus of reciprocal greeting answered him.

"You must all be dry," cried Manton. "Be upstandin', all of you!"

Eagerly they seized the cups and pannikins, jars, and other vessels which had been filled with beer. The big man rapped for silence.

"To the Kelly gang. Long life to 'em!"

Never was a toast more whole-heartedly honored. They raised their cups and pannikins and jars above their heads, and most of them drank the contents at one gulp.

Amid their shouts the big voice of Manton was heard in the opening bars of "For They Are Jolly Good Fellows!" The others took up the refrain, which was sung with a vigor that compensated for its lack of harmony.

"Fill 'em up again, boys!"

Again they lifted their drinking cups. Manton was about to speak, when Regan cut in,

"To the police - may they never be where they're wanted!"

With shouts of laughter they drank again. "Speech, Ned!" Harry Young called.

"Yes, come on, Ned. Up on your hind legs!" The shrill voice of Sam Jackson rose above the din.

It was a curious scene, the more remarkable when it was realised that the men whose health they had been drinking were the proclaimed enemies of society, outlaws with prices on their heads.

"Three cheers for Ned!" someone shouted. Their roar made the rafters ring.

"Thanks, boys," said the bushranger. "We owe a lot to you. You don't know what a night like this means to us. We're not likely to be disturbed, because' the police are somewhere else. When you've been hunted day and night for months it's fine to feel you can let up. They've kept us on the move, I can tell you. If any of you've been away in the bush for long stretches, you know what it means to get back, even for a little while, to your friends. It makes up for a lot. If it hadn't been for your help they'd have had us long ago."

"They'll never get you, Ned!" shouted Stevens. "Hear, hear!" they chorused.

Ned smiled a twisted sort of smile. "I hope not, Tom. We're planning something big, but I can't let you know what it is yet. When it comes off it'll show Hare and Standish and Sadlier that we're not done yet. And it'll show them that the people are behind us - they don't hold with police persecution."

"You're right there!" cried McCullagh.

"'Course he's right!" yelled Young.

"You've all stuck to us up to now," Ned resumed, "and we're looking to you to keep on. You've shown that none of you want to get rich out of blood money."

"Anyone what did that'd make it warm for himself!" exclaimed Jaensch, with an ugly grimace.

"We've been out for months now," Ned continued, "and you boys have fed us and put the troopers off the scent."

"Huh!" cried Young. "They couldn't pick up the scent of a paddock full of dead horses!"

"Don't make any mistake about that," counselled Cavendish, the schoolmaster. "There are many brave and clever men among the police. If we value Ned's safety we mustn't underate them."

"You're right there, John," Ned agreed; "they've given us a taste of their quality before now. We've had some close shaves, I can tell you, and once or twice it's been where things looked pretty safe. There's some fine bushmen among them. It doesn't do to get too cocky. The way you've all stuck to us has been grand, and some day we hope to show you in another way what we think of it."

"We're only too glad to be able to help you - aren't we, boys?" said Wicks.

The roar of assent that went up left no doubt in the minds of Ned and his men as to the sincerity of their queerly assorted allies.

"There's one thing I'd like to tell you," the outlaw leader added. "The police know of the plant near the Big Bend and at Clancy's Crossing. Don't leave anything more there. I'm not sure about Shelly's, but anyone who takes anything there wants to keep his eyes about him."

Once more they drank success to the gang. Dan Kelly drained his panni kin at a gulp and held it up for more.

"That's enough, Dan!" cried his brother.

"Git away wid yez!" cried O'Rourke. "A dhrop more won't hurt the bhoy."

"He's had enough." There was a commanding note in the outlaw's voice. Dan scowled, and O'Rourke put down the bottle. Steve Hart and Joe Byrne, whose mugs were about to be replenished, at once refused another drink. Ned's leadership amounted to a dictatorship. His word was law with his three associates, from whom he exacted implicit obedience.

During a temporary lull in the conversation one of the horses outside whinnied. Instantly every man was on the alert.

"D'ye hear that?" asked O'Rourke.

Manton. laughed. "It's all right. Nobody can get within coo-ee of this place while Larry's about. Did you hear anything, Larry?"

A big shaggy dog rose from a corner of the room, and put its nose on Manton's knee.

"He wouldn't let anyone come near without letting us know, would you, old boy?"

Larry's tail wagged in a way that showed if he didn't know exactly what was said he had some idea of what his master meant to convey.

"You ought to have a dog like that with you, Ned," someone suggested.

The bushranger shook his head. "No; a dog's dangerous - the best of them. He's likely to talk at the wrong time."

"Anyone seen Jacobson lately?" McCullagh inquired.

"I called there a day or two ago," Steve Hart replied.

"They tell me there's been a hell of a lot of troopers round his place lately," McCullagh continued. "It's just as well to watch him."

"I don't believe he's square," Tom Stevens announced.

"What makes you think that?" Ned asked.

"Well, as Mac says, the police is gettin' too friendly with 'im."

"We're lookin' after Jacobson," Jackson told them.

Then he related how he had induced Jack Briant to take a job there.

"That's the boy I met in the bush," said Ned. "He's all right."

"Are you sure?" Cavendish inquired.

"I'd bank on that boy," Ned retorted.

"Yes, but Jacobson's got two girls, and you never know how a girl can get round a young fellow.

A smile flickered round the corners of Steve Hart's mouth.

"Did you see this young chap the other day?" Cavendish turned to Steve.

"He was there when I got some matches."

"How did he strike you?"

"Oh, all right."

"Of course he's all right!" snapped jackson. "Didn't he work for me best part of a week?"

"I know we can trust him," said Ned, with such confidence that they expected something further, but the bush ranger said no more.

Larry pricked up his ears and emitted a low growl.

Instantly every eye was on the dog.

"What is it, boy?" Manton asked, a little anxiously. Larry growled again.

"Stay here boys," said the big fellow, as accompanied by the dog, he went outside.

The bush rangers exchanged glances, and instinctively the right hands of Dan Kelly and Joe Byrne went to their revolver holsters. Ned's easy confidence was less apparent, and into Steve Hart's dark eyes there crept a look that signified defiance more than dismay.

"We've been making too much row," remarked Robertson, fearfully.

"Let 'em come!" boasted Harry Young. "We'd give 'em a go for it!"

"Don't talk like a fool!" admonished Cavendish.

"The police aren't likely to come tonight." All the same, there was a trace of anxiety in Ned's voice.

"You never know when they'll come," retorted Cavendish. "We can't be too careful."

"Let's go and have a look," suggested McCullagh.

With several others he moved to the door, but before they reached it Manton burst into the room, his eyes' dilated with excitement. "Ned's horse is gone!"

Without a word Ned Kelly rushed from the hut, with the others at his heels.

"By God, they've been here after all!" cried McCullagh.

An angry bark from Larry added to the general alarm.

An examination by lantern of the spot where the horse was tied to a tree gave them no clue.

"Give me the light a minute," said Sam Jackson. He dropped on his knees and carefully inspected the ground. "Something scared him," he added, as he pointed to the hoof-prints.

"But how did he get away?" asked Regan.

"Pulled the reins loose," replied Jackson, indicating a slight abrasion on the bark of the tree.

Ned scrutinised it closely. "You might be right," he said, in a relieved tone. "Let's beat the bush a bit."

They separated and scoured the scrub for some distance round the clearing, but there was no sign of the missing animal.

"You'd better take my moke, Ned," 'said Jim Kerry, when they met again.

"Or mine," chorused the others.

The bushranger shook his head. "Thank's, boys, but I'd sooner find him."

Again they searched the bush, Manton keeping a close eye on Larry for any sign of warning. Twice the dog stopped and sniffed the air, but made no sound.

"Listen!" Young's quick ear had detected some noise on the hill beyond the creek. "There you are again. There's a horse over there, or I'll eat my hat. Let me go - it might be a trap."

Anxiously they waited while Young plunged into the scrub. He seemed to be gone for hours, but in reality it was only a few minutes when they heard his excited call, "I got him!"

Ned ran to meet him, and took the reins from him.

He breathed a sigh of relief. While he doubted the possibility of police interference after such care had been taken to put them off the scent, experience had taught him always to be on his guard, and the absence of his horse had looked decidedly suspicious. It took the edge off the enjoyment he had derived from the company of his friends. His voice was much less cheery, therefore, when he announced that they had better be going.

"I was reckonin' on the four of you stayin' the night," said Manton, ruefully.

"Not tonight," Ned replied. "Come one, Dan, Joe and Steve."

"Well, let's have another drink before ye go," O'Rourke suggested.

Ned shook his head. "It's time we made a move. Good-night, boys, and thanks again."

They pressed him to stay longer, but he was obdurate, and to the accompaniment of their good wishes, the four horsemen rode into the night. They watched them grow dimmer and dimmer, until the shadows closed round them.

"Ned seemed a bit shook up over that horse breakin' away," remarked McCullagh.

"No wonder!" muttered John Cavendish. "My God, what a life!"

14

"I Love You Nita!"

TWO days later, Jack carted his first load of wood into Benalla. On the way he overtook the tramp he had encountered on the road to Jacobson's. "Hullo," he said, "I thought you went to Melbourne.'

"I'd - I'd been there before now only I hurt me foot," was the hesitant reply. "You got a job, I see."

"Yes."

"How d'you like it at Ja - at the place you're workin' at?"

"Oh, all right."

"Better than Jackson's, I reckon."

"In a way, yes."

"Better company, eh? Two fine girls, ain't they?"

He looked as though he regretted that remark.

"Look here," said Jack, "you seem to know a good bit about the people round here."

"Er-yes, I've been through these parts once or twice before."

"As a swaggie or as something else?"

The man started perceptibly, and he was slow to reply. "Of course, what else?"

Briant laughed. "Sure you weren't wearing uniform the other times?"

"Uniform ?" - with a gasp of surprise.

Jack eyed him up and down. "You're the worst imitation of a swaggie I've ever seen. You don't know how to carry your bluey, and no tramp ever walked like you walk. The Superintendent should have got someone to school you properly."

The tramp laughed a mirthless laugh. "Gord! you don't take me for a copper, do you?"

"As a matter of fact, I do, I did the first time I met you."

"You're like everyone else, I guess - this 'ere Kelly business has got on your nerves. You're fancyin' things. I believe I saw Ned the other day."

"Yes? - and what did you do - run?"

The tramp's eyes flashed angrily, but he managed to control himself. "There wasn't no need to run. The gang wouldn't do me no 'ann. I got nothin' for 'em to rob either. 'UlIo, 'oo's this comin'?"

A horseman appeared round the bend of the road - a bearded man with one side of his head bandaged. He rode a jaded-looking bay gelding.

"Look's like a trooper," Jack commented.

"Does a bit, don't 'e?"

When the rider came up, Briant was struck by his familiar appearance, although his head bandages gave his mouth a peculiar twist. He pulled up a few yards from the dray and beckoned the tramp over to him.

"I'm Coombes from headquarters," he said in an undertone. "Haven't seen anything suspicious, I suppose?" Without waiting for a reply he asked, "Who's the young chap?"

"Used to work at Sam Jackson's, one of the Kelly mob, now with Jacobson," the tramp answered.

"Is he all right?"

"I don't know. Wants watching, I should say."

"I'll have a yarn to him. I want you to give this to Superintendent Hare as soon as you can. It's important, and no one else is to see it. Be as quick as you can." He gave the other man a letter and then rode over to Briant. "Know me?" he asked.

"Damned if it isn't Ned!" exclaimed Jack in amazement. "I suppose you know that tramp's a policeman?"

"Oh, yes," with a laugh. "I've given him a letter for Hare, inviting him to come and take me."

"Do you think--"

"That he knew me? I'm certain he didn't. These rags alter me a bit, don't they?"

"They certainly do. I wasn't sure of you myself till you spoke. You're taking a bit of a risk, aren't you?"

"It's a risk all the time. Was Nita home when you left?"

"No; she went along the bush track on the black mare a good while ago."

Ned's eyes showed the satisfaction the news gave him, and with a hurried "Must be off now," he galloped away.

What were the relations between the outlaw and Jacobson's daughter? Was she the girl whom rumour declared Ned met clandestinely from time to time? Was it possible that while the father plotted against the bushranger, one of his own flesh and blood was secretly in love with him?

The suggestion did not please Briant. He wondered why. Was he in love with her himself?

He asked himself that question a dozen times as he drove along the road without being able to supply a satisfactory answer. There was something about Nita that made a strong appeal. Possibly it was that her curious two-sided nature constituted a challenge. She was a difficult girl to understand, and her attitude toward him, at times frankly affectionate and at other times coldly indifferent, set him a puzzle that demanded a solution.

On two other occasions he had seen her ride away alone, and late one night he heard, or fancied he heard, her voice and a man's at the sliprails at the back of his sleeping quarters.

He made up his mind to try that night to find whether there was any ground for his suspicions. On his return from Benalla he asked Jacobson if he might have a horse to ride over to Jackson's, being careful to add that it was as well to keep in touch with the old man, who seemed to know a good deal of the gang's movements. His employer readily assented.

"I'm riding across to Jackson's tonight," he told Nita when he found her alone. "Like to come?"

She accepted his invitation with obvious eagerness.

"Remember our last ride?" he asked, when they had gained the track.

"Of course I do. Why?"

"I was just wondering."

"Wondering what?"

"What someone else would say if he knew."

"But father knew I came with you," she replied without a moment's hesitation.

Briant laughed.

"You're a clever girl, Nita."

"Thank you for the compliment."

"Is your father the only one who has a right to be concerned?"

"Well, there's Frank, but he's younger than I am, and you'd hardly expect me to be responsible to him, would you?"

"No, I suppose not," he admitted. "I say, let's sit on that log for a while and talk."

The suggestion seemed to please her. They tethered their horses to a tree. When they were seated she asked:

"What made you mention our last ride?"

"Well, I just wondered whether I might be treading on someone's corns. I say, can you guess whom I saw this afternoon?"

"Ned Kelly! I saw him myself!"

Her frankness astonished him.

"Y-yes."

"Yes, I was riding over to Jennie O'Donnell's. She's my cousin, you know."

"You've never told me that before," he said sharply.

"No. Well, does it matter'?"

"Perhaps not. Go on. Did you speak to Ned?"

"Yes. I said 'Hullo, Ned,' and he said 'Hullo!'"

"You know him pretty well, then?"

"Oh, yes."

"I suppose you didn't by any chance feel you'd like to ride into Benalla and tell the police?"

"I certainly did not."

"Why not?"

"Well, for one reason, by the time I'd have reached Benalla Ned would have been miles away, and, for another reason- "

"Yes - yes."

Her reply was to jump to her feet with a startled cry.

"What is it?" he asked in alarm.

"I thought I saw a man move from behind that tree. Perhaps I was wrong."

"Shall I have a look?"

"Oh, no. I must have been mistaken. There are funny shadows in the bush at times."

A little later he turned to her intently. "Nita, you didn't answer my question."

"What question?"

"You didn't tell me the second reason why you didn't try to tell the police Ned was in the district."

"Didn't I? Well, perhaps there wasn't any other reason."

"But there was. You said so yourself. You said 'and for another reason.'"

"Did I really? I say, don't you think Frank's getting more morbid? I'm afraid of my brother."

He saw that it was useless to pursue the Kelly topic, so he said: "Frank is fretting his heart out here. He wants to get back to town. Don't you, Nita?"

"Yes - and no."

"Do you mind explaining the reservation?"

She laughed. "It's a pretty dull sort of life here, as you know, yet -"

"Yet there's someone who makes you want to stay?"

"Yes, there's something about the bush that seems to grip you. You wouldn't feel like that, of course, as you haven't known it long enough."

"Nita, you're wonderful the way you sidetrack a direct question. I didn't say 'something.' I said 'someone.'"

"Oh, there are my father, brother and sister, of course."

"And, me?"

"Oh, of course," with a merry chuckle.

"No one else?" he asked.

"Surely those are enough." Suddenly her manner changed. "Jack, do you mind if I don't talk for a little while? I want to think."

"Of course not. Lean against me - you'll be more comfortable."

With a scarcely audible sigh she allowed her head to rest against his shoulder. Instinctively his arm went round her.

"Is that better?" he asked.

"Much, thank you."

Neither spoke for a few minutes. The warmth of her body thrilled him, and he drew her closer.

"Nita!" he whispered.

She did not reply. He saw that her eyes were shut, but her lips were smiling. He bent down and kissed her lightly, but she did not stir. Again he kissed her, this time passionately, almost savagely. With a little cry of delight, she threw her arms around his neck and her lips clung to his.

"Nita, Nita!" he murmured.

"Oh, Jack!" she answered, snuggling still closer to him.

"Do you love me, Nita?" he whispered.

"I do-oh, I do!" she cried. "Do you want me dear?"

"God, how I want you!"

He crushed her to him and rained kisses upon her responsive lips.

"Take me away from here, Jack," she pleaded. She noticed his surprise, and added, a little hysterically,

"I can't stay here without you-it-it would be unbearable!"

"I'm sorry!" he said in a half whisper.

She freed herself from his embrace.

"Sorry for what?" she asked tremulously. "Forgive me, Nita. It was wrong of me."

She sat staring in front of her. Then she rose from the log.

"We had better be moving if we are going to Jackson's."

It was now the other Nita who spoke - the cold, unemotional girl whose moods had so astonished him. Her voice was calm and steady, and bore no trace of the passion which a few moments previously had shaken it. He was so amazed at her sudden change that without a word he followed her to the horses.

Neither spoke for some time as they rode along.

They were too full of their own thoughts for conversation. Inwardly Jack cursed his impulsiveness. He did not wish to fall in love with Nita Jacobson, yet there were times when he felt her attractions irresistible.

Did she really care for him? he wondered. Had she, like himself, merely acted on the impulse of the moment, or had she been stirred by a deeper emotion? Surely her display of feeling towards him was sufficient proof that his suspicions concerning Ned Kelly were unfounded - unless she was a sort of girl he did not for a moment believe her to be.

"Nita," he said at last, "are you sorry for what occurred just now?'"

"Please forget that it ever happened," she replied, with a little catch in her voice.

"You're a strange girl, Nita."

"I know I am - so strange that often I don't understand myself. Sometimes, I do things which a little later I hate myself for doing. That isn't the sort of nature to make one very happy, I assure you."

"Then aren't you happy?"

"At times without a care in the world, at other times the most miserable creature living. Who was it said: 'As high as we have mounted in our delight, in our dejection do we sink as low'."

"That was Wordsworth."

"That's one of the reasons why I like you so much, Jack," she said. "It is a treat to be able to talk to someone who knows other things than the price of wheat and stock, and the sort of bush talk that one gets so frightfully tired of."

"So my chief attraction is the education I received as a youth," he bantered.

"Don't be unkind, Jack. You know it isn't only that."

"You told' me just now that you loved me."

"And you said you wanted me."

"Well?"

She reached over and laid her hand on his arm.

"Please, Jack, let us forget."

"But supposing I didn't want to forget?"

Her answer was a sigh.

"What would you say then, Nita?" he persisted.

"Don't, Jack, don't!" she pleaded, as though the suggestion hurt her.

They had now reached Jackson's, but no dogs greeted them. The hut was in darkness.

"Queer!" Jack muttered.

"Even bush folk don't always stay at home," Nita reminded him.

"No, I suppose not."

He knocked at the door, but there was no response.

The harness and dray were missing from the shed.

"They've gone' to one of the neighbors, I suppose," said Nita.

"Perhaps a bush party somewhere?" he suggested.

"Perhaps."

"With distinguished guests."

She made no comment:

"The old man's pretty friendly with the gang, isn't he?" Briant went on.

"You should know whether he is or not, you lived with him," was her non-committal rejoinder.

"Well, what's your opinion?"

"I have heard lots of things. People will talk, you know."

"If you were called as a witness to give evidence if Jackson were charged as a Kelly syrnpathiser, what would you say?"

"My evidence would be useless because it would be only hearsay.' Jack laughed.

"You're much too clever for me. Nita. Well, as Sam and the old lady aren't home, I suppose we'd' better be getting back."

"Yes; it must be getting late."

Both were strangely silent on the homeward journey. When they had put away the horses and they stood at the door Jack took her hand, but she pulled it away.

"Not one good-night kiss, Nita?" he asked.

"Don't- don't torture me!" she cried, as she ran from him.

15

Arrested!

As Briant awoke next morning the familiar figure of Constable Costello stood beside his bunk.

"What the- "

"Get your clothes on and come with me!" The trooper's command was peremptory.

"I'll see you damned first!"

"I've a warrant for your arrest."

Jack gasped. "For my arrest! What for?"

"Highway robbery." Costello produced a blue paper from his pocket, and read its startling contents - official jargon which, translated into plain English, charged Jack Briant with having, on the previous night, while under arms, robbed John Cleggett, a neighboring farmer, of £7. The stereotyped warning as to anything he might say being used in evidence against him, followed.

"So hurry into your clothes, and come along - with me." added Costello.

"You've put this up on me, you dirty skunk!" cried Briant.

To his surprise, the trooper merely smiled.

Attracted by their voices, Jacobson came up. "Why this early call, Costello?"

Costello told him, adding with evident relish that the penalty for that sort of crime was at least seven years' gaol.

"You're mad, man," laughed Jacobson. "He rode across to Jackson's last night, and Nita went with him. Here, Nita!"

The girl came running over. She started at the sight of the policeman.

"I suppose you didn't know that while I was with you last night I was also over the Winton road robbing old John Cleggett," Briant said. "Costello says so, and he's got a warrant to arrest me."

"Arrest you!" Nita's face lost some of its color. "Cleggett got a good look at the man who bailed him up, and his description tallies with Briant," Costello told her.

"But I was with him last night."

"What time did you get back from Jackson's?" The trooper turned from one to the other.

"Honestly, I don't know," Jack replied.

"But I do," cut in Nita. "I looked at the clock - it was twenty-five to 10,"

"Oh, was it? Well, Cleggett was robbed about half past 10, and it doesn't take more than twenty minutes to get from here to where he was bailed up." There was a note of triumph in his voice.

"It's absurd," cried the girl.

"That'll be for the magistrate to say," snapped the trooper. "Hurry up there!"

"Look here, Costello, if you weren't a policeman, I'd punch your head."

Jacobson jumped forward in alarm. "Don't do anything foolish. Interfering with a trooper is serious business."

"But, father," protested Nita, "Constable Costello is mistaken. Jack wouldn't do such a thing if he had the chance."

"If you're so cocksure, perhaps you'll come and give evidence for him," sneered the trooper.

"I certainly shall," she flashed at him.

"Court sits tomorrow, so you won't have long to wait.

Come on, Briant, I'm not going to wait here all day for the likes of you."

"You'll wait here till I've had my breakfast, anyway." Costello was about to make an angry retort, when Jacobson led him up the yard. They talked earnestly for a few minutes.

"It won't do any harm to go with him," Jack's employer remarked on their return. "You can easily prove where you were last night. He's going to wait till you've had your breakfast, though. It's rough on you, I know, but lots of people suffer through policemen's mistakes."

"Costello has a set on me, but I'll get even with him yet," said Briant, as he went inside.

The trooper interrupted the meal by saying he had waited long enough, and didn't intend to wait any longer.

"Very well, then, you'd better be going," jeered Briant. "I am going, and you're coming, too."

"When I've finished my breakfast. Take your ugly mug out of this - it spoils my digestion."

Costello, purple with rage, whipped out his handcuffs, but Jacobson stepped in front of him.

"Put those away, Costello, you know they're not needed."

"Don't you interfere with me in the execution of my duty!"

"I'll have no high-handed business in my house," Jacobson shot at him.

"You know what it means to interfere with the police?" cried the enraged young trooper.

"I also know what happens to a silly young fool who loses his head and tries to exceed his duty. The boy's going in with you when he's finished his breakfast, and there's no need for all this flashness."

"Will you have another cup of coffee, Jack?" Nita asked.

"Thanks, Nita, I will," he replied, not because he wanted it, but because the delay would annoy Costello.

It did annoy him, to the extent of declaring that Briant had had enough and he didn't intend to wait any longer

"So you're going to say how much I'm to eat and drink, are you?" Jack jeered. "Really, your interest in my welfare is quite touching. If I'm keeping you from duty, just go along. I'll follow you later."

Almost beside himself with rage, Costello stepped in front of Nita as she brought Jack's refilled cup. With a snarl of anger Jacobson roughly pushed him aside.

"You remember, Costello, your business is with Briant.

Don't you dare interfere with my daughter!"

"Thank you, father," laughed Nita. "You saved me the trouble of throwing this coffee in his face."

"I'll make all of you sorry for this," Costello blurted, trembling with rage.

"You're a fool, Costello," exclaimed Jacobson.

"Hear, hear to that!" laughed Briant.

Costello glared at both of them. "You know what happened at the Kellys when they assaulted Fitzpatrick," he reminded them.

"I do happen to know," rejoined Jacobson. "I know a woman was sent to gaol on the word of a drunken policeman."

The trooper's eyes gleamed.

"A policeman's word is always accepted."

"Not always," Jack cut in. It wasn't in Donnellan's case. It mightn't be in Costello's. Donnellan was a silly young fool like yourself, and did things that even Headquarters couldn't stand."

"I'm not waiting here all day," snapped Costello, who obviously was impressed by the reference to the hotheaded young trooper who had been dismissed for many acts of arrogant brutality, which culminated in an attack on an old man named Thompson.

"I'm ready now," Jack announced, as he rose from the table. "How do you propose to take me?"

"You'll walk alongside my horse with the darbies on," replied Costello, again producing his handcuffs.

Briant smiled and shook his head. "Not that way."

Costello took a step forward. Nita took Jack's arm, "Come on," she said, "I'll drive you in."

"No you won't."

Nita walked up to the trooper, and staring him full in the eyes, said; "That's the way he's going in, Constable Costello. If you've any objection you can tell the magistrate all about it. Help me to get the horse in, Jack."

Not quite sure of himself Costello followed them into the yard. Briant shot an amused glance in his direction.

"Haven't you forgotten something? You can't tell the Bench tomorrow that you searched the prisoner and his bedroom, but failed to find any trace of the stolen money or the robber's revolver. By the way, what sort of revolver was it? I'm curious to know the kind of weapon my criminal half uses while my law-abiding half lies snugly in bed. Not only am I a criminal part of my time, but I seem to possess the extraordinary power of being in two places at once. You'll have an interesting story to tell the Bench. Why not have a look round for the plunder while you're waiting?"

Costello gritted his teeth, but did not move or speak.

Jack continued his banter.

"To make sure you won't be shot while I'm driving alongside of you, I'll show you I haven't a pistol on me."

He turned out all his pockets, removing a few shillings from one and several letters from another.

"Oh, this isn't any of Cleggett's money. This is part of last week's wages."

The horse had now been harnessed, and Nita had taken her seat in the buggy. Jack climbed up beside her.

"I shan't be long, Mr. Jacobson," he shouted to his employer as they drove through the gate.

"You go ahead," Costello commanded.

"That's very good of you," remarked Briant. "It'll save us the unpleasantness of having to look at you for the whole trip."

"By God! You'll be sorry for all this!" If looks could kill, Briant would have died on the spot.

"No; it'll be you who'll be sorry, Costello, in about a week's time."

"What do you mean by that?"

"Wait and see."

Costello said very little during the rest of the journey, except occasionally to demand a better pace. Nita, too, mostly was silent. Jack talked to her at intervals. but she replied in monosyllables.

Their arrival at Benalla caused some stir, and when they drove up to the police station a group of idlers gathered round the door.

"That ain't Joe Byrne 'e's got, is it?" one old fellow laughed.

Briant overheard the remark.

"Bless you, no," he laughed. "I'm Ned Kelly!"

The old man, with a startled gasp, hid himself behind his companions.

"Pooh! That ain't Ned Kelly!" exclaimed a boy. "Ned's got whiskers you could 'ide in!"

This rather reassured the old chap, who timidly emerged from his hiding place.

"Who you got there?" Costello was asked.

"Highway robber," he replied, with some show of pride.

To Jack - "Now then, step lively."

To the crowd's astonishment Briant turned to the trooper and said: "Don't be rude, Costello."

"By God! E's a 'arc un!" exclaimed a bystander. Costello, feeling that he was being humiliated, seized Jack by the shoulder. The appearance of a sergeant of police put an end to his contemplated demonstration, however.

"Is this your man?" asked the sergeant, closely scrutinising the prisoner, "What are you doing here, Miss Jacobson?"

"Constable Costello behaved so badly at our place that I thought I'd like to come," she replied.

The sergeant looked at Costello, who said with an angry frown: "The whole lot of them interfered with me, Sergeant. I had hard work to get the prisoner here,"

"You damned liar!" cried Briant.

"Here, here, that language won't do," the sergeant remonstrated. "You clear out, the lot of you!" he added to the little knot of excited spectators who surged round the door.

Inside the police station were several officers and a venerable-looking bearded man, whom Jack recognised from photographs he had seen as Superintendent Hare. A tall, grizzled countryman looked Jack up and down with a puzzled expression on his well-tanned face. He came forward and looked intently at him.

"Is that the man?" asked Hare, after the formal charge had been read.

"Oh, I say," Briant protested, "this method of identification is rather irregular."

"Have you ever been identified before?" sharply 'inquired the Superintendent.

"I have not, but I know something of legal procedure! Still, go ahead if it suits you."

Superintendent Hare frowned.

The old man, whom Jack took to be John Cleggett, his supposed victim, walked round him slowly, and then whispered to the sergeant, who in turn, said something in an undertone to the Superintendent.

"I want you," said that official to Jack, "to go up to this man and say, 'Your money or your life!'" Unhesitatingly Briant carried out these instructions. "That's not 'im!" cried Cleggett.

Nita muttered "Thank God!" under her breath, and Costello scowled.

"Are you certain?" Hare demanded.

"Certain," replied Cleggett. "'E's about the same build, but 'is voice ain't a bit like."

With a smile on his lips Jack waited for the next move.

It came from the Superintendent. He beckoned Cleggett over and talked earnestly with him for a few minutes. Then he announced: "Apparently some mistake had been made. Cleggett is certain that it was not this man, who robbed him."

"When this robbery took place," said Jack, "I was in bed. With Miss Jacobson I had ridden over to Jackson's, and we got back about half-past nine. I went straight to bed."

At the mention of Jackson's name, Superintendent Hare stiffened perceptibly. "I suppose you know that Jackson is a notorious Kelly sympathiser."

"I know that the police worried him a lot while I worked for him," Jack responded.

"And from your observations would you say he was a Kelly sympathiser?"

"It is evident, sir, that you don't know old Sam Jackson. If you did you would realise that he's the sort of man who doesn't tell any more than suits him."

"The police came to his hut one night when Ned Kelly was seen to ride in that direction. They found you and the old couple playing cards. Did Kelly visit them that night?"

Realising that any hesitancy on his part might arouse suspicion, Briant replied quickly: "At that time I was a cripple. I sprained my ankle and couldn't get about much. Of course, the whole gang could have come there without my seeing them, but if I were a betting man, or rather, if I had anything to bet with - I'd lay a shade of odds that they didn't."

"Constable Costello says that you behaved suspiciously on more than one occasion while he was at Jackson's," the Superintendent went on.

Briant smiled.

"Judging by his own behavior, I should say that Costello is a pretty poor judge of what is suspicious or of anything else. He is one of the bumptious young men who do so much to discredit the police and make Kelly sympathisers all over the country."

Hare's eyes widened.

"That is a very serious statement to make, young man."

"But, nevertheless, true. Still, you needn't worry very much about that. Within a week Costello will be transferred to some obscure district where his methods will be less mischievous."

A gasp of astonishment went round the room. Hare's face was a study, and so was Costello's.

"What do you mean by that?" demanded the Superintendent.

"Just what I said. In a few days you will receive notice of Costello's transfer."

"But, but, who are you, and how do you know what Headquarters will do or will not do?"

"Jack Briant, tramp, of no fixed address. As to Headquarters' intentions I can only say 'Wait and see.' As Mr. Cleggett has definitely stated that I didn't rob him on the Winton road at a time when I was home and in bed, I suppose I may go?"

Hare, who was still puzzling over what Briant had said, made no reply.

"Is there any reason for my staying here any longer?" Jack asked again.

"H'm-er-no. Mr. Cleggett is so certain that a mistake has been made that we cannot any longer detain you."

"Thank you." Then, walking up to Costello, Jack said in a voice that was loud enough for everyone to hear, "If you weren't a policeman, Costello, I'd give a few years of my life to have five minutes alone with you. Your own mother wouldn't know you when I'd done with you! As you'll be leaving this district shortly, I'm not likely to see you again, so goodbye, and may you get everything that sooner or later is bound to come to your sort!"

Before they had recovered from their surprise, he was through the door, followed by Nita.

"Oh, Jack!" she gasped, when they reached the buggy. Without a word he helped her up, and took his seat beside her. The loungers outside watched them drive away, while the station windows framed the perplexed faces of six astonished policemen.

Nita laid her hand on his arm. "Jack, what does this mean?" she asked.

"What does what mean?"

"What you said about Costello."

He laughed. "Just a bit of bluff, that's all."

Apparently it was more than that, however, for four days later Super-intendent Hare was officially informed that Constable Costello had been transferred to a small township in Gippsland, and was to report forthwith for duty at his new station!

Briant smiled,"I'm not going that way!"

16

Briant Disappears

THE fulfilment of Briant's extraordinary prophecy became a topic which temporarily overshadowed discussion of the Kellys. Who was this young stranger who was able to say, days in advance, what the Melbourne authorities intended to do? everyone asked. Was he himself a highly-placed officer from Headquarters?

Next day Superintendent Hare personally rode out to Jacobson's to question him.

"I'm a clairvoyant," Jack laughed; "I can see future events quite clearly at times."

"Please don't fool with me," said Hare sternly.

"Well, what do you wish me to say?"

"I want to know who you are."

"I told you that yesterday. My name's Briant, and I'm a tramp."

"Where did you come from?"

"Melbourne, four months ago."

"How did you know that Constable Costello was to be transferred?"

"Well, he deserved to be, didn't he?"

"That's no answer to my question."

"Don't you understand clairvoyance?"

Superintendent Hare made no attempt to conceal his annoyance.

"Don't trifle with me, young man! I demand to know where you got your informafion!"

"You forget yourself, Superintendent Hare!"

"Forget myself! Forget myself! Don't you dare to talk to me like that! Do you know what I could do to you if I wished?"

"Yes - nothing!"

"I could gaol you for this."

"Gaol me for refusing to give information to an inquisitive official who has no right to demand it? No, sir. The law may be an ass, but it isn't as big an ass as that."

Hare spluttered. "W-what do you know about the law?"

"Quite a lot of things. Now, why all this bother about Costello? I assure you he isn't worth it."

Hare drew himself up to his full height.

"Do I understand, then, that you refuse to give me any information?"

"I've already told you all you asked."

The Superintendent angrily turned on his heel.

"You'll hear more of this!" he snorted.

"Just another word," Jack shouted after him. "Costello made himself objectionable, and Costello's gone somewhere else!"

Hare could hardly believe his ears. Was this young man actually suggesting that even he might be transferred? Never before had he been subjected to such indignity. It was preposterous, unbearable. He - Viciously digging his spurs into his horse's side, he rode away at a hard gallop.

Nita, who had overheard the whole conversation, went thoughtfully inside, fear in her eyes.

Jacobson followed Briant across the paddock. "Tell me, boy," he pleaded.

"Tell you what, Mr. Jacobson?"

"What it means, what everybody is saying. Are you from-from Headquarters?"

"Oh, rather," laughed Jack. "I'm the Commissioner in disguise."

"I could help you a lot, you know," Jacobson continued, insinuatingly.

"You've already helped me a good deal in giving me a job, and I'm very grateful."

"But I don't mean in that way."

"No?"

"About the Kellys. You know I- "

"I know you want that reward very badly, Mr. Jacobson. Well, you go ahead and get the gang, and I'm sure they'll willingly give you the money."

"And you will help me, won't you ?" - eagerly.

"Oh, of course," replied Briant, moving away. Jacobson stood scratching his head in perplexity, then slowly walked back to the house.

There was little attempt at conversation at the tea table that night. Nita and Julie watched Jack with new interest - an interest not unmixed with fear it seemed and Frank stole covert glances at him. Several times Jacobson looked as though he was about to speak, but each time he thought better of it and remained silent.

"I say," Jack laughed, "We're a merry party, aren't we?"

No one answered him. He looked from one to the other.

"What's on all your minds?"

Again there was no response.' Briant got up.

"I don't seem to be very popular here, Mr. Jacobson. Would it inconvenience you very much if I cleared out tomorrow morning?" .

His employer and his elder daughter looked at him in dismay.

"You're not going away?" Nita faltered.

"You don't mean that?" Jacobson asked.

"I never stay where I'm not wanted," he told them. "I'll be off tomorrow."

"But you are wanted - isn't he, Father?" Nita said tremulously.

"Of course he is," declared Jacobson.

"We'd like you to stay," volunteered Frank. This was the first real friendly advance that young man had made since the fight, and Jack was unable to conceal his surprise. He noticed, however, that Julie maintained the attitude of hostility which she had assumed ever since the transfer of Costello had given him his unwelcome notoriety.

The same afternoon old Sam Jackson passed Jacobson's, and when Jack waved him a greeting deliberately he turned his head away. Briant ran after him.

"I say, Mr Jackson--"

The old fellow wheeled round sharply.

"I don't want to talk to the likes o' you!" he snapped.

"Why, what's the matter?"

"I took a snake to me bosom when I took you in that's what I done!"

"Don't be foolish, Mr Jackson. I suppose you think that because I told them Costello would be removed I'm a policeman."

"What I think I keep to meself!" And, kicking his horse viciously in the ribs, he galloped away in a cloud of dust.

Briant watched him with curious feelings. Hard and rough. as he was, there was something about Sam Jackson that he liked. He admired his courage and reverenced his loyalty to the outlaws whom he befriended at considerable personal risk. He wondered whether Mrs Jackson also would think him a spy. And Kate Kelly? He ached to know how she regarded him.

There was considerable police activity round Jacobson's that day and the following day. Jack caught a glimpse of someone watching him through the trees while he was stacking wood. When at night he took the gun for the purpose of shooting a few possums for the rug Nita was making he felt that he was being followed.

"Damn them!" he muttered. "I'll give them something to remember." A dark figure moved about a hundred yards in front of him, and Briant emptied both barrels in its direction.

"Don't, you fool!" shouted a voice. A man ran towards him, and when he came up he recognised Constable Martin.

"You might have shot me!" he complained.

"I thought you were a 'roo," Jack explained. "What are you doing here, anyway, spying on me?"

Martin laughed mirthlessly. "Oh, come now, why should I spy on you?"

"I've been watched all day, and I'm full of it! You go back and tell Hare that he might follow Costello if he's not careful."

Obviously, the trooper was impressed. "You don't mean to say you could get the Superintendent transferred, too?"

Briant smiled to himself as he replied: "A word in the right direction might do even that."

"I'd give something to know who you are," Martin ventured after a pause.

"Everyone knows who I am - just a tramp."

Martin laughed incredulously.

"That story won't do me. Do you know, all the boys are glad Costello's gone? He was a silly young fool and did us a lot of harm."

"Well, he won't do much harm where he is now."

"No, I'll bet he won't."

"When are you going to catch Ned Kelly?"

"I'm damned if I know," the other returned. "Sometimes—"

"Sometimes you feel you wouldn't like him caught, eh?"

"I didn't say that. I'm doing my best."

"You were pretty decent at Jackson's the other day, although you did try to bribe me to become a spy," Briant said.

Martin winced. "I only did my duty."

"Perhaps you did. Some of you have a queer way of interpreting it, though."

"Macguire lost his head, as he often does. You can't always blame the police if they cut up rough at times.

We're only human, you know, and we're always being jeered at."

"I know that. Look here, Martin, will you do me a favor?"

"I will if I can. What is it?"

"I know Hare's having me watched. Tomorrow night I'd like you to try and put them off the scent. Tell them you heard I was going to Jackson's and get them all to watch his hut. I want to go somewhere else for a while, and I don't want to be disturbed."

Martin hesitated. Then he held out his hand and said, "I'll do my best." "Thanks. I thought I could rely on you. It won't do if any of the others see me talking to you. I'll go. Good night!"

"Good night, Mr Briant."

Jack chuckled as he walked away. He was Mr Briant now. Evidently Martin had been impressed by the Costello incident. He did not continue his possum hunt, but went straight back to Jacobson's.

Frank met him in the yard. "What's up? No possums?"

"No, but plenty of troopers. They are watching me pretty closely, and that sort of thing doesn't appeal to me. Tell Nita I'm sorry I didn't get any skins for her rug. I'm off to bed. Good night!"

Frank hesitated as though he wished to talk, but contented himself with "Good night," and went inside.

As they worked in the wood paddock next day he pressed Jack for details of what happened at the police station.

"Didn't Nita tell you?"

"She did tell me a little, but she was a bit too excited to know what happened, I reckon."

Jack related the whole of the proceedings. At the end he said, "Frank, if the police asked you to say, 'Bail up, money or your life!' to anyone, how would you say it?"

Frank recoiled as though someone had struck him, and his face paled.

"W-what do you mean?" he gasped.

"Tell, how would you say it?"

"I'd just say it, of course."

"Let me hear you. Supposing I was someone you wanted to rob, how would you go about it?"

Frank's eyes showed the tumult that was surging through his brain. "What's the game?" he asked.

"There's no game," Jack replied. "I just wanted to know. Of course, if there's any reason why you shouldn't, then don't. What's the matter?"

Briant caught his arms as he staggered towards him and seemed about to fall. With staring eyes and quivering lips, Frank clung to him. "You know it was me!" he sobbed. "I want to get away from here, and old Cleggett's rich enough not to miss it - so's Josh Herman. You won't put me away, will you? Say you won't, Jack, for God's sake!"

Jack gripped his hand. "Of course I won't."

"They might have potted you for it, too. Oh, why did I do it? Why did I do it?"

Briant led him to a log and they both sat down. "You've got to be careful or you might give yourself away. Don't try it again. You'll find some other way of leaving here if you're patient."

"Patient! I can't be patient! This place is killing me! I've got to get away. I can't stay here!"

"You'll get away all right if you go on like this, but it mightn't be farther than the Benalla gaol."

Frank threw up his hands as though to ward off a blow.

"Don't say that, Jack!"

"Look here, you've got to pull yourself together. You can't clear out and leave your father and sisters."

"Can't I? Can't I? I'll show 'em I can. What do they want to stay here for?"

"Your father can't afford to throw this place away, and nobody wants to buy it. You must be patient like the rest of them. It hurts Nita and Julie just as much as it does you."

"No, it doesn't. Julie doesn't want to go while Steve Hart's here. She told me so."

"So Julie's in love with Steve Hart, is she?" remarked Jack.

"Course she is. And Nita's in love with you."

"Did Nita tell you that?" Jack asked, with quickened pulses.

"No, she didn't, but I can see it. She's been like that ever since you came here."

"No, Nita isn't in love with me. She might be in love with Ned Kelly, though."

Frank snorted. "Hugh! Don't you know Ned's sweet on my cousin, Jennie O'Donnell? She and Uncle Joe live over near McCullagh's."

Jack's heart sang for joy. For many reasons he hated to think that Nita might be infatuated with the notorious outlaw. Only tragedy could result from such an attachment. He felt sorry for the other girl, but he was glad for Nita's sake. And for his own? Yes, he was glad for himself. There were times when he felt that life without Nita would be a blank. There were other times when he was sorry he had ever met her. Was Frank right when he said she loved him?

"Perhaps I oughtn't to have told you all these things," said Frank.

"They're quite safe with me, old chap. I say, where's your revolver?"

"I've got it planted in the shed. Why?"

"Take my tip, and get rid of it. It might tempt you again. Throw it away where it won't be found. If the police discovered it they might ask awkward questions."

"By God, I will! I'll try to be patient, Jack; but it hurts, it hurts like hell!"

"That's the spirit!" cried Briant, slapping him on the shoulder.

Frank hung his head shamefacedly. "I-I don't know why you're doing this for me, after what I tried to do to you."

"I've forgotten that long ago, so don't let it worry you. I'd hate to think you were nabbed for trying a bit of amateur bushranging. Give up the silly idea of making money that way. It can't be done. Now, let's get that wood ready for tomorrow."

Briant was strangely silent at tea that night. Nita asked him what was wrong, and he said he had a headache.

"Poor boy!" she smiled sympathetically.

"I think I'll get off to bed early," he announced at the end of the meal.

"That's right," Jacobson approved. "Nothing like a good rest for a headache."

Jack did not go to bed, however. Instead, he gathered his scanty belongings together in a bundle, crept cautiously across the yard, and disappeared into the night.

17

T he Outlaws' Hiding Place

THERE was consternation at Jacobson's next morning when Jack failed to appear and investigation proved that his bed had not been slept in. Only Julie was unperturbed; indeed, her expression showed that she was relieved rather than dismayed. She sneered at her sister's troubled face.

"Oh, Julie, he didn't even say goodbye!" cried Nita, chokingly.

"Good job, too!" snapped Julie, walking away.

"I can't make it out," Jacobson remarked. "He didn't say anything about going, at least not since he agreed to stay the other day."

"He worked like a nigger yesterday afternoon, getting the wood ready for today," Frank told them. "He must have made up his mind all of a sudden. I suppose he's all right."

Fear gripped Nita's heart, but she did not speak.

"Serves you right for taking on any stranger who asks for a job!" Julie sneered. "I suppose you'll find all sorts of things missing when you look round."

"You musn't say that!" cried Nita, a hurt expression in her eyes.

"But I did say it, and I'll say it again."

Jacobson regarded his daughter in amazement. "But I thought you liked him, Julie?"

"So I did until- "

"Until you thought he was a policeman, eh?" cut in Frank. "Well, he isn't."

Julie turned upon her brother almost fiercely. "You'll see whether he isn't when Sam Jackson and Mrs Jackson and all the rest of us are arrested!"

"Well, I happen to know he isn't," Frank persisted. "That's all!"

Julie was unconvinced, however. "If you're all fools enough to believe a swaggie knows what the police down in Melbourne are going to do, I don't. I thought you had more sense."

Two days passed without tidings of Briant. On the third day Frank, returning from Benalla, brought in a letter.

"Here's something for him," he said. "Looks flash too."
Nita almost snatched it from him. It was a high quality envelope, and the writing was a woman's. With a little sob she put it on the mantelpiece and left the room.

It remained there for a whole day. It seemed to have a peculiar fascination for Nita, who never entered the room without examining it. Once, with anger in her heart, she was about to throw it into the fire when Julie's sudden appearance deterred her.

"Still nursing his letter!" jeered her sister. "I suppose it's from one of his swell lady friends in Melbourne. I knew he was only playing with you. Open it and see what a fool you've been!"

"Open it! Open it!" These words sang in Nita's ears all day. Her conscience rebelled at the suggestion, yet- He had run away without even saying goodbye. Why should she consider him? With trembling fingers she tore the envelope, and noted the embossed address at the head of the paper. Through a mist she read:

My own Jack,

Your uncle has given me your address, and I am writing to implore you to come back. It was all a terrible mistake. Why did you leave me, dearest? I am still yours. Oh, how I want you, jack! Write at once and say you are returning to me. I shall count the hours till I hear from you.

Your loving, but heart-broken,

Jessie.

Nita read it again, and each word stabbed her deeper than before. Then, with blazing eyes, she tore it, envelope and all, into little pieces and threw them into the fireplace.

"Hullo, where's the precious letter?" asked Julie, coming into the room a little later.

"I- I burnt it!"

Nita's distress was so pathetic that her sister's heart melted. Julie threw an affectionate arm around her.

"I'm sorry, sis, I didn't mean the nasty things I said to you. Forgive me, dear."

Nita did not cling to her sister and find relief in tears, as most girls would have done. Instead, she said, in a voice that contained not the slightest trace of emotion, "One hates to have one's ideals shattered, and I'm afraid I acted like a fool. All the same, I don't share your ideas about Jack and the police."

She was now the Nita - who had so often puzzled Briant - coldly impersonal - and there was no trace of the feeling which, a few minutes before, she had betrayed. Even Julie, accustomed to her changing moods, was amazed.

"I wish I could hide my feelings like you can," she observed.

"I am not hiding them."

"Oh, don't be silly! When I came in you were nearly crying, and now you're talking as if Jack were nothing more to you than a stranger. What was in the letter?"

Nita told her.

"There you are!" cried Julie, triumphantly. "I knew he wasn't straight."

"Don't say that. Because a woman who evidently loves him has written asking him to comeback it does not mean that he is a policeman in disguise. It does show why he came to the bush, though. I'm sorry now I burnt the letter."

"Surely you wouldn't give it to him if you could?"

Julie's eyes were wide with surprise.

"Of course. It may mean his future happiness. I'll try to find him and let him know what she said."

Julie could not understand such magnanimity.

"If I loved a man do you think I'd give him up like that?" she asked, almost fiercely. "Not if a hundred other women wrote asking him to come back! I'd fight for him against them all!"

There was a lot that was frankly elemental about Julie Jacobson.

Nita smiled a little wanly.

"You take it for granted that I love Jack Briant?"

Julie's astonishment was written on every feature.

"You've got me beaten," she said, as though it was useless further to try to understand her strange sister.

"Still," Nita went on, "I'd like to know where he is at this moment."

"That's an easy one. Back with his loving Jessie, of course."

Julie's guess was much wider than she imagined, however. At that moment Jack was crouching in the undergrowth at the foot of the ranges, intently watching the movements of a girl who left the little hut that nestled amid the trees. As a matter of fact, he had been watching that hut for two days and two nights.

She carried a half-filled sugar-bag and was coming his way. As she drew nearer he noticed how her red-brown hair glinted in the sun. Her eyes seemed bluer than when, a pathetic figure of abject fear, she had burst dramatically into Jackson's hut. Though shorter, she bore some resemblance to her cousin Nita. She had the same purposeful poise, the same confident air.

She left the track and began to ascend the hill which stood between the hut and the ranges proper. Cautiously, Briant followed at a safe distance. Once or twice he lost sight of her, but later discovered her picking her way among the boulders half way up the rise. She disappeared behind the rocks, and when, a minute or two later, she came into view again she was empty handed.

Jack watched the hut door close behind her before he moved. Then he followed the track taken by the girl until he found himself in the middle of a curious rock formation, a circle of giant boulders evenly spaced by apertures less than two feet wide. Through out of these holes he squeezed.

Inside was a circular patch of flat ground, bare in places and grassed in other places to which the sun had access between the boulders. It was a natural fortress, which only needed strengthening between the rocks to make it impregnable. The boulders varied in height from ten to fifteen feet, and the ground enclosed by them was roughly twelve feet in diameter.

There was no sign of the bag which Jennie had left there. Briant searched every possible hiding place without success. He knew there was food in it, and that was what he mostly needed. He had taken some tinned stuff and some biscuits with him when he left Jacobson's provisions he had bought in Benalla as an emergency ration against just such an adventure as that upon which he was now engaged. All that food had gone, however, and he was feeling ravenously hungry.

He turned over every stone it was possible to move, searched in every crevice that could conceal anything, and examined the earth to see whether it had been disturbed. For a long while he continued to search, hunger adding vigor to the quest. He had not expected that the mission on which he was engaged would last as long as it had, and consequently his provisions had run out. For several reasons he did not wish to seek food at any of the homesteads, the main one being that he was anxious not to be seen by anyone. Now there was nothing to do but wait.

For the rest of the day he crouched there, well hidden in the scrub, but in a position from which it was impossible to miss anyone who might visit the rocky hiding place.

It was a tedious vigil, but eventually it was rewarded.

Just as darkness had thrown the ring of boulders into ghostly relief, the figure of a man emerged from the undergrowth, halted, looked round cautiously, and then squeezed through the aperture between two of the rocks. He reappeared soon after, carrying the bag which all of Briant's efforts had failed to find.

Jack followed him as he climbed the hill. The w ind f avored h im, but for all that he picked his way very carefully. Twice the man in front stopped suddenly and looked round him, and each time Jack dropped down amongst the undergrowth.

Suddenly he disappeared. When Jack reached the spot he found himself confronted by a semi-circular clump of stunted trees, the trunks growing closely together, and the undergrowth between them so thick that he could not find an opening. He worked his way round them to the right, and came upon a solid wall of rock, at the end of which was a dizzy precipice.

Possibly there was an opening on the left. Cautiously he investigated. Again he found himself faced by rock. It was as if Nature, in a playful mood, had fashioned a theatre, the arc of timber representing the auditorium, and the rock formation the sides of the proscenium. What was on the other side of the trees? There must be some way of getting through them, even by the light of the stars. Several times he failed, but at last, after bruising himself and tearing his clothes, he penetrated the jungle. Fearing that a false step might mean disaster, he worked his way with infinite care.

Presently he heard voices, which suddenly ceased as he stumbled and snapped a dry bough that he had clutched for support. After what seemed hours to Briant, who crouched in a cramped and painful position, the talking was resumed, and he crept further forward. It was possible to move only by inches at a time, but presently, he came upon a narrow track. That it was man-made was obvious from the cut boughs that lined either side of it. It was too dark to see them, but as he groped his way he could feel that the leaves were dry.

The track took a sudden turn; and before he realised it he had come to the end of the timber and was standing on the edge of a small plateau. At the same instant he was confronted by four men, each with a levelled revolver in his hand.

"It's all right - don't shoot!" he cried, as he stepped forward to meet them.

One of them picked up a lantern, half of which was covered by black cloth, and held it close to Briant's face.

"What are you doing here, boy?" demanded the familiar voice of Ned Kelly.

"I told you I'd come some day, and I'm here," Jack answered

"How did you find your way?"

There was a note of irritation in the outlaw's voice.

"Followed you."

"We ought to shoot you!" snapped one of the others.

"That wouldn't do much good," laughed Briant. "I told you I wanted to help you, Ned, and now I'm going to."

The other three were talking in undertones, and from chance words which tie caught Jack could tell that his intrusion was resented.

"First of all I'm hungry enough to eat the four of *you*," he went on. "What have you got to eat? What was in the bag, Ned?"

Ned did not reply, and one of the others remarked:

"He knows too damn much."

Ned Kelly joined the other members of the gang, and for several minutes they talked earnestly. Then they came over to Briant. "As you're here, you'd better stay till morning, at any rate," the leader said. "Then you can go back - on one condition."

"I know what that condition is," Jack retorted. "You're a fool, Ned Kelly!"

Briant heard the bushranger's surprised intake of breath.

"Are you going to let him talk to you like that?" Dan demanded.

Jack laughed. "Ned ought to know I'm square. Still, I suppose I can't blame him for being suspicious. I found this place by hiding in the bush for two days. Do you think I'd have come alone if I wanted to trap you?"

"What about Costello?" broke in Steve Hart.

So the gang were familiar with that incident, too. How perfect was their organisation which kept them so well posted.

"Yes, what about Costello?" It was now Joe Byrne who spoke.

"I'll tell you all I know about him later on. First of all, I want something to eat."

"Food's hard enough to get for ourselves," grumbled Dan Kelly.

"Oh, I'll get you plenty more," Briant assured them.

"Look here, the longer we talk the hungrier I'm getting, so don't let us waste any time, or there won't be any left for you fellows."

"I wouldn't like to have to eat you, anyway," observed Byrne - "you're hide's too tough!"

Jack laughed. "Well, as the Chows say, 'No cheek, no Clismas box.' "

The lantern was placed on a flat rock, and into the small arc of light which it gave Ned set out the contents of the bag - a huge piece of corned beef, pickles, bread, butter and cheese. He cut five junks of beef and liberal helpings of bread, and opened the pickle bottle. "There you are," he said.

It was a curious meal. The five of them were in darkness except for the lantern light and the light which the stars afforded, and they ate in silence. Ned, he noticed, carried his leadership even to the extent of rationing the provisions. Never had food tasted sweeter to Jack than the rough fare which he held in his fingers, and devoured with the relish which acute hunger induced.

"By jove," he exclaimed. "Wouldn't a billy of tea go good now!"

"How can we light a fire?" said Dan, irritably.

"You can if you know the way."

"And have a mob of troopers down on us," growled Hart.

"It's easy to hide a fire if you go about it in the right way. Do you mean to say you never have anything warm?"

"Only when we go to our friends," replied Ned.

"Well, tomorrow I'll show you how to do it. Any of you like a small wager?"

There was no response.

"I was going to say that I'm willing to bet you'll all have hot meat and tea tomorrow, that is if you've got any tea and sugar."

"Plenty," said Ned.

"All right. Are there any takers?"

"But I said you were going back tomorrow," Ned reminded him.

"And I said I was going to stay," laughed Briant.

Dan Kelly made an impatient gesture. "I suppose you've come to show Ned how to run this show?"

"Ned's shown he can do that very effectively. Still, there might be some things that I could show him. As you don't have tea regularly it is pretty clear you don't know how to conceal a fire."

"Look here," Byrne interrupted, "what were you going to tell us about Costello?"

"Costello seems to have got on everybody's nerves, and I'm afraid my lucky guess is the cause of it."

"Lucky guess!" exclaimed Ned.

"It was only that. I saw enough of Costello at Sam Jackson's to know he was a silly young fool, who couldn't last long, but I didn't know I hit the bullseye like I did."

Ned leaned over towards Jack. "Is that the truth you're telling us?"

"Why should I tell you a lie, Ned?"

The outlaw did not reply immediately. He thought for some time, then he said with a reverence that rather surprised Briant:

"Will you swear by the good name of the mother who bore you, by the Almighty God above you, that you aren't working with the police?"

"I will," responded Jack.

"If I thought you were a spy I'd shoot you like a dog."

"And I wouldn't blame you," agreed Briant.

18

The Tragedy at Stringybark Creek

THEY talked far into the night. Jack was anxious to hear from Ned his version of the tragedy of Stringybark Creek, and he adroitly led the conversation in that direction.

"I know you didn't murder those three policemen in cold blood," he added.

"Of course, we didn't," cried Ned, with some show of feeling. "We could have shot them the day before if we wanted to. We watched the four troopers pitch their camp, and it would have been easy to have put a bullet through any of them. We did want their guns and ammunition and food, though. That's why we bailed up McIntyre and Lonergan when Kennedy and Scanlon were down the creek. Lonergan showed fight, and was shot.

"We promised McIntyre if he would tell the other two to surrender when they came back everything would be all right. I'm sorry Lonergan was killed, but he shouldn't have tried to draw his revolver."

"What about the report that you told McIntyre you mistook him for Constable Flood, and that if it had been Flood you'd have roasted him alive?" Briant interrupted.

"All lies," replied the bush ranger, with some vehemence.

"I believe the police would have shot us on sight if they'd had a chance, but I didn't want murder on my hands. I did talk a bit to McIntyre to scare him, but if the other two had put up their hands when he asked them to they'd have been alive today."

"McIntyre did beg them to surrender?"

"We all heard him. We told them to bail up, but they refused."

"Did Kennedy fire at you?"

"He did and he was a good shot, too. One of his bullets went through my beard, and another grazed Dan's cheek. Scanlon was unslinging his rifle when we got him."

"It was a terrible business, Ned."

"My God, it was!" the outlaw assented. "We'd had a rough time from the police, and my mother was in gaol because Fitzpatrick lied about what happened when he came to our place, but we weren't murderers. Supposing we hadn't shot them, where would we have been? It was a fair fight, and we won."

"Kennedy and Scanlon were brave men," Jack ventured. "Brave, but foolish. McIntyre had pluck, too. We might have shot him, too, when he jumped on Kennedy's horse and galloped off."

"You did fire at him?"

"We did, and some of the bullets went pretty close.

We could tell by the way he kept ducking."

"If you were anxious to kill him, too, you would have followed him.

"We didn't want any more bloodshed," said Ned, with a little quaver in his voice. "That was over two months ago, and since then the police have kept us moving. It was a bad business, and the man responsible for it was Fitzpatrick. His lies put my mother in gaol, and drove Dan and me into the bush. Now, we'd better get some sleep. We've got a few bags, and you can have a couple of mine."

"No, you keep them," Jack protested. "You'll need all yours."

"It gets cold in these hills even at this time of year. Get under these." And Ned tossed him two sacks slit down the centre.

"Do you all sleep at once?" Jack asked, as he noticed that Dan, Hart and Byrne also were preparing to rest.

"There's someone else watching tonight," replied Ned. "We won't be disturbed. Good-night to you, boy!'"

"Good night, Ned. And you three, too!"

"Night!" gruffly responded Byrne, the only one of the three to speak.

Tired as he was, Briant's brain refused to rest. Here he was in the bush rangers' camp. Within a few feet of him lay the four men for whom the whole Victorian force was searching-outlaws with a price upon their heads. The regular breathing of Ned and Joe Byrne told him that they were asleep. He was not so certain about Dan and Steve Hart. He had an idea that the younger Kelly was watching him from the shadow of the rock under which he lay.

Suppose by some miracle the gang were captured that night, what would his position be? With some misgiving he recalled that section of the Felons' Apprehension Act which provided for a maximum penalty of fifteen years' imprisonment for anyone giving assistance in any form to the outlaws.

The countryside had been liberally plastered with proclamations concerning the Kellys, and he almost knew the text of some of them by heart. There was one clause which had impressed him particularly-that which made it lawful for "any of Her Majesty's subjects whether a constable or not and without being accountable for the using of any deadly weapon in aid of such apprehension whether its use be preceded by a demand of surrender or not to apprehend and take such outlaws alive or dead."

For hours he lay awake. There was a faint light in the eastern sky when eventually he managed to get to sleep, and it seemed to him that he had just closed his eyes when the voices of the gang awakened him.

"Good Lord, daylight already!" he exclaimed, sitting up and rubbing his eyes. "I don't believe I've slept an hour."

"Wasn't like the feather beds you've been used to, I suppose?" There was a sneer in Dan Kelly's voice.

"My bed's been just as hard as yours lately, except when I was at Jacobson's. Heavens, what a view!"

Jack walked to the edge of the plateau. At his feet yawned a chasm hundreds of feet deep. Across the purple abyss the hills were tipped by the glow of the rising sun, and the sky beyond them ranged in color from deep red to pearl-grey.

There is a glory in sunrise in the Australian bush unequalled in any other part of the world. Never before had Jack seen it in such arresting beauty. To the others it had no such appeal. It meant the beginning of another day of peril - of nerve-racking vigilance - of doubts and fears.

As Briant surveyed the scene he was struck, too, by the fact that if Nature had purposely fashioned a hiding place she could scarcely have improved upon that rocky platform perched dizzily on the mountainside.

Access was possible only through the belt of timber which he had found so difficult to penetrate. That was the only vulnerable spot, for no one could climb the sides of the mountain, which rose straight from the gully, hundreds of feet below. The plateau was open only to the hills a mile away, and as it was higher than the highest mountain top it is doubtful if any part of it was visible, even through powerful glasses.

"Why, Ned, you're as safe here as if half Australia was guarding you," said Briant. "There's only one danger spot - that clump of timber. You could light a bonfire in the daytime and no one see it."

Ned silently shook his head.

"I'm going to give you tea for breakfast this morning if you can find some water. May I use that billy?"

"It's too dangerous."

"It isn't dangerous at all. Let me show you."

With a tomahawk which lay amongst a miscellaneous collection of food and clothes under a ledge of rock, Jack cut four forked sticks about three feet long, after being shown by Ned how to deaden the sound of the chopping. Driving these into the ground so as to forma square, he cut a number of light boughs, and constructed a roof.

"If we built a fire under that," he exclaimed, "the leaves will filter the smoke and make it invisible at the height of a few feet. You watch."

He placed a bough under the shelter and set alight to it, the others watching him with keen interest. Blue smoke rose from it in a cloud, but the leafy screen broke it up so effectively that the tiny spirals which came through it were quickly absorbed in the air, and were invisible almost immediately.

"Who taught you that?" asked Ned, admiringly.

"That was a trick I learnt from a book I read as a boy. Now what about some water, and then for some steaming hot tea."

Steve Hart took the billy and disappeared into the scrub belt, returning a few minutes later with it full of crystal liquid.

"You seem to have water laid on here," Jack remarked.

"There's a spring a few feet lower down, but it takes some getting at," Ned told him.

"Don't put too much on the fire at once."

Briant laughed away his fears as he carefully built up a fire from the embers of the experimental bough.

From the improvised storehouse under the rock ledge Joe Byrne produced four pannikins. "Had beer in 'em," he said, sniffing one of them. "Never mind - give the tea a flavor."

"Better rinse them out when the water boils," said Ned. It was not long before the tea was ready, and they drank it with relish, Ned insisting that Jack should have a pannikin while he used the lid of the billy.

"Sorry I came along?" Briant grinned, as he noted their appreciation. "It does warm you up, doesn't it? Remember our last drink of tea together, Ned?"

"It does warm you up, doesn't it? Remember our last drink of tea together, Ned?"

The bushranger smiled at the recollection of his meeting with this audacious youngster, and of the startling trick that had been played upon him. Dan Kelly, Steve Hart and Joe Byrne showed by their expressions that Ned had not told them of that memorable encounter.

"Any wallabies round here?" Jack asked.

"Millions," replied Byrne.

"Well, what's wrong with roast meat today?"

"How can we shoot wallabies?" asked Dan querulously.

"You can hear gunshots for miles round these hills."

"What did they use before guns were invented?"

Steve Hart laughed. "What you going to do - spear 'em, or club 'em, or shoot 'em with arrows?"

"If you can get close enough it isn't hard to kill a wallaby with an arrow."

"We can always get meat," Ned cut in. "We've never bothered about fresh meat because we couldn't cook it, but now you've shown us the way it'll be different. We'll get some tonight."

"Why not today?"

Dan made an impatient gesture. "If you think it's easy dodging troopers in the daytime you're- "

"Couldn't I go for it?" Jack interrupted.

"It wouldn't be safe," Ned assured him.

Their breakfast was much the same as the evening meal had been-junks of corned beef and bread and butter, but the hot tea added relish, and the five of them ate heartily.

"What do you do when it rains?" Jack asked, looking round and noting the poor shelter which the rock ledges afforded.

"Get wet," replied Dan.

Briant grinned. "Don't think I want to criticise your bushcraft too severely, but the man who gets wet in a place like this doesn't know, well, he doesn't know how to get in out of the rain!"

"You do, I suppose?" sneered Steve Hart.

"I most certainly do. Here's a ledge of rock about three feet high, about fifteen feet long, and jutting out more than two feet. At a pinch two of you could sleep under it. Supposing you dug out the earth four or five feet and covered the ground with bracken you'd all be as snug as a bug in a rug. I suppose it'd be easy to borrow spades from your friends?"

"Dead easy," assented Dan.

"Then if you want shelter, why not?"

"We've got to move on," said Ned, after a pause.

"All the same it'd be handy to have a place like this to fall back on."

"We won't be in this district much longer," Ned volunteered. The glances of the others showed that they considered the remark indiscreet.

"I'll tell you what I'll do," said Jack. "I'll fix it up for you while you're away."

"Supposing we don't come back this way?" suggested Hart.

"Then I'll use it myself as a summer residence. Say, where do you keep your horses?"

The question surprised the gang, and none of them seemed disposed to answer it. Briant laughed at this reticence. "I see I'm still not to be trusted."

"It isn't that, only- "

"Never mind, Ned. I was merely curious."

"They're safe where no damned trooper's likely to find 'em," declared Dan.

"I didn't suppose you kept them at the livery stable in Benalla. Going away, Ned?"

With the exception of Byrne, all the outlaws were strapping on their revolvers.

"Yes, we've got something to do. Joe's staying here. You'd better get away, too."

"No, I'm staying."

Dan looked first at Jack and then at his brother. "He's the only man I've heard you let talk like that. What's coming over you?"

Ned did not reply, He picked up a sack, threw it over his arm, and disappeared into the scrub, Dan and Hart following.

Sam Jackson lurched forward on his horse's neck.

19

Joe Byrne's Remorse

"DAN'S got a set on me," remarked Briant, as he watched them go. "I suppose it isn't to be wondered at. This sort of life isn't likely to make one very amiable."

Byrne's lips parted in a mirthless smile. "You're right there, Dan's always a bit irritable. There'd be trouble with him but for Ned."

"Ned's a fine fellow."

"One of the best."

"It seems such a hell of a pity."

"What do you mean?" asked Byrne, wheeling round.

"You know what I mean, Joe. Why don't you all clear out of the country? It's your only chance. They'll get you if you don't."

"There's things to do first."

Jack made an impatient gesture. "Surely there's nothing as important to you as your lives."

Byrne thought for a moment before replying. "You don't understand. We couldn't get away if we had the money."

"Of course you could. My people are in the shipping line, and I could fix it. I've told Ned that already, but he says it can't be done - yet. It's foolish - it's suicidal!"

Byrne's gaze was very searching as he asked, "Didn't Ned tell you why?"

"No. Why?"

The other remained silent.

"If there are reasons that I shouldn't know, all right. All the same, Ned seems damned obstinate. Once you got to the coast you'd be safe. I'd see to that."

"But we mightn't get to the coast."

Noticing Briant's perplexity he added: "About here things are different. We've got plenty of good friends to keep an eye on the troopers and on those who mightn't be as friendly as they seem. There's a fair bit of money to be had for putting us away, and money counts a lot with some people."

"Yes, I know that, but how does staying round here help?"

"We're not staying round here. We've got other things to do."

Jack was beginning to see a little clearer. "Now I see daylight. Some of your supposed friends might be willing to forgo the Government reward if you could satisfy them in another way. The banks, eh?"

"I didn't say that!" - sharply.

Briant smiled.

"You really did, Joe. Bank robbery's a dangerous game, though."

"Isn't this dangerous?"

Jack laid a sympathetic hand on his shoulder.

"Of course it is, and I wish you'd let me get you out. If you hadn't shot those policemen!"

Byrne went to the cliff edge and stood with bowed head. He remained there for fully a minute, then slowly turned, walked to a rock, and buried his face in his hands. "God, it was awful!" he said, without looking up.

Briant seated himself beside him and put his arm round his shoulders.

"None of us wanted to kill," the young bushranger went on in a voice that showed the remorse he was feeling. "We expected them to surrender, and when they didn't - well, we fired, because in some way or other, it was impossible to do anything else. Oh God! why did it happen?"

"Don't talk about it, Joe," said Jack.

"But I've got to talk about it, or I'll go mad! Ned won't let us mention it, and I feel unless someone will listen to me I won't be able to stand it. They call us murderers, the troopers tell my mother her son's a murderer - but we're not. I'd give the rest of my life to bring back those three men! We could have shot a dozen troopers at different times if we'd wanted to."

"You've got to get away and make a fresh start in a new country," Briant persisted. "There's no other way."

"Not yet - not yet!"

"You could go over to Sydney. If you lie low for a while the police would be certain to let up a bit, and you could easily cross the Murray."

"I wish we could. What's that?"

He turned sharply as his keen eyes caught a slight rustle in the scrub. Motioning Jack to remain where he was, he parted the foliage and looked about him. Then he cautiously picked his way through the trees. When he had been gone several moments Briant followed him.

Presently he found the path, and with careful footsteps made his way towards the edge of the timber belt. There he found Byrne, who started violently at the sound of his approach. He put his finger to his lips and pointed down the hill.

"Police?" Jack whispered.

"Looks like them. Two of them are going over to O'Donnell's."

"What about Ned, Dan and Steve?" Jack asked in alarm.

"They're all right. Still, I don't like them knocking about so close to us. Look, there's Steve, and the troopers are coming his way!"

Briant saw with dismay the young outlaw creeping among the rocks at the foot of the circle of giant boulders. His heart almost stood still at the sight of the two tall men coming up the hill in his direction. Once they hesitated and looked as though they intended to turn back, and for a second he breathed more freely.

Then, to his horror, he saw them approach the boulders.

Steve had seen them, too, for he was flattening himself against the rocks.

"If they separate, he's done for!" gasped Byrne, pushing aside the foliage.

"Where are you going?" asked Jack in frightened accents.

"If he's got to make a fight for it, I'm going to be with him!"

Jack pulled him back. "For God's sake, Joe, no more bloodshed! Look! They're keeping together."

They saw the troopers circle the boulders, and one of them squeezed himself into the space inside. Presently he emerged, and Hart came into view again as he played this desperate game of hide-and-seek. Twice they circled the rock, Steve always a few yards ahead of them. The troopers remained for a moment with their backs to the scrub. Then one of them retraced his steps, while the other stood still.

In mute despair Jack and Joe exchanged glances. If the policeman, who by this time had disappeared, went round the other side, Hart's discovery would be certain. With pounding hearts they watched and waited. God, there he was! He had completed the circle again.

But where was Steve? Where had he managed to hide? Where? From the gully below came the faint echo of a shriek, followed by a woman's cry of "Help!" The troopers listened, and it was repeated. They ran down the hill, taking the fallen timber in their stride. What new horror was this?' Jack's face was as white as that of his companion and great beads of perspiration stood out on his forehead.

"Look, there's Steve!"

Hart had emerged from the boulders and was cautiously coming towards them. When he reached the timber he almost fell at their feet. They helped him along the path to their hiding place. Panting with excitement, he flung himself on the ground. Presently he sat up. "Hell! that was c-close!" he stammered.

"Where did you hide when the trooper came round again?" asked Briant in amazement.

"I squeezed in and lay down just on the other side of the rock where the second man was standing. Did you hear a woman scream? It came from O'Donnell's way?"

"Isn't the girl who lives there a friend of Ned's?" Briant asked.

Neither of them answered him, but he saw by their faces that he was right. "I'm going down to see what's wrong," he added.

"But- "

Jack cut Byrne short. "It's all right. I'll work well round the hill, and they won't see the direction I come from. The chances are I'll be back soon."

20

Jennie O'Donnell

WHEN he reached the edge of the timber Jack worked his way amongst the scrub until he was almost level with the tiny hut that nestled at the foot of the hills. Further to disguise the direction in which he came he cut a diagonal course so that he would leave the scrub at the back of O'Donnell's, thus giving the impression that he had come due south instead of from the east.

At the edge of the clearing he paused. No sound came from the hut. As he approached still closer, however, he heard voices, amongst them a woman's. They were talking in quiet, even tones, so that if some danger had prompted the scream and the call for help it seemed to have passed. The back door was open, and through it he saw Jennie and two big men. One he recognised as Constable Martin, but the other was a stranger. Martin looked up as he approached.

"Here comes Mr Briant," he exclaimed, going out to meet him. Jack could scarcely suppress a smile. It was evident that Martin was going out of his way to be respectful. The Costello incident had impressed him very deeply.

"I heard someone call for help when I was away back in the scrub, and I hurried over. What was wrong?"

"Miss O'Donnell trod on a snake, and it curled itself round her leg. She grabbed it near the head before it could bite her, and unwound it. Then, just like a woman, she screamed when all danger was over."

"Did she kill it?"

"No, it got away."

"That's a pity. You must have been close by when she called out."

"Oh, y-yes," replied Martin, a little hesitatingly. "We weren't far away."

"Still hunting for the Kellys, eh? What made you come here when everyone knows they were seen at Wangaratta two days ago?"

Martin's eyes widened. "I never heard that. Who told you?"

"I heard it in Benalla last night, and an old chap I met on the road said he expected they'd soon be caught now that they were making north."

"Who was he?" was the trooper's eager inquiry.

"I don't know. A sandy-whiskered old fellow, riding a flea-bitten grey mare."

Martin rubbed his chin reflectively. "Was he a tall man?"

"N-no, inclined to be short, with a bit of a cast in one eye."

Martin thought again. "That's queer--I can't place anyone like that. Maybe a stranger."

"I shouldn't say so from his conversation."

The other man came out of the hut, and Martin introduced him as Constable Treloar. He was a tall, rangy man with a big black moustache.

"I've heard a bit about you," he grinned, as he extended a long, knobby hand.

Jack laughed. "That guess of mine about Costello seems to have attracted a lot of attention."

"I was sent up from Melbourne to take Costello's place," Treloar volunteered.

"You're lucky."

"How do you mean?"

"Well, it'll be easy to prove yourself a better man. Costello seemed to imagine that because he was a policeman he owned the country. He said things to Sam Jackson that no constable has a right to say to any old man."

"Jackson's the Kelly sympathiser I told you about," Martin interposed.

"How do you know that?" asked Jack.

Martin smiled. "We all know that."

"Then why don't you arrest him?"

"We're sure he's helping the Kellys in some way, but we can't get anything on him."

"You mean he's too clever for you."

Martin winced "Well, we haven't been able to get any direct evidence against him - yet."

"Still hopeful?"

"Of course we are. If you told us all you knew, now- "

"I'm afraid that wouldn't help you very much. If you knew old Sam as well as I do you would know that he doesn't usually advertise his business before the world."

"He's as cunning as a wharf rat, but - well, you never can tell. What's the matter?"

A gasp of surprise came from Briant, who, looking towards the hut, saw the face of Ned Kelly momentarily framed in the window!

"An eagle – the biggest one I've ever seen," he replied, pointing over the roof of the house. "Look! He may come over the trees again."

The two troopers turned and watched the sky for a minute or two.

"Must be flying low. I'd no idea they grew so big," Briant went on.

"I've seen 'em with a seven-foot wing spread," said Treloar. "A fellow like that can carry off a pretty big lamb."

"Which way are you making for now?" Martin asked, after a pause. "Going back to Jacobson's, by any chance?"

"I'm not sure," Jack replied. "I'm a wanderer, you know, and like change. I wonder if old O'Donnell would give me a job?"

Martin nudged his companion. "Trust him to look for a job where there's a pretty girl about."

"Is there a pretty girl here? They told me O'Donnell had a daughter, but I imagined she was over forty. Thanks for the tip. By jove, you're right!" he added, as Jennie O'Donnell came through the door towards them.

"Good afternoon," she said to Jack, with a smile that revealed her glistening teeth.

"This is Mr Briant," said Martin.

"I've heard my cousin, Nita Jacobson, speak of you."

Nita! Jack felt a tug at his heartstrings. He had treated her badly in running away without a word of farewell, and he felt a little ashamed of himself. .

"I hope she didn't give me too bad a character," he laughed.

"Nita wouldn't do that," she replied.

Martin looked meaningly at Treloar. "We'd better be getting away."

A shade of annoyance crossed the girl's face.

"I was wondering," she said, "whether you would do something for me before you go. It isn't often we have three strong men here at one time. Dad and I have tried for days to shift that log over there, but it's too heavy for us. We're going to build a shed there when we clear the tree away."

"Always at the service of the ladies," replied Martin with an exaggerated bow.

The fallen tree indicated by the girl was a big one.

The branches had been lopped off, so that only the trunk remained.

"I don't know what Dad did with the poles we tried to roll it with," Jennie said, looking around.

"We mightn't need them," said Treloar, stooping down and placing his hands on the log. "Now then, all together."

Their combined strength failed to move it an inch. "It's heavier than you think," laughed the girl.

"We'll shift it, never fear," said Martin, looking about him. "Ah! here we are." Walking over to where a heap of saplings lay, he pulled out a thick one. "If we can find a couple more we'll be right."

Eventually three suitable poles were found, and the log was levered into the position desired by Jennie, who every now and then stole anxious glances in the direction of the hills. As the three men paused for breath she looked again, and what she saw evidently pleased her, for she turned to them with grateful smiles.

"Thank you very much. It's very good of you."

Martin waved a deprecatory hand.

"It was nothing - only too pleased to help you."

When they had gone Jack turned eagerly to her.

"Did Ned get away?"

"How did you know?" she asked wonderingly.

"I saw him look out of the window. I guessed your log-rolling scheme was to delay the troopers. You're a clever girl, Miss O'Donnell."

She beamed her pleasure. "Won't you call me Jennie?"

"By all means. Was Ned in the house all the time those two were here?"

"Ned and Dan, too."

"Wasn't, that risky?"

She laughed merrily. "They'd never think I'd call them if we had bushrangers in the house."

Big-eyed he said: "Then the snake was a fake, too?"

She smiled again.

"You see," she explained, as she led Jack inside, "Steve Hart was here, too. He went to go back to the hills just as the troopers came along. They must have caught sight of him because they followed him. We watched them. It looked dangerous, so I called for help."

"That was very clever of you," said Briant, admiringly. "And when they came to your rescue you told them the snake yarn."

"Don't give me any credit for that," she laughed. "That was Ned's idea."

21

Uncle Joe

"ARE you going back to Uncle's?" Jennie asked.

"I don't know…"

"You left pretty suddenly, didn't you? What made you do it?"

"To spy on you!"

She sat up with a start. "To spy on me?"

"Don't be alarmed at that," he laughed. "I did it for Ned's sake." He saw, with some misgiving, how her eyes lighted at the mention of the outlaw's name. "I wanted to help Ned, but he wouldn't let me go with him. I knew he came to see you- "

"How did you know that?"- with heightened color.

"The usual little bird. I watched this place for two days and two nights, and I can tell you it was dreary work. It isn't all honey hiding in the bush during a cold spell like this, although it is November."

He saw the pity in her eyes, and knew that it was of Ned and not of himself that she was thinking.

"I watched you hide that bag of food, and when Ned came for it I followed him up the mountain. I spent last night with them."

"Did they let you see The Ledge?"

"The Ledge?' Oh, is that what you call it? They couldn't have got rid of me - unless they threw me over the cliff. This morning I showed them how to light a fire without the smoke showing, and we had some steaming hot tea."

"That was very good of you, Mr- "

"Jack."

"Jack, then why did you do this for Ned?"

"Because I like him." There was a world of gratitude in her big blue eyes. "I want to help him, but he won't let me. They'll have to leave Australia - it's their only chance. He could send for you later," he added, as he noticed her dismay.

She shook her head. "Ned can't go yet!"

"Everyone says that, but I don't see why," he said, a little irritably. "I could arrange the whole thing if they'd let me."

"Oh, if you only could!"

"I can, I tell you--"

Something sounded like a footstep outside. Jennie looked at him in a way that signified a warning. They had been talking in undertones, but now she raised her voice.

"So you like the bush, Mr. Briant, in spite of its roughness?"

"I do, Miss O'Donnell," he replied.

She laughed. "I thought you might have been scared by the Kellys."

"Oh, no By the way, what's Ned like? I'd like to see him."

"Oh, a big chap with a brown beard."

"Have you ever seen him?"

"Many a time before he became a bushranger."

"And never since?"

She hesitated before replying.

"I'm - I'm not quite sure. One day my cousin pointed out a man to me and said he was Ned Kelly, but I believe she made a mistake."

"Aren't you scared of him?"

Jennie laughed. "Not a bit. None of them ever interferes with a woman."

"So they tell me. It's a shame to see a chap like Ned going to the devil."

She winced, but her tone was quite casual as she replied, "It is, isn't it. Let's talk of something pleasant. Did you like my cousin Nita?"

"Very much. She's a hard girl to understand, though."

"She is," Jennie agreed. "She's fearfully moody, yet- "

There was a knock at the door. In response to her "Come in!" Constable Martin entered the room.

"I'm sorry to disturb you," he said, "but I've lost my notebook. I wondered if I dropped it here."

"I don't think so, but we'll have a look."

144

The three of them made a careful, but unsuccessful, search.

"It doesn't seem to be here," remarked Jack. "Perhaps it fell out of your pocket when we were shifting that log."

And he led the way outside. There was still no sign of it, and Martin turned to them with an apologetic air.

"I'm sorry to have been a nuisance, but it had some notes in it I wouldn't like to lose."

They watched him go through the slip panel before re-entering the hut.

"He was listening," said Jennie, a little anxiously.

"I don't think he heard until you so smartly changed the conversation. Jennie, is every bush girl as clever as you and Nita and Kate?"

She flushed with pleasure.

"You pay me a great compliment when you speak of me in the same breath as Nita and Kate."

"You're all so wonderful!" he exclaimed. "You're so unlike-so unlike- "

"So unlike the city girls you know. Is that what you were going to say? I'm sorry" -as she noted his changed expression.

"You're quite unlike them, I'm glad to say."

The bitterness of his tone did not escape her.

"I shouldn't have asked you that, because I see it hurt you."

"There are memories that hurt me very much, Jennie, I'm ashamed to admit. When I left Melbourne I swore I'd forget everything, but it's hard, damned hard."

"You're not going to stay in the bush, are you?" she asked after a long silence, her eyes softened by pity.

"I don't know. The chances are I will, though. There are very few in Melbourne who care - now. Here I am free to do as I like, if the police only let me," he added with a mirthless laugh.

"I wish I could help you," she said. He turned to her eagerly.

"You can help me, and Ned, and yourself. Try to persuade them to clear out before the police get too strong. The black trackers- "

The girl uttered a despairing cry, and covered her face with her hands.

"We mustn't let them get him, Jennie. They must get away! You'll have to part with him for a while."

She turned her tear-dimmed eyes to him: "I'd do anything to save him! If he'd be safe I'd part with him tomorrow, even if it meant I'd never see him again. Never-see-him-again." She whispered it shudderingly.

"Don't let us look on the black side of things. There's a way out, I'm sure."

"I wonder if there is a bright side?" she said; more to herself than to him.

"Of course there is! I've made you gloomy, and I'm sorry. You can rely on me to do all I can. And I'm sure I can succeed. I'll go back to Ned and try again to persuade him to leave the country."

He rose, but she laid a detaining hand on his arm. "You won't find Ned."

"Won't he be at The Ledge?"

She shook her head.

"They told me they were moving on."

"They'll be getting ready now, and tonight they ride away."

"Must they go?" Jack asked.

"Ned says they must," she replied, in a way that indicated that nothing further need be added. He recalled Kate Kelly's "Ned knows best" as further evidence of the complete faith which all his friends reposed in this masterful outlaw leader.

"The blacks have been round here," Jennie said, with fear in her eyes; as though she realised what added danger the employment of those uncannily skilful trackers meant to her lover. "Some of them are not trying, I know, for fear the gang will shoot them, and we're all doing our best to let them know that the boys have sworn to kill everyone they set eyes on. Oh! but they're so clever. It was hard enough with the police scouring the bush night and day, but the trackers are making it ten times harder. They're more than human. I saw one of them just glance at the ground and say, 'Big doe kangaroo come along two, three hour ago?' "

"But he mightn't have been right."

"He was right. Dad saw the 'roo himself just about that time."

"Do you mean to tell me that a black fellow can tell from tracks which we wouldn't even notice the sex of the animal and when it made them?"

"They can do it easily. Every time I see or hear of a tracker my blood runs cold."

"Ned told me that they could sleep undisturbed last night, because someone was on guard," said Jack.

"There were four of us watching last night - Dad, Red Regan, Tom Stevens, and me."

Briant looked as though he had not heard aright.

"Do you mean to say you were out in the bush all night?"

Her lips parted in a wan smile.

"We all take our turn," she said simply.

"You stagger me! You amazing girl!"

"Is that very much to do for the man I love?"

"It is something that very few girls would do," he replied, with a trace of bitterness in his voice.

"We're only poor, simple bush people, but we do stick to our friends."

"Assuredly you do!" he exclaimed. "It's a pity- "

"I know what' you are going to say," she interrupted.

"It's a pity you are not doing this for better men."

"I didn't mean that. Ned and the others aren't saints, but- "

"Ned never was a saint, I know. Even before this trouble he sold horses that didn't belong to him. Dozens of others did the same thing. I don't care if he did. He's the bravest, kindest man that ever breathed, and I love him. He never did anyone real harm until that terrible affair in the Wombat Ranges, and then the police brought it on themselves. He was driven to the bush by the police. Their lies put his mother in gaol. I hate every trooper in the force!" Her eyes blazed and her bosom heaved.

"The police are like every other sort of people – there are good and bad ones," he remarked.

"If I saw a policeman drowning and could save him, I wouldn't move an inch!" she declared with bitterness.

"Oh, yes, you would."

"I would not!"

Jack put his hands on her shoulders and looked squarely into her eyes.

"A girl like you couldn't be mean and ungenerous. If a trooper was drowning you'd be the first to go to his rescue."

"I'd like to shoot everyone of them!" she snapped, pushing his hands away.

"Wrong again, Jennie," he smiled.

A heavy step was heard outside. A big form darkened the doorway, and Joe O'Donnell stepped inside. He was one of these young-old men often met with in the bush - tall and broad, with a tangled red beard and bushy eyebrows, giving him a fierceness that the kindly quirk at the corners of the mouth belied.

"Didn't know there was anybody here," he remarked, looking Jack up and down.

"This is Mr Briant, Dad," said Jennie.

Jack held out his hand, but O'Donnell ignored it.

"Oi've heard about ye and Costello," he said, with a scowl.

Briant laughed.

"Your father shares the general opinion that I'm a policeman, Jennie. He looked at me just like Dan, Steve and Joe did at The Ledge last night."

O'Donnell gasped. "At The Ledge?"

"Yes," Jennie interposed, "he spent last night with the boys, and this morning showed them how to build a fire and hide the smoke."

"Who told you that?"

"Ned did."

"Mr. O'Donnell," said Jack, going up to the big Irishman, "if I'd wanted to put Ned away I could have' done it weeks ago. Why, the first time I met him I could have shot him dead." He related the incident.

Jennie smiled. "Ned told me that, too."

"Then who the divil are ye?" O'Donnell demanded. "At present a swaggie, doing odd jobs wherever I can find them."

O'Donnell's face showed how curiously mixed were his feelings. He had heard enough about this mysterious youngster who was able to tell several days in advance what was going to happen to a policeman to share the suspicion of half the countryside; yet, if what he had just heard about Ned Kelly were true it was impossible that Briant had any connection with officialdom. The boy didn't look like a sneak, and Jennie, with her uncanny intuition concerning people who were and people who were not to be trusted, had accepted him.

"You've got Dad puzzled," laughed the girl.

"Looks like it. That was an unlucky guess of mine about Costello. You see, I knew that young fool would strike trouble sooner or later, but I had no idea I was such a good prophet," he added in response to O'Donnell's inquiring glance.

At last the big Irishman came to a decision. He held out a hand that looked like a mallee root.

"If Jennie says ye're right ye can't be far wrong. We're goin' to hav' a boite to ate, and Oi'd like ye to join us."

"That's very good of you. A swaggie never refuses a meal, you know."

"He's a funny swaggie, isn't he, Dad?" smiled Jennie.

"Oi've seen his loikes before," her father responded. "He's not the first mahn to lave the city and come to the bush because somethin' happened. But if ye're a frind av Ned's ye're a frind of moine."

"I'm very glad to hear you say that, Mr. O'Donnell. I say, I wonder whether Martin will take my tip that the gang is heading north?"

"Whin they're goin' south," grinned O'Donnell.

"By jove, I'd like to be with them!" exclaimed Briant. "Ye wouldn't."

"Why?"

"Because it wouldn't be good for yez. Do ye know what it manes, bhoy, to be hunted all the toime? Do ye know pwhat it manes to watch ivery sthip ye take, to hoide in holes in the daytime, and crape out at noight loike a dingo? Do ye know phwat it manes not to be sure of ivery one who calls himself a frind. Do you know pwhat it manes to have to snake loike a thafe to the people ye can trust only whin it's certain the coast's clear? Do ye know phwat it manes to be min that the law says annyone can take dead or alive? Do ye know phwat it manes to long for the friendly voices of the people ye love? If ye don't, ye don't know pwhat those poor bhoys are goin' through - God help them!"

With a gesture of despair, O'Donnell walked to the window and looked out on the over lasting hills, into whose safe keeping so many strange secrets had been entrusted.

22

Sticking Up Younghusband's

THERE was greater activity than ever at the Benalla police station when Constable Martin came in with Briant's story of the bush rangers going north.

Every station as far as Wodonga was warned, and the New South Wales authorities were advised that an attempt might be made to cross the border.

Every road leading north was closely guarded that night, and scores of troopers scoured the bush. The men they were looking for were riding in another direction, however; Ned and Byrne about half a mile ahead of Dan and Hart. They talked at long intervals, for each of them seemed impressed by the seriousness of the undertaking upon which they were engaged.

Twice they rode into the bush to avoid travelers - first a horseman, then a man and woman in a spring cart.

Sunrise found them on the outskirts of the little township of Euroa. Concealing their horses in a thick clump of timber, they walked to a small rise from which a clear view was obtained of the homestead of Younghusband's Faithful Creek Station. For over an hour they watched and waited.

"What's the good of hanging around any longer?" said Dan irritably. "Let's go over now."

"Not yet," replied Ned.

Half an hour later a train puffed its way over the main railway line, which was a short distance from the collection of buildings which constituted the homestead, and in full view of them.

"Why not ride over together?" suggested Steve Hart, as the guard's van disappeared round a curve.

"No!" cried Ned.

There was a mutinous glitter in Hart's dark eyes, and Dan and Byrne also were showing signs of restlessness partly due to excitement, which the idleness insisted upon by their leader did not allay.

Ned recognised the symptoms and frowned.

"This has all been carefully planned, and I'm not going to run any risk by rushing things. About midday's the time."

"I don't see why we can't go now," grumbled Dan. "I can, and we're staying here till the right time!"

There was a dangerous glint in the outlaw's eyes, and the others, recognising the futility of further protest, remained silent.

The hours dragged slowly by. At last Ned untethered his horse and mounted.

"Follow me in a few minutes," he said, as he rode away.

Except for a dog, which growled at his approach, there was no sign of life at the homestead when he dismounted and walked round the back to a hut with a smoking chimney.

Two men and a woman were eating their midday meal in the room, which he rightly guessed was the kitchen.

"Is Mr McCauley, the manager, about?" he asked. The woman replied that he was not, and Ned, saying he would wait until he returned, went to the front of the house, where his companions were tying up their horses.

When the four of them appeared at the kitchen door and announced whom they were, the two men jumped to their feet, but the woman went on with her meal.

"We want food for ourselves and our horses," said Ned. "No harm'll come to you if you do as you're told."

The eagerness with which the two station hands fed the horses showed that the warning had been effective.

"What you goin' to do with us?" asked the more youthful attendant, as though uncertain of what terrible fate awaited him.

When told that he would be locked up with everyone else who came along, his relief was so profound that Dan laughed.

"Think we were going to roast you alive?" he grinned.

"N-no, I didn't think that," the youth gasped.

The two men were put under lock and key in the storeroom, a long, wooden iron-roofed building.

At intervals arrived other employes, whose astonishment when they learned that the station was in the hands of the Kellys was expressed in a variety of ways. One old man fell on his knees and prayed to the good Lord to defend him. A red-headed youth with freckles the size of threepenny bits walked into the storeroom with head erect and chest expanded, as if he fully appreciated the importance of the occasion and felt the reflected glory of association with such' notorious outlaws.

When Mr McCauley arrived he was inclined to treat the matter as a, joke, but when he saw the revolvers carried by the bush rangers he realised that it was serious business.

He was a broad-shouldered man with a pair of kindly grey eyes. "Oh, well," he said, when he was certain that the intruders were the Kellys, "you might as well make yourselves comfortable. Come in and have tea." Ned and Hart followed him inside, while Dan and Byrne kept guard.

"I thought you fellows had crossed into New South Wales," remarked McCauley, as he filled up their plates, and the housekeeper poured out tea. "Don't wait," he added, as the bushrangers showed no inclination to begin their meal.

"After you," said Ned, significantly.

"Oh, the food's safe enough," McCauley laughed, as he proceeded to eat. Thus reassured, Ned and Dan set to with a will.

"You've beaten the police for over seven months now," remarked McCauley. "Whatever's one's feelings might be, no one can help admiring your bushcraft."

A gratified smile parted Ned's lips. He liked admiration, and praise of his leadership flattered him more than anything else.

"It hasn't been too easy, either," he replied. "Judging by the crowd of troopers about, a fellow would think every second man in the colony was a policeman."

"And you've given them all the slip."

"Up to now."

"They'll never get us - alive!" exclaimed Steve Hart.

Ned's glance was a rebuke, and Hart took no further part in the conversation. The bush ranger had found that his companions, particularly Dan and Steve, were inclined to be reckless of speech, and he preferred to do most of the talking himself.

With some hesitancy, as though uncertain as to how the topic would be received, McCauley remarked that Sergeant Kennedy, one of the victims of the Wombat Ranges tragedy, had been a friend of his, and his death had shocked him.

"Kennedy shouldn't have shown fight," Ned replied.

"He brought it on himself. We were four to two, and they hadn't a dog's chance. He should have seen that."

"It was a bad business, and I'm as sorry as anybody else. If we hadn't shot him, he would have got one of us, perhaps more, and when it meant his life or ours we couldn't do anything else. They call it murder. It was a fair fight."

"But - but the law gave the police the right to shoot and didn't give it to you."

"The Law!" Ned spat out the words. "The law believed Fitzpatrick's lies and sent my mother to gaol. The law drove us to the bush. If you were Ned Kelly and I was a trooper, and we met in the bush, wouldn't you shoot first if you believed I'd get you if you didn't?"

McCauley thought for a moment and then frankly admitted that he believed he would.

"Well, that's what happened on the Wombat. It's easy to call us murderers - it isn't so easy to tell us how we could have done anything else."

"Now you put it that way, it isn't," McCauley agreed. Ned and Steve ate quickly, and when they had finished their meal they exchanged places with Dan and Joe Byrne.

"You'd better stay here till they're through," Ned told the manager, who, while betraying no fear, obviously was impressed with the necessity for obedience.

He talked freely to Dan and Joe, but failed to draw them out. Beyond a few non-committal replies to the questions with which he plied them, they were uncommunicative.

By dusk the prisoners in the storeroom numbered 30.

They included a travelling hawker named Gloster - whose van yielded the outlaws a much-needed change of clothing - the boy who accompanied him, and an old man whose features were almost hidden by bandages which swathed his head. There was a miscellaneous assortment of station requisites in the storeroom, and the eyes of one bearded giant, with huge hairy arms, turned longingly to a half-dozen axes which lay in a corner.

"Why not give 'em a go for it?" he suggested.

Two others - an undersized youth with rat-like features, and a gaunt-visaged Scotsman with fiery red hair - at once announced their readiness. "If we r-rush 'em when they open the door, we'd hae a chance," the latter declared. "They'd drop a few of us, nae doot, but there'd be muckle siller for those wha the guid Lord presairved."

The old man with the bandaged face ran to him in terror. "Man!" he shrieked. "Ye're mad! You don't know the Kellys as I do. They'd burn down the shed and all of us in it! We wouldn't have a chance! We can't do nothin' but stay where we are."

The Scotsman shot a pitying glance in his direction.

"Oot o' this, ye wheedlin' auld fool!" He turned to the others. "Are ye men, or what are ye?" he demanded.

"We ain't damned lunatics, anyway," observed a young station hand.

"No more we ain't," cut in the bandaged man.

"D'ye know there's two thoosand poons waitin' for the capture o' the Kellys?" the Scotsman came back at them.

"Two thousand or twenty thousand ain't much good to dead men!" counselled a middle-aged man with a cast in his eye.

"It wouldna be to ye because ye couldna see it unless it was roond the corner," retorted the Scotsman.

This sally provoked a roar of laughter. As it subsided the door opened and Ned Kelly put his head inside.

"You'll need a bit of fresh air before we lock you up for the night," he said. "You can all come out together, but, mind you, no funny business." He tapped his revolver to give emphasis to the warning.

The prisoners eagerly availed themselves of the respite.

As Ned walked a few steps away and the three other bush rangers, each with a revolver in his hand, kept the captives under close view, the old man with the bandaged head managed to slip behind them.

"Better be careful, Ned," he whispered. "Some of 'em wanted to fight."

As Kelly leaned forward to get a closer view, the old fellow pushed aside his bandages sufficiently to reveal the grinning countenance of Sam Jackson.

"I thought I'd surprise you," he chuckled. "It's risky for four men to hold up a mob, so I thought I'd come along in case you wanted any help. You just treat me like the rest, and if there's any danger I'll find a way to let you know."

And before the astonished outlaw could voice his amazement Jackson had moved away to join the rest of the captives.

When the prisoners were finally locked up for the night, Ned told the womenfolk - who were not included among the occupants of the store-room, but went about their duties unhindered - that they might go to bed, and no harm would come to them.

The bush rangers slept two at a time, Ned and Byrne being the first to seek much-needed rest in more comfortable quarters than they had been accustomed to for a long time.

Many of the prisoners were still sleeping in all sorts of extraordinary attitudes when Dan and Joe Byrne cut the telegraph wires along the railway line to prevent communication with the police at Benalla.

A little later three Melbourne men and a local resident, who had been kangaroo shooting in the Strathbogie Ranges, drove up to Faithful Creek. Ned met them with the news that the station was stuck up by the Kellys, and told them to turn their horse round. The occupants of the spring cart, which contained shotguns and a rifle, got down, but the suggestion by one of them that they should get the weapons and put up a fight against the bushrangers was discouraged by Ned.

"I believe you're Ned Kelly," he said to the owner of the cart, named Casement. "You've stolen that outfit."

Casement nearly exploded with indignation, and his fellow sportsmen hotly resented the imputation.

"Even if you are a policeman, you needn't insult honest men," cried one of them.

"None of your cheek, or I'll put the bracelets on you!" threatened Ned, who was thoroughly enjoying the joke.

"It's no wonder the police are unpopular!" declared another. "Much more of this, my man, and I'll report you to your superior officer!"

Winking at Dan, who had come up, Ned induced the sportsmen to follow him to the homestead, where the groom, who had been allowed out of the storeroom to attend to the horses, amazed them by saying, "In case you don't know, this is Ned Kelly!"

"My God!" gasped Casement, while his companion, who had threatened the vengeance of police officialdom, recalled his temerity and went sickly white about the gills. His fears were unfounded, for the only inconvenience he and his fellow sportsmen suffered was to be locked up with the rest of the prisoners herded in the storeroom.

A little later Ned, Dan and Steve Hart, attired in the new clothes taken from the hawker's van, set out upon another expedition which thrilled Australia from Cooktown to the Leeuwin.

"I want you to write me a small cheque, Mr McCauley," said Kelly to the station manager. "A couple of pounds will do."

McCauley hesitated for a moment before complying, but the look in the outlaw's eyes speeded his pen.

Then, with Joe Byrne in sole charge of the homestead, the trio, accompanied by Gloster's boy, left the station. Ned drove the hawker's hooded van, and Dan the hunting party's spring cart, while Steve Hart, riding one of the station horses, brought up the rear.

2 3

Robbing the Bank

THE gang had laid their plans with remarkable precision, A funeral on the outskirts had taken many residents from the township, and a licensing court was engaging the attention of a number of others. There were, therefore, few people in the vicinity of the National Bank when the outlaws pulled up in front of it.

"You can't come in - it's after hours," said one of the clerks through the closed door in response to a knock.

"I've a cheque of Mr McCauley's, and I'm anxious to get it cashed," the bushranger pleaded.

"We're not allowed to do business after three," replied the voice from inside.

"Surely you can oblige me," persisted Ned.　　"It'll be a great convenience if I can cash this cheque now."

The teller half opened the door, and Ned and Hart, brushing him aside, entered the bank.

"I'm Ned Kelly, and I want all your money!"

It was a startling announcement, and two revolvers levelled at the clerk's head added poignancy to it. Mr Scott, the manager, was brought from his room, and forced to surrender the key of the strong-room, and into a gunny bag its contents were shovelled. It was a handsome haul, about £2000 in cash, and nearly 30 ounces of gold dust, but Ned was disappointed.

"I expected fully £10,000," he told the manager. "I'm going to burn all these books and bills."

Scott, alarmed at the destruction of the whole of the bank records, pleaded eloquently for their preservation. "They're no good to you," he said, "so why not let them alone?"

"Oh, very well then," Ned replied. "I want everyone here to come with me to McCauley's."

The occupants of the household were mustered—Mrs Scott, seven children, and two servants. The bank manager's wife shared none of the fear exhibited by her maids.

She smiled at Ned, and remarked, "You're a much handsomer and better-dressed man that I expected, and you don't look a bit blood-thirsty."

This flattery was not lost on the outlaw leader, and he was in the most genial of moods when Scott invited him to take a glass of whisky with him.

"Your health!" said the banker.

"Good luck!" responded Kelly, who, after waiting for Scott to drink first, drained his glass at a gulp. "No, no more, thanks," he added, as the banker tilted the bottle again."

"We'll want your buggy to take the family to McCauley's," Ned said. "You'd better put the horse in."

"If you want the trap you'll have to harness the horse yourself - my groom's away," was Scott's unexpected reply.

This was talk that Ned was unaccustomed to, but he merely smiled, and went into the yard. While he got the horse out of the stable, Dan, who had been guarding the back door, took his place in the bank.

A little later, the strange cavalcade set out for Younghusband's station. Ned, with Scott and the money, drove the hawker's van, Mrs Scott, the family buggy with some of the children, and Dan, Casement's cart with the rest of the household, Hart riding the horse on which he came to the township.

A mile up the road they encountered the funeral party returning from the cemetery. As they approached the bushrangers warned their prisoners that if they attempted to make any sign they would be instantly shot. It was an anxious moment, but none of the mourners appeared to notice anything unusual in the procession, and Scott, his family, and the bank clerks looked straight ahead of them as the other vehicles passed.

Joe Byrne's vigil at the homestead had not been without incident. One of the trains which passed close to the. station slowed down, and almost pulled, up. Byrne watched it with anxious eyes, and there was great excitement amongst the prisoners in the storeroom. One of them wished to break a window and signal to the passengers, but Sam Jackson warned him that any attempt to attract attention meant death - possibly to all of them.

One man got off the train - a telegraph linesman, who had come to look for the cause of the interrupted service.

When he walked over to the homestead he was promptly bailed up by Byrne, and added to the prisoners. Scott and the bank clerks also were locked up, and the bushrangers set about preparations for their departure.

They were in no hurry to leave, however, and when they had had another meal they announced that the prisoners would see something worth watching.

Their horses were saddled, and while one kept guard the others indulged in equestrian feats that made the spectators gasp with amazement. Ned Kelly's reputation as a rider was well earned, as all who formed that strange group of spectators could testify. Setting his horse at full gallop, he picked up small objects from the ground, stood up on the saddle, lay outstretched on the horse's back, dismounted and mounted, and jumped two fences while in a kneeling position.

"To think that a man like that is throwing his life away!" remarked Mrs Scott.

"It's a terrible business!" the station housekeeper agreed. "If ever I had a chance to do him a good turn I believe I'd do it!"

"I'm sure you're one of very many."

One of the Scott children who stood by her side, her cheeks flushed with excitement at the outlaw leader's surprising feats, looked up into her mother's eyes.

"Mummy, a man who can do those clever things can't be very wicked, can he?"

"He must be," exclaimed a boy a few years older than herself. "He pointed a big pistol at Daddy. A good man wouldn't do that."

"Anyway, he can ride better than the man we saw in the circus!'" declared his sister.

"He's coming over here!" said the boy in a frightened voice.

While two of his companions rounded up the prisoners and ordered them back into the storeroom, Ned, leading his horse, walked over to where the women and children stood.

"I must congratulate you on your riding," said Mrs Scott.

The bushranger smiled awkwardly. "I - thanks," he stammered. "I hope we haven't put you to any great inconvenience," he added.

"It's been quite a pleasant experience," she assured him.

Dan Kelly and Steve Hart, who were impatient to get away with the bank's money, rode up.

"Hadn't we better be going, Ned?" asked Dan.

"In a little while."

Kelly had other things to attend to. First, he gave Gloster's boy, who had accompanied them to Euroa, £2 and the watch taken from the body of Constable Lonergan. The servants of the homestead were presented with several pounds between them. His last act, before riding away, was to ask McCauley and a man named McDougall for their watches.

"That was given me by my mother, and I'd be sorry to lose it," pleaded McDougall.

"I know what a good mother is, and I wouldn't think of taking it," was the bushranger's unexpected reply.

Meanwhile, Byrne had appropriated the bank manager's watch.

"We're off now," announced Ned, addressing the prisoners from the-door of the storeroom. "You all stay here for three hours. If anyone of you leave before then, we'll track you down and shoot you dead! I look to you, Mr McCauley, to see that no one makes a fool of himself!"

A few moments later the sound of hoof-beats told that the outlaws were riding away with their booty.

24

The Police Outwitted

BY the time O'Donnell, Jennie and Briant had finished their plain but plentiful meal, it was dark.

"Well, I suppose, I'd better be moving on," Jack remarked, as he rose from the table. "I'm much obliged to you both. It isn't often I get a banquet like that, and I'm very grateful."

Jennie laughed. "I'm sorry for your banquet. But-" with a more serious face - "you haven't anywhere to go, have you?"

"Oh, any amount of places, I assure you," he returned with a grin. "You, Jennie, can't appreciate a bed in the bracken, a shakedown under a log, or the luxury of a wombat's hole. Did you ever sleep in a wombat's hole, Mr. O'Donnell?"

"Indade I did wanst, but o'im not after cravin' for any more av it. Ye see, it was a convenient place for me at the toime, because- well there were gintlemin in the neighborhood o'i wasn't anxious to mate - not nearly as anxious as they were to mate me, if ye git the drift av it."

"I quite understand."

And Jack winked at the girl, who turned to him with troubled eyes. "You mustn't sleep in the bush tonight. We can easily find you a shake-down, can't we, Dad?"

"We can- that, and ye're welcome to it," assented her father.

"That's really very kind of you. Someday, I may be able to pay this debt."

"If ye've been av service to Ned the debt's paid beforehand," O'Donnell declared with considerable feeling.

"Ned's unfortunate in some respects, but in one at least he's the luckiest of men. No one ever had more loyal friends, prepared to sacrifice so much to help him."

"If ye knew him as well as we do, ye'd say he desarved it," said O'Donnell. Jennie shot him a grateful glance, and Briant remarked that he was sure he was a good fellow at heart.

"I wonder where he is now?" he added. "Ye'll hear in a day or two." Jack looked at him inquiringly, but the old man was disinclined to be more communicative.

"It must be a terrible strain on you, Jennie," said Briant.

"It is. I know only too well the danger he's in every day of his life. Yet-yet somehow I feel he is safe for some time. Something tells me he'll be successful in what he's going to do tomorrow."

"You know why the gang rode south, then?"

She inclined her head ever so slightly.

"It's the future that worries me," she went on. "Oh, if they could only get away!"

"That's what I've said all along," cried Briant. "They must clear out of Australia."

"'Tis asier said than done," remarked O'Donnell.

"I can't see that. I could help quite a lot, but Ned's so darned obstinate- "

"Ned knows best."

"I'm not so sure of that. It would be a simple matter to lie low for a few months, and at the same time let all his friends spread the news that the gang had reached the coast and taken ship for some other country. Then, when the police really believed it, they could go to Melbourne or Sydney and get away unnoticed. Two of them could go to one port and two to the other."

O'Donnell pulled his straggly whiskers.

"That moightn't be aisy. Ye see, whin Ned's at the head things is all roight, but if they separated there moight be throuble."

"Dan and Steve Hart would be inclined to kick over the traces, eh?"

"They're only bhoys, and the good Lord knows how they moight let their tongues run away wid their brains, 'specially if they had a dhrop av dhrink. They moight talk boastin' loike, and put thimselves away."

"Dan's a bit of a harum-scarum, I know, and Steve's inclined to be erratic. Joe Byrne struck me as being more level-headed."

O'Donnell grinned.

"Oi don't know so much about that. Joe only joined the gang for the excitement av it. A broth av a bhoy is Joe, believe me. Ned's head is worth the three av 'em put together."

Jennie, flushed with pleasure, stroked her father's scanty locks.

They talked on for an hour or so, and then went to bed, Jack being given a shakedown in a little cubby off the kitchen that served as a store-room. The possums seemed to be holding a race meeting on its tin roof, but the noise they made troubled him very little, and he was soon asleep.

"Oi was thinkin'," said O'Donnell next morning, "that Oi could do wid yer hilp for a day or two if ye haven't anything better."

Briant accepted the offer with grateful eagerness. He wished to learn more of Ned Kelly, and Jennie was the most likely source of information. For several reasons he was not anxious to go back to Jacobson's. For one thing he felt he hadn't been quite fair to Nita. For another, Jacobson's treachery angered him, and during the last few days he was there he found it increasingly difficult to be civil to him.

Jennie made no secret of her pleasure when he announced his intention of staying. She was a bright girl, in spite of the sorrow that at times made her silent and depressed. She was easier to understand than Nita, whose moods were as changeable as the weather.

During the morning, as he was assisting O'Donnell with a line of fencing, a swirl of dust along the track heralded the approach of visitors. There were two of them, both women, and Jack noticed, with a slight quickening of his pulses, that one was Kate Kelly. Mrs Skillion, her sister, accompanied her. He noticed, too, the packs in front of their saddles, which indicated either that they were taking something to the gang, or that they had made provision to stay at whatever destination they had chosen.

Jennie ran out to meet them, and O'Donnell dropped his tools and walked to the slip rails. They talked for some time, and then, to Briant's surprise, he saw Kate dismount and walk in his direction. He hurried to meet her.

"So you've changed your quarters?" she smiled.

"Yes, moving on again," he replied. "Have you seen Ned lately?"

"Yesterday, and I'll see him again tomorrow night, please God." Her manner showed the excitement which she was trying to suppress.

"There's something afoot, I take it," he ventured.

"Something big," she replied. "Something that will give the police a lot to think about."

"Well, I hope it comes off. Tell him, will you, that I'll have The Ledge ready for him when he comes back."

"You're very good, but you mustn't take any risks. There'll be a bigger hunt than ever after - Listen!"

Briant strained his ears, but could not detect a sound except the faint murmur of voices at the slip rails.

"Horses!" cried Kate. "Troopers most likely. It won't do for them to see you talking to me. Good-bye!"

Keeping the hut between her and the track for most of the way, she rejoined her sister and the O'Donnells. It was several moments later when Jack heard the hoof-beats that had caught the girl's sensitive ear. Her surmise was correct. One of the horsemen was Constable Martin, but the other was a stranger.

"Good morning!" said Jennie genially, as they came up. "Trust you fellows for knowing when there's tea about. We're just going to have a cup, so you'd better come inside."

Martin and his companion, who had been very interested in the saddle packs of the two Kelly girls, expressed their thanks and followed the others into the hut.

"Come on, Jack - tea-oh!" Jennie called, and Briant promptly obeyed the summons.

"You look hot, Mr Briant," remarked Martin.

"Digging postholes isn't the softest job in the world, believe me."

"There's not many soft jobs round these parts," remarked the stranger, a tall, wiry fellow, whom Martin introduced as Constable Fuller.

From the kitchen came the clatter of crockery and the sound of three womanly voices. Jack, who was seated opposite the door, looked up to see Jennie making signs which he interpreted as instructions to keep the troopers talking. He turned to Fuller. "Weren't you the policeman who jumped off a bridge and rescued a woman from the Yarra five or six months ago?"

"That was my brother," Fuller announced with a flush of pride. "Did you see it?"

"Yes. I was one of the crowd that looked on. Too cowardly to do anything, I suppose. It was the pluckiest thing I ever saw. Is your brother still in the force?"

Fuller's face clouded. "No. He's dead- stopped a bullet in a street row."

"I'm sorry to hear it. He was too good a man to end up like that. Still, I suppose stopping a bullet is a danger that faces every policeman."

Martin and Fuller exchanged glances. "Yes, I suppose so," assented the latter.

"Did either of you ever know Big Jack Doolan?"

"He was one of the most popular policemen in Melbourne some years ago, before my time, but I've often heard my father speak of him. He, too, went out to a bullet fired by a dirty weedy little foreigner from a window in Fitzroy during a brawl. Big Jack once arrested four men from the middle of a drink-maddened mob. He just ploughed his way through the crowd, hitting every head that came his way. He was the fellow, too, who went into a burning shanty in Little Bourke Street, and rescued three stupefied Chinamen. There were fine men in the force in those days - just as there are today."

Martin and Fuller acknowledged the tribute by gratified smiles. "I won't keep you waiting long," said Jennie, putting her head round the door.

"That's all right, we've plenty of time," Martin assured her. The sound of voices in the kitchen was interspersed with merry peals of girlish laughter. Presently Jennie emerged, carrying a huge teapot in one hand while she balanced several cups in the other.

"The fire was cranky, but I coaxed it," she announced.

She returned for more cups, which she proceeded to fill.

Martin jumped up. "Where's the Kelly girls?"

Jennie looked around in well-simulated surprise. "They just went outside. Kate! Kate!"

Martin rushed to the door, followed by Fuller. The only horses in sight were their own! "By God, they're tricked us!" he cried, red with rage.

"Aren't you staying for a cup of tea after I've gone to the trouble of making it?" asked Jennie in an injured tone.

"No!" snorted the trooper, as he dashed from the hut with his companion at his heels.

Briant took the girl's hands in his.

"Jennie, you're the cleverest woman I've ever met! Your brain works much quicker than a policeman's. How long were you talking and laugh-ing to yourself after Kate and her sister left?"

"Oh, just for a minute or two."

"Mr. O'Donnell," said Jack, "you ought to be proud of a daughter like that!"

"And be the powers, there's no man prouder!" he declared, drawing the girl to him. "She has the brains av her mother, God rist her sowl!"

25

Briant's Misgiving

"WELL, I guess we've given them the slip."

Mrs Skillion reigned her horse and looked back through the timber, a break in which revealed a ribbon of track many feet below them.

"Martin'll be roaring mad," Kate laughed.

They rode on through the scrub, which was so dense in places that they had to zig-zag to find openings. Once Kate's horse reared on its haunches with a frightened snort, and a big black snake glided into the bushes.

"A six-footer, I should say," the bushranger's sister remarked quite casually, patting the neck of her still panting steed.

"They ought to be at the bank about now," said her sister.

"I hope their haul's worthwhile," Kate remarked. "Sure to be. God knows, some of us could do with it! Look out! Someone putting on the pace. Perhaps it's Martin."

Both girls turned their horses behind a thick clump of timber and through the foliage looked down on the track, along which a man galloped at breakneck speed. Twenty paces behind him came another horseman.

"Looks like him and the other trooper. Martin's a good bushman. Lucky we were careful getting off the road."

Before Kate Kelly and her sister left the track they circled their horses so as to leave a maze of hoof-prints, selected a hard piece of roadside, dismounted, and led their hacks for a short distance, and then rode straight into the bush. Their tracks were plainly visible up to the point where they criss-crossed the soft surface of the road, but it was impossible to say what direction they had then taken, whether they had ridden to the right or to the left.

With a smile on their lips they watched Martin and Fuller stop, get off their horses, and closely examine the ground. Once Martin pointed in their direction, and instinctively they crouched closer to the bushes. Then the policemen walked to the other side of the road. For a while they stood, as if undecided which way to proceed, and finally rode straight ahead.

"That's funny," remarked Mrs. Skillion. "Martin's a cunning devil, so we'd better watch out."

"You stay here for a while, and I'll see if I can spot them from the top of the hill," said Kate, handing her reins to her sister.

Carefully she made her way to the crown of the rise, always keeping herself well hidden from the track. From the hilltop the road was visible at intervals for a mile or two. There was no sign of either trooper. Presently she uttered a muffled cry of surprise, and hurried back to Mrs Skillion.

"I saw them through the trees making for Carter's. We can't go there now."

"That's awkward. Let's go on. If we hide near the three big gums we can see whether they stay. At any rate, the boys won't be along for a good while yet. If the worst comes to the worst we can give them the signal when they reach the ford, and then they can go to Thorpe's. I'm not so sure that isn't the safest place after all."

"I think you're right," Kate laughed. "Billy's a wonder the way he bluffs the police."

"He's all that and more," assented her sister.

Thorpe, a farmer with a considerable holding, a man of substance compared with most of his fellow-settlers, was one of the most valued of the bush rangers' allies, because he appeared to be the most violent of their enemies. Several times he had reported the loss of horses, and each time he had accused the Kellys of stealing them. He never neglected an opportunity of publicly vowing vengeance for the wrongs he had suffered at the outlaws' hands.

"I wouldn't talk too freely if I were you," Superintendent Hare had once warned him. "The Kellys and their friends have a way of making things uncomfortable for those who are known to be against them."

Thorpe laughed at his fears. "I'm not frightened of them. They know if they came to my place they'd get a warm reception. There isn't a better shot in all Victoria than my Tom, and Sam isn't far behind him."

"All the same, I think I'd be more discreet," replied Hare.

"Oh, that's all right!" remarked Thorpe, with an amused twist at the corners of his mouth.

The objective of the Kelly girls was a little knoll, on which three giant gums grew in inspiring majesty, topping all their fellows by twenty or thirty feet. On the hillside across the gully, in the centre of a small clearing, stood a hut, typical of the rude homesteads which sheltered the big-hearted men and women who, unmindful of hardship, were fighting a grim battle with Nature for the right to live.

Kate Kelly's surmise was correct. Martin and Fuller were going to Carter's. From their vantage-point the girls watched them approach the hut from the opposite sides, tether their horses, and shoo off the dogs that snarled at their approach. A short man came out of the hut, and they followed him inside.

Half an hour elapsed without their reappearing. The sun had long since set, but their horses could still be discerned across the darkening gully,

"I wonder what's keeping them," said Kate, with a trace of anxiety in her voice. "Supposing I go over, and see what they're doing?" I'll find a way of letting you know if it's better for the boys to go to Thorpe's."

"Right."

Both packs were transferred to the saddle of Mrs Skillion, who rode off in the direction of the road, while her sister's horse picked its way unerringly down the rough hillside toward's Carter's hut.

There was a light inside when she reached it. Warned by the barking of the dogs, Carter came to the door. The look of fear in his eyes partly vanished as Kate whispered, "Everything's all right."

The two troopers were astonished to see the outlaw leader's sister, and made no effort to conceal it. Both looked at her intently without speaking.

"I didn't know you had visitors till I saw the horses outside," she observed.

"That reminds me," said Martin, going to the door, "that nag of mine gets a bit restless when he's tied up for any time. I'll just slip out and see if he's all right."

Kate laughed to herself. She knew that he wanted to see what was in her saddle pack, and she chuckled as she thought how disappointed he was going to be. Martin went straight to her horse, and when he saw that the pack which had excited his suspicions earlier in the day had disappeared, he relieved his feelings by cursing loudly.

"Horse all right?" asked Kate, as he re-entered the hut.

"Yes," he gruffly responded.

"I don't suppose you noticed whether mine was well-tied?"

Martin's expression was eloquent of the anger he felt, but he did not make any reply.

"Where's Mrs Carter?" asked Kate, looking round.

"Our gal over the ranges ain't too well," the old man replied, "so she went acrost there this mornin'."

"That's a pity. I wanted to see her."

"If it's very partic'ler."

"Oh, no, nothing very important. I may come over again tomorrow."

"We'd better be moving, Fuller," said Martin.

"I'm goin' to 'ave a bite to eat presently, and I thought you might stay," invited Carter.

"No, thanks; time we were off."

Carter stood at the door and watched them ride away.

Then he hurried in to Kate.

"My God. When you came I thought it was the boys!" he exclaimed.

"I wonder if they know anything?'" she said, a trifle apprehensively.

"The boys– "

"They'll go to Thorpe's. My sister will signal them at the ford. I've got to let her know. Martin's going to watch me, and I'll have to give him the slip. They'll be back in a few minutes, listening, so we must be careful what we say. If you're going to have something to eat, I'll get it for you."

While she was busying herself over the fire a low growl from one of the dogs caused her to glance significantly at the old man.

"There's something about that chap Martin I like," she announced a little later. "He's up against my brothers, still he's a man."

"I like him, too," responded Carter, raising his voice for the benefit of the eavesdroppers. "I don't s'pose 'e'll worry Ned very much, seein' as the boys 'as gone to Noo South Wales."

"No, I don't suppose so. Ned didn't tell me much before he cleared out, but he's going to write me from Sydney. I wonder why those policemen came here. They must know that if you are friendly to our family you can't do anything to help the gang."

"Of course I ain't able, but I suppose you can't blame 'em. They've got their job to do, same as other people."

"That's right and some of them are pretty decent about it, but not all of them."

"No, it's a pity they ain't all like Martin. Are you gain' straight back 'orne, Kate?"

"Yes, just as soon as I get you some tea."

When they had finished their frugal meal and Kate had put the dishes a way, a slight noise outside the hut indicated that the eavesdroppers were anxious to get away well before her.

There was no sign of them when she rode up the hillside. She was certain she was being followed, however. When she gained the road a movement amongst the trees told her that the troopers were within easy distance. Galloping furiously along the track for a mile, she jumped from the saddle and ran into the scrub. A few minutes later Martin and Fuller came upon her riderless horse.

"Well, that beats Gallagher!" exclaimed the former.

"What's to be done now?" asked his companion.

Martin scratched his head. "I'm damned if I know. We had a hope of keeping up to her while she was mounted, but now she's hiding somewhere we've as much chance of finding her as we have of riding to heaven."

"She's clever!"

"She's more than that!"

"Why not follow her horse?"

"That wouldn't be much good. He's sure to go home."

"Not if we take him with us. I say, she might find it harder to help the gang if we took it."

"Not a bit of it. There's plenty of other horses. Still, I suppose- "

At the moment a rabbit, scurrying across the track, frightened the abandoned animal, which, with a snort, galloped into the bush. Both troopers dashed in pursuit. It was a hopeless race. The riderless horse, further scared by the hoof-beats behind it, increased its speed, and, dodging the trees in a way which the troopers' mounts could not emulate, was soon lost to sight.

"Come on," said Martin, as he turned back in the direction of the road, "we might as well give it up."

As they disappeared around a bend of the track Kate Kelly emerged from the bushes where she had been hiding, not a dozen yards from the edge of the road, and followed the direction in which her horse had gone.

It was a clear, starlit night. Sure of foot and strong of limb, Kate walked quickly, avoiding obstacles with almost uncanny precision. Once some strange sound caught her ear, and she stopped to listen.

At a spot where the tall timber gave way to scrubby undergrowth, she paused. Throwing back her head and pursing her lips, she uttered the plaintive call of the curlew, a weird cry like the despairing wail of some soul from whom all hope had gone. Back came an answering call, and Kate hurried in its direction. She found her sister waiting near a spot at which a ford crossed the sluggish creek. By the side of Mrs Skillion's horse stood her own. It neighed a welcome, and she threw a loving arm round its glossy neck.

"So you didn't run away far, you beauty?" she crooned.

"I found him up the creek," her sister explained. "Gave me bit' of a scare at first. I wondered what had become of you."

Briefly Kate recounted her experiences since they had parted.

"I'm glad you piled it on thick about Martin," remarked Mrs Skillion. "He's one of the troopers we've got to watch. He never seems to let up, and you never know where he'll turn up next. If we flatter him a bit it might help. I suppose he heard all you said to Carter?"

"I'm certain he was listening. I wish the boys would come. This hanging about makes me nervous."

Her sister shivered slightly. "I wonder if they're all right?"

"It's risky, but we can trust Ned. Listen! Someone coming now."

Hoof-beats were heard in the distance, and the girls hid their horses in the scrub.

"Only one," said Kate, inclining her ear. "I wonder- "

She did not complete the sentence, but peered anxiously into the darkness.

Presently the rider came into view. With quickened pulses they watched from behind the trees. Whoever he was, he was not in a hurry. He came along at an easy canter, and when he reached the ford he pulled up to give his horse a drink.

"Looks like Jack Webber," whispered Kate.

"That's who it is," responded her sister, "I could tell the mare anywhere."

When he had ridden away the girls emerged. Mrs Skillion sat on a stump, but Kate's anxiety kept her on the move.

"It won't do any good walking up and down like that."

"I know, but I can't help it. I wish they'd come."

A long silence followed, broken only by the ripple of the creek and the distant hoot of a mopoke. Both girls' nerves were at high tension. They knew the dangers the gang had been facing, and their failure to appear at the appointed time opened up all sorts of tragic possibilities.

"Hark!" The exclamation came simultaneously from both of them.

"Two!" cried Kate, listening to the distant sound of horses' hoofs. The eerie cry of a curlew was borne on the clear night air. The girls answered it together. Then, with fast-beating hearts, they waited.

Mrs Skillion gave a little cry of delight. "It's Ned!"

It was. And with him rode Steve Hart. Kate and her sister ran to meet them. Ned jumped from his horse and embraced them with almost savage fervor.

"We thought something must have happened!" cried Mrs Skillion, as she clung to him.

"Where's Dan?" asked Kate.

"We pick him and Joe up at the burnt bridge."

"How – "

The bushranger, anticipating his sister's query, and tapping the bag strapped to his saddle, laughed gaily.

"All the bank had, though we expected more."

As the four of them rode through the bush Ned told his sisters many of the incidents connected with the sticking up of Younghusband's station and the robbery of the bank.

Mention of Sam Jackson's presence among the prisoners caused a mist to rise before Kate's eyes.

"That old man's one in a million!" she cried.   "You mustn't forget him, 'Ned, when you're cutting, up that- " pointing to his saddle pack.

"I'm not likely to forget him. Seen anything of young Briant the last day or two?"

"Oh, yes. He's at O'Donnell's now."

Ned frowned and dug his heels into his horse's ribs. Kate laughed softly. "I believe you're jealous."

"Don't be a fool!" he snapped. It was evident that the news displeased him, however, for he said very little during the rest of the journey, although the girls plied him with questions.

At the burnt bridge - a place where a bush fire had destroyed a rough wooden structure which spanned the creek - Dan and Joe Byrne joined them. The banks of the stream were high and steep; but the horses negotiated them without effort, and the shallow water gave them no trouble. On the other side they halted while Ned gave a few brief instructions.

Then they separated, the girls riding together, while the four others spread out fan-wise. All of them rode cautiously, but when they converged and finally met at the homestead of Bill Thorpe nothing had occurred to arouse their suspicions.

Thorpe's house was a more substantial structure than the homes of most of the settlers in the district. It stood in the centre of a clearing of considerable acreage, and its well-built sheds and yards and two big haystacks gave it an air of rural prosperity.

At the first warning bark of the dogs the door opened, and a girl ran to meet the visitors. Ned Kelly, throwing his reins to Dan, leapt from his horse and hurried to meet her.

"Jennie!"

"Ned!"

In a moment she was in his arms, and he was raining kisses upon her. Oblivious of everything, the outlaw held her to him, each too happy for words.

"When you've finished love-making," came a laughing voice from the house, and hand in hand they walked to the door.

Inside were Thorpe, his wife and two fine upstanding sons, Jack Briant, Big Manton and Tom Stevens.

Dan banged on the table the bag containing the bank's money.

"There you are- thousands!" he cried with a dramatic gesture. "Look at it!"

With fingers that trembled with excitement he opened the valise and took up two great handfuls of notes, gold and silver.

The sight of the money had a strange effect upon Briant. In helping the bushrangers he knew that he had been breaking the law, but this seemed different. This was robbery, something he hardly had bargained for. He stood deep in thought while the others crowded round the dazzling heap.

Thorpe's big voice disturbed his reverie. "Eyes must be sharp tonight," it said.

Thorpe's two sons had put on their hats and taken up their guns. Manton reached for a weapon which stood in the corner.

"There ought to be four," said Thorpe.

Jack had now divined their purpose. "If you're going to guard the house, let me help," he said.

"No, I'll be the other," said Tom Stevens, picking up a gun which lay near his chair.

"What are the guns for?" asked Briant, not quite clear as to whether it was intended to put up a fight if the police appeared.

"We're possuming," laughed Sam Thorpe, "one north, one south, one east, one west. If we see a trooper we fire up into the trees. When they hear the shot here they'll know what to do."

"But supposing a dozen of them turned up?"

"Well, they wouldn't find the gang," was Sam's confident rejoinder.

Briant held out his hands for Steven's gun. "Better let me be in this."

The old man looked inquiringly at Ned and then parted with the weapon.

"Mind, not a shot unless there's danger," admonished Thorpe, as the four vigilants passed out into the night.

26

Guarding the Gang

JACK Briant was allotted a post on the eastern side of the homestead, and as he walked up the slope on which the timber had been thinned he felt no elation over his self-imposed task. He was just as anxious as ever that no harm should come to Ned and his companions, but the sight of that bagful of stolen money seemed to set his nerves a-jangle. Then his thoughts flew to Nita, and he realised with some misgivings, that he had missed her very much since he had left her father's employ. In spite of the companionship of Jennie O'Donnell and the relief afforded by his parting with the treacherous Jacobson, he felt singularly lonely.

Could it be that really he loved Nita? Was it possible that her varying moods were prompted by her love for him, which at times she might be bravely struggling to suppress? That possibility pleased him more than he cared to admit. After all, she was good and brave and, damn it! Why shouldn't he love her? Why shouldn't he forget the wretched past and the girl who had driven him to the bush?

Click! What was that? He sprang round with a start. It sounded for all the world like the cocking of a gun. Click! There it was again. Why was his heart pounding so? Could it be that he was losing his nerve? Rebellion at such a thought steadied him momentarily, and he peered into the darkness which the white trunks of the gumtrees but faintly relieved.

A moment later he was laughing softly to himself. An old man kangaroo, bent on enjoyment of the succulent juices of Thorpe's growing crops; came into view, a ghostly figure that covered the ground in giant hops.

"Shoo!" Briant cried.

The intruder paused as though resentful of this interruption of its plans, and then disappeared in the gloom.

The hours dragged slowly by. No lights were visible in Thorpe's windows, and Jack judged either that they had been carefully shaded or that the strangely assorted party had retired for the night.

That house that lay dimly shadowed before him held a fortune. In it were the four men for whose capture there was a substantial reward that in all probability would be largely increased as a result of their latest exploit. In it lay the money belonging to the bank. If he crept to the stables and saddled one of the horses he could reach Benalla and be back with a squad of troopers long before daylight. If, as a result of his resource, the whole gang were captured, and the bank's money restored, he would be the most-talked-of man in Victoria.

Almost as soon as it came to him he thrust the treacherous thought aside, inwardly cursing the disloyalty that had prompted it. From over the hill came the hooting of a mopoke. "Trait-or! Trait-or!" it seemed to say. When he remembered how his soul had revolted at Jacobson's suggestion regarding this blood money, he wondered how he had given it a moment's thought.

At intervals he set out on his prescribed beat of about half a mile square, always taking the precaution to look up into the tree-tops in simulation of a genuine possum shooter, in case his movements were being watched.

The rosy fingers of dawn were creeping over the hills and the birds were waking from their slumbers when he heard his name called from the house, and saw someone beckoning him. His vigil had ended.

The three other watchers had come in, but when he entered the house there was no sign of the bushrangers or the Kelly sisters. Jennie, too, had disappeared.

"Where's Ned and the rest of them?" he asked.

"Went away an hour ago," he was told.

Again he wondered at the wizardry of these intrepid bushmen and their equally skilled sisters who could secure their horses and ride away without betraying their movements. He was strangely depressed when, after being given a substantial breakfast, he walked slowly back to O'Donnell's. To his surprise he, found both the old man and his daughter astir, Jennie's bright cheeks and sparkling eyes giving no indication of the little sleep she had enjoyed.

"Hullo, Jack!" she greeted him. "You don't look very lively this morning. Staying up all night doesn't seem to agree with you. Still, it was good of you to help."

"Oh, that was nothing," he replied awkwardly. "When did you come home?"

"About four."

"And. the boys left at the same time?"

"Yes."

"They'll' need to be very careful after this. The Government's bound to increase the reward, and the police will be busier than ever."

Elation at her lover's successful exploit had given the girl new confidence, and she laughingly replied, "They can be as busy as they like, they'll never catch them."

"I wish I could think so."

As Jack, an hour or two later, joined O'Donnell on the fencing job at which they had both been working, he had made up his mind he would leave next day. He wished to get away from all these associations for a while.

The situation was becoming far too involved. He felt that he had committed a criminal act, the seriousness of which appalled him. Did it matter very much, though? He had chosen this life in preference to a very different existence, and had espoused the outlaws' cause, so he might just as well go through with it. All the same, he was young, and the possibility of imprisonment and disgrace was not a pleasant prospect.

O'Donnell looked at him keenly when on two occasions he was too absorbed in his own gloomy thoughts to hear the remarks addressed to him.

"Phwat's the mather wid ye?" asked the big Irishman. "Is it dramin' that ye are"

"I'm sorry," Jack replied with a forced laugh. "I must have been."

Long years in the bush had robbed O'Donnell of his garrulity, and he was a dull companion at the best of times. Briant was glad of that, for he was in no mood for conversation. Very few words passed between them except those that were necessary in connection with their work.

Half way through the morning it was usual for Jennie to bring them a billy of tea and some damper. As Jack was having trouble with a particularly knotty rail. he heard footsteps, but did not look up.

"Too busy for a snack?" said a voice that was not Jennie's.

He turned sharply.

"Nita!"

It was Jacobson's daughter, who held a steaming billy and two pannikins in one hand and a tin plate of buttered damper in the other. Jack snatched them from her, put them down on a log, and put his eager arms around her.

He kissed her rapturously.

"Mr. O'Donnell's looking!" said Nita, struggling half-heartedly, but with bright lights of happiness shining in her eyes.

"I don't care if all the O'Donnells in Victoria, or Ireland, or anywhere else are looking!" he cried, as his lips sought hers again and again.

But O'Donnell wasn't looking. Grinning widely, he was walking towards the hut.

"Nita, it was good of you to come," Briant whispered. "I wanted you! God! How I wanted you!"

"Then why didn't you come for me?"

"Because I was a fool! But I'll never let you go again. Kiss me, dear."

Her lips clung to his, and his arms held her so tightly that they hurt.

"Please, let me go now," she panted, but with laughter on her lips. "There's a time and place for everything, you know."

"The time and place to love you, Nita, is all the time, everywhere!"

His fervor surprised her, but happiness was singing in her heart.

"Why did you go away, Jack?" she asked as he sat beside her on a log.

"Because of your father. I couldn't stand his treachery towards the Kellys. I don't mind an open enemy, but- "

"I know, I know!" she interrupted. "Sometimes I almost hate him myself! He wants so badly to get away from here!"

"Is blood money the only way?" Briant asked bitterly.

"It tempts him. And he'll be tempted still more when they make the reward bigger. Of course, you know all about the Euroa bank affair?"

"Yes; the Kellys were at Thorpe's last night, and I helped to keep watch."

She flashed a gratified smile at him, and he kissed her again.

"What about your tea? It'll get cold if you don't have it now."

"Oh, all right," he laughingly replied, taking the pannikin which she handed him. "You'd better have the old man's share. He'll be having his at the house."

"You scared him with your love-making," admonished Nita.

He looked tenderly into her eyes. "I didn't scare you, did I, dear?"

"You made me very happy," she whispered.

They were silent for a little while. Then her hand stole into his.

"Are you going to stay here, Jack?" she asked.

"Before you came I had made up my mind to clear out. Now, all the police in Victoria couldn't get me away from this district!"

"Father would be glad to have you back," she said slowly, as though afraid of how he would take it. "So would Frank, who says he misses you very much. Even Julie misses you, but the stubborn little wretch won't admit it."

"Anyone else in the family who has missed me?" he asked, slyly.

Nita threw herself into his arms.

"Missed you! I've missed you every minute! I thought you didn't care, dear, and the sun just seemed to sink forever! There wasn't anything left in life without you!"

"I'd like to go back to be near you, but it's hard to be civil to a man who's trying to betray those one's trying to help shield."

"I know it's very hard, but- "

She hesitated, and the color left her cheeks. In her happiness she had forgotten the letter she had destroyed, and the sudden thought of it, and what it might mean to Jack, sent a chill to her heart.

"Do you really love me?" she asked him.

"Better than anyone in the whole world!"

"Supposing- supposing, someone you- you once loved asked you to come back?" Breathlessly she waited for his answer.

He took both her hands in his. "There is no one who could take your place, Nita. I didn't know what love was till I met you."

"And yet the other love drove you away?"

"It was pride more than love. I was a conceited young fool with the idea that the world was made just for me, and when I found it wasn't, well, it hurt. No, 'Nita, there's no one but you now."

"And at one time I was rather afraid of Kate Kelly." She watched him closely as he spoke, but his face gave no clue to his feelings.

"I was very much attracted to Kate, and I still think she's a wonderful girl, so different from those I'd associated with, but- well, she isn't Nita!"

She snuggled closer to him, Should she tell him about the letter? Many times she had regretted having destroyed it, yet Jack meant so much to her that she couldn't risk losing him in that way. She would have to tell him sooner or later. It would be a relief to her conscience to confess what she had done. At the same time, she was uncertain as to how he would regard her deceit.

The reappearance of O'Donnell, still wearing a broad grin, interrupted her thoughts. She jumped down from the log and went to meet him.

"I'm sorry if we drove you away, Uncle Joe," she said. "And, another thing, I've drunk your tea and eaten your damper."

"If the young fellow manes well boi ye, 'tis all roight," he replied.

"I haven't seen Nita for so long," said Jack with an apologetic air, as he joined them, "that I felt- "

"Bedad ! Oi saw how ye felt!" laughed the old man.

"I love her, and- "

"Well, if ye don't ye gave a damn foine imitation!"

"And we drank your tea."

"Ah! Ye're a divil an' all, to be sure! Jennie was watchin' ye through the windy, and she says, say she, ye did it well!"

Nita shot a mischievous glance at Briant. "Jack does everything well."

O'Donnell scratched his head.

"Oi'm not so sure. Look at that post there, that's lanin' loike the sphoire at Ballyrnannock."

She followed his gaze to a part of the fence which was badly out of alignment.

"That'll be all right when I've finished," Briant assured him.

"I must leave you two to your work," said Nita, gathering up the billy and pannikins. "I'll see you later, Jack."

When Jennie called them in to their midday meal she mischievously put Nita's chair on one side of the table and Briant's on the other.

"The light gets in my eyes from here - I think I'll go round where it isn't so strong," Jack remarked, as he picked up his chair. Nita rewarded him with a ravishing smile, Jennie laughed joyously, and her father grinned.

Jack was happier than he had been for a long time. With Nita at his side life seemed very good to him. Even his misgivings concerning the bank robbery were forgotten. It was a merry meal, and the hut rang with their laughter.

"Nita's walking home presently," Jack said, as they rose from the table, "and I was wondering whether I could have an hour or two off to go with her. You know," he added, with a twinkle in his eyes, "it isn't safe for her with all these bushrangers about;"

"Och, go 'long wid ye," responded O'Donnell, "and if ye sthay away too long Oi'll dock yer wages!"

Briant disregarded his warning, for he stayed away most of the afternoon. Neither he nor Nita was in any hurry over their walk through the fragrant, sunlit bush, and when they reached her home and found Jacobson absent, he tarried long, happy in his reunion with the girl whose love meant so much to him.

When at last he bade her a reluctant farewell his mind was made up. Life with Jacobson, the traitor, would be preferable to an existence without Nita. He would go back as soon as the fencing job was finished and O'Donnell could spare him.

27

"Greater Love -"

BRIANT was correct in his surmise that the Euroa Bank robbery would result in an increased reward for the capture of the Kellys being offered by the Government, and that the police would redouble their efforts.

Australia was thrilled by the news of their impudent exploits, and the press demanded to know how much longer four men were to be allowed to defy the law with impunity.

Superintendent Hare sat in earnest conclave with half a dozen of his senior officers at his headquarters at Benalla, and the plan of campaign then formulated was more daring and comprehensive than any that hitherto had been put into operation.

The home of every known Kelly sympathiser was watched each night, while scores of troopers beat the bush in daylight and darkness in all localities that might contain a possible hiding place of the gang.

One night about a week after the bank robbery, Sam Jackson saddled a smart-looking black gelding whose presence in his paddock had mystified Kenny and Fuller, who had been deputed to watch his hut.

"I wonder where he got that horse from?" remarked Kenny. "No one's reported any theft, and Jackson's too dog poor to buy a nag like that."

"A gift from the Kellys, perhaps," suggested Fuller. From the shadows they saw the old man ride through the slip-rails. Mounting their own horses, they followed him at a safe distance. Their pursuit led them over miles of scrub country, up hills, through gullies, and along the bed of several dry creeks. Once or twice they lost sight of him, but were able to pick him up again soon after. In one thick clump of timber, however, he seemed to disappear altogether.

"Steady!" whispered Kenny, as Fuller's horse stumbled noisily in a tangle of dry boughs. "You go that way, and I'll go this. We'll meet at the top of the hill."

As they separated, Jackson, chuckling to himself, emerged from the bushes that had hidden him, and rode back in the direction from which he came. After going a few hundred yards he turned sharply at a right angle and set his horse at a gallop over the rock-strewn hillside.

At the top he halted and listened. Satisfied with what he heard, or at the absence of sound, he slid from the saddle, tied his horse to a tree, and crept cautiously down the hill.

In a treeless space at the foot he stood for a moment, peering into the darkness. Then he took off his hat and let it drop to the ground. Two figures emerged from the scrub and went to meet him.

"The troopers are about, Ned," he whispered to the taller of the two men. "Two of 'em followed me for miles. 'Taint safe here. Best be gettin' away."

"Where did you leave them?" asked Ned Kelly, with an uneasy inflection in his lowered voice.

"Back a couple o' mile. Better be off. The bush has been swarmin' with 'em' for nights."

"Got you scared, have they?" laughed Joe Byrne. "'Taint me I'm thinkin' of."

Ned thrust a roll of notes into the old man's hand.

"Take these, Sam, you'll find them useful."

"You was always good to me, boy," he replied, as he put the money into his pocket.

"Not half as good as you've been to us .... Listen!"

In the bush behind them a twig snapped. To the right of them there was a rustling of dry leaves that was ominous on such a still night.

"You two hide quick - I'll make a run for it! They'll follow me, and you can get away when the coast's clear."

"No, no, Sam!" cried Ned. "It's too risky, you might get shot!"

Heedless of the warning, the old man plunged into the scrub, and the listening outlaws heard his crashing through the undergrowth.

"They're after him!" whispered Byrne, as other sounds reached his ears.

Jackson ran on until his failing breath compelled him to rest at length in a thick clump of bushes that completely enveloped him. Eagerly he listened for sounds of pursuit, but none came. Believing that the troopers had passed on, he crawled from his shelter and turned in the direction in which he had left his horse.

Halfway up the hill he heard them coming behind him and again he looked round for shelter. It was harder to find on that less thickly covered hillside. Despairing of its security, he slipped behind the trunk of a giant gum. Luck was with him, for although his two pursuers halted within a few feet of him, they did not discover his hiding place.

"Must have gone straight on," said a voice which he recognised as Kenny's. "Martin and Macguire are over in the gully, so he's not likely to get away!"

Jackson's heart missed a beat. He might be able to dodge two of them, but two others blocking his way. If he could only reach his horse he believed he could easily outdistance them.

"It's too risky- you might get shot!"

Ned's warning came back to him, and he shivered apprehensively. Scarcely daring to breathe, he crept up the hill.

His horse was still in the bushes where he had left it.   Relief gave him renewed vigor, and he was in the saddle in an instant. For a moment he hesitated, and then, deciding that it would be better to make a dash for it, went down the hill at a pace that would have meant disaster for a less sure-footed mount.

As he reached the road he paused to look behind.

Simultaneously a dark figure rose, it seemed, almost in front of his horse's head, and a stern voice demanded, "Stop, or I'll fire!"

Without a moment's hesitation, he charged straight at the intruder, who sprang to one side and raised his arm. The report of a revolver rang out sharply on the clear night air, and Jackson flung himself forward on his horse's neck. Another shot followed, but the horse galloped madly on.

A shout ahead of him sent a chill to his heart. He turned his horse's head as though to ride into the bush, thought better of it, and kept to the road.

Jackson had a blurred vision of two other figures that rose up from the roadside, and of two spurts of flame. As the crack! crack! of the revolvers reached him he lurched forward and maintained his seat only by grasping the pommel of the saddle. The stab of pain in his chest told him that one of the bullets had hot gone astray. He put up his hand, and when he withdrew if, it was wet and sticky.

Could he reach his home in time? The singing noises in his head were growing louder, and a peculiar numbness was creeping over him. It was becoming increasingly difficult to keep his seat. Once he found himself lying almost on the horse's neck and realised that momentarily he had lost consciousness.

What had become of his horse's head? It seemed to have disappeared altogether. He turned his eyes to the right, and the trees that should have been there were missing, too. God! he was blind!

No! he was able to distinguish a faint blur, which gradually became clearer, and in a few moments the shapely head of his fast-galloping gelding had come into sight again.

The noises in his head were less intense, but he realised to his horror that the numbness of his injured side had spread down his leg, so that when he tried to move it, it felt as though it were no longer there.

Just round the bend lay his home, but how far it seemed! Why was his horse going so slow, although its hoof-beats told him that it was still galloping strongly? Now he seemed to be going round in circles. Now he appeared to be suspended in mid-air and could no longer feel the saddle under him. Now he was falling - down! down! down!

The barking of the dogs brought Mrs Jackson to the door, and as she saw the horse with a huddled-up figure crumpled at its feet she ran out with a cry of alarm.

"Sam! Sam! What is it? For the love of God, speak to me, my husband!"

No response came from him, and with fear in her eyes, and terror gripping her heart, she half-carried, half-dragged him inside. The red patch on his coat told its own tale. With trembling fingers she threw back his clothes and shuddered at the small dark mark from which the blood slowly ebbed.

With her head on his chest she listened for the beating of his heart. Then she bathed his wound and bandaged it as well as she was able.

In a little while Sam opened his eyes and looked about him.

"Did I manage to get home, Mum?" he whispered. "I'm done for, Mum. In me pocket's a roll of notes that Ned gave me. Put them away - you'll need 'em."

He closed his eyes again, and his lips twitched in an effort to speak.

"Who did it, Sam, tell me who did it?" She bent over him with the light of vengeance blazing in her eyes. "Sam! Sam!"

With an agonised sob the wizened little woman threw herself across his prostrate body. One of the dogs thrust its muzzle under her arm. The other crawled to the side of the master it would know no more.

Sam Jackson's tragic fate - the first death since the tragedy in the Wombat Ranges, in the never-ceasing struggle between officialdom and outlawry - brought a demand for vengeance from many Kelly sympathisers, who threatened to shoot every trooper on sight.

Jack Briant was shocked by the news. Jackson never had become reconciled to him since the Costello incident had aroused his suspicions, and the thought that the old man had gone forever dismayed him.

They buried him a hundred yards from the rude home where for years he had battled for a living in a spot where Nature had decreed none was to be won. Jackson had acknowledged no creed, but as most of his associates had been Roman Catholics, it was a priest who spoke the last sad words that must be uttered over all of us sooner or later.

Dry-eyed and with firm-set lips, the woman who had shared his hard life stood in the group of stern-faced men who had come from near and far to see the last of the man they were proud to call friend.

Jack Briant, who had ridden over with O'Donnell, gasped as he saw a tall, bearded man take his place at her side. Ned Kelly! Good heavens! Did he know the risks he was taking?

This was loyalty in its most magnificent form, but - He gasped again. A few yards from the bushranger, with bowed head, stood Constable Macguire - Macguire the fire-eater, who of all the North-Eastern troopers had been loudest in his denunciation of the man to whose memory he now paid tribute!

Briant noted that many of the mourners were casting covert glances at the strange intruder, as if resentful of his presence. Ned Kelly, however, did not notice him, or, if he did, he gave no outward sign of recognition.

Neither did the trooper show any interest in his enemy, who was almost within arm's length of him.

Through the trees at the front of the hut Jack saw, with dismay, that three horsemen were stationed. Were they policemen, and was Macguire's presence at the graveside merely a subterfuge? Or were they the three other bushrangers acting as surety that Ned would honor his old friend unmolested? If they were troopers, Macguire's acting was superb. Of all the mourners none was more affected than he, none apparently more genuinely emotional.

"Eternal rest give unto him, O Lord!" chanted in Latin the voice of Father Phelan.

The shoulders of Red Regan quivered, and Big Manton's hairy hand wiped from his eye the moisture he made no effort to conceal.

"And let perpetual light shine upon him!"

O'Rourke, keeper of the shanty on the rise, allowed the tears to trickle down his furrowed cheek unchecked.

"I am the Resurrection and the Life; he that believeth in Me, though he be dead, shall live, and everyone that liveth and believeth in Me shall not die forever!"

Ned Kelly felt the wizened little hand of Mrs Jackson seek his own, and his fingers closed round it in silent sympathy.

"May his soul and the souls of all the departed, through the mercy of God, rest in peace! Amen!"

As the last sad words of the priest died away Briant looked again at the bereaved old woman. She had crumpled up into the arms of the bushranger, who, without glancing at the other mourners, carried her tenderly to her lonely home.

All eyes were now turned on Macguire. Wonderingly they watched him reverently cross himself over the little mound of earth, replace his hat, and walk to the slip-rails, and mount the horse that stood tethered there. In another moment he had ridden away.

Briant's first thoughts were of Ned Kelly, and he led those who hurried over to the hut. Mrs Jackson was alone, staring ahead of her with eyes that betrayed a sorrow too deep for tears. The outlaw had disappeared.

28

Crippled!

SAM JACKSON'S death made a deep impression on the whole countryside. It brought home to the outlaws' friends the desperate nature of the game they were playing. Although they had known for months that the hills and gullies were full of armed men with authority to shoot to kill, this was the first time death had stalked in their midst. Some wavered In their allegiance to the gang, but none of them had the courage to go over to the enemy.

When it was found that Jackson had given his life to save the men on whose behalf he had endured hardship and persecution, it was felt that while friends could only pray for the rest of his soul, something could be done for his widow.

But Mrs Jackson was not to be found. When Angus McCullagh, Jim Kerry and Charlie Wicks called at her hut to find out how best they could help, the place was deserted. Where she had gone was not certain, although it was believed that she joined a married daughter in Sydney.

Macguire's attendance at the funeral was talked of everywhere. It formed the subject of a serious interview between the constable and Superintendent Hare.

"Yes, sorr, Oi wint," Macguire confessed. "Oi believe 'twas moi bullet that killed him, and Oi just had to be there!"

"I don't see that."

Macguire looked at him as though he had not heard aright. "D'ye mane to say, sorr -"

"I mean to say that it was a most extraordinary procedure," snapped his superior officer. "I am told that Ned Kelly was there also, and you made no attempt to capture him."

"Oi wint to pray for the soul av a mahn Oi belave Oi'd kilt. Twas a toime av pace, sorr, and we were in the prisence av a servant av God."

"That is no excuse why you should neglect your duty."

Macguire's red whiskers began to bristle. "Is it moi resigna-a-tion you'd loike, Mr. Superintendent?"

Hare had not bargained for this. Macguire was a good officer in spite of his fiery temper, and he had more intimate knowledge of the mountains than any other man in the force.

"I- I won't go as far as that, Macguire, but all the same I wish you to know that I think your conduct very, very irregular, to say the least."

"The -- old fool!" muttered the trooper when he left the office. "Made no iffort to capture him, eh? Wid half a hoondered thaves and murderers ready to tear me to paces! Bah!"

The more Macguire thought of his chief's censure the more it rankled. He was still brooding over it when Briant, returning from a visit to Benalla to purchase stores, met him.

"Good day," said Jack genially. "Might I congratulate you upon your fine action the other day?"

The big trooper disliked and distrusted this stranger from the city concerning whom there was so much mystery, but he was bubbling over with resentment at the Superintendent, and he felt he had to talk to someone.

"It was a fine, manly thing to do," Briant added.

"'Tis a pity other people don't take it that way," growled the trooper.

Then he unburdened himself, cursing with picturesque emphasis his superior officer and all his relatives for many generations. When he spoke of Sam Jackson, however; it was with something akin to reverence.

"Why," exclaimed Briant, "I thought you were his greatest enemy."

"Oi'm the inimy of no mahn who's paid for his sins. The hand av God was in this. Jackson was punished, just as ye'll be punished, bhoy, if ye don't keep clear av that murderin' gang."

Jack pondered deeply over that warning next day when, misjudging the fall of a tree he was helping O'Donnell to cut, he was smothered in its crashing descent. He tried to rise, but a big limb kept him prisoner. When eventually O'Donnell cut it away, he found that his right leg was useless.

Jennie and her father carried him into the house.

"The damn thing's broken," declared Briant, wincing with pain. "That means that I've got to go to Melbourne, somehow. I'll be weeks on my back. Curse the luck!"

"Of course, you'd be more comfortable in the city," said Jennie.

"It isn't a question of comfort. I'll need a lot of waiting on, won't be able to do a thing for myself. If there was a hospital in Benalla where I could go to I'd prefer that. I don't want to go to Melbourne, but there doesn't seem any other way."

Jennie looked at her father. "Couldn't you and I look after him, Dad? Nita'd come as often as she could, I know."

Jack flushed with pleasure. If he went away that would mean separation, and the thought hurt him.

"Oi'rn as rough asa currycomb mesilf," said O'Donnell, "but Jennie's as tinder as a chicken. We'd be glad to hey ye sthay here if ye could sthand it."

Jack shook his head. "It'd be asking too much, couldn't think of it."

"Well," said O'Donnell with a grin, "if ye've made up your moind to go a way' divil a wan'll sthop ye!"

"In other words," laughed Briant" "if I want to go a way you're not going to help me?"

"Look at that now! The mahn's brain works like a stame ingin!" The old fellow winked at his daughter.

"We'll be glad, to do anything we can for you, you know that, Jack." There was an unmistakable note of sincerity in the girl's voice.

"You don't know what it'd mean. I'm a rotten patient, anyhow."

"Well, thin, be off wid yez !" cried O'Donnell, waving his arms as though shooing away a depredatory hen.

Jennie had taken off her apron. "I'm going to Benalla for a doctor. Your leg's got to be set. I broke mine once, and I know the pain of it."

In a surprisingly short time they heard galloping hoof-beats. Without a word O'Donnell left the room. He was back in a minute with a cup in his hand.

"Ye're lookin' a bit whoite about the gills. A dhrop of the cratur won't do ye anny harm."

"You've a heart as big as an elephant's. Good luck!

By jove! that's good whisky!"

"Is there anny bad whisky?" demanded O'Donnell with such vehemence that Jack had to smile in spite of the pain that racked him. "You lay quoiet there. Jennie'll be back in a jiffy wid a dochter if she has to drag him here be the scruff av his neck."

It was a very long "jiffy" before she returned, however. To Briant it seemed hours. At last she came, and with her Dr Frost, a little fat man with a very red face and very white whiskers.

He frowned at his patient.

"What do you mean by breaking your leg and dragging me out here? Don't you know I've been hard at it since early this morning? Broken arms, broken noses, sprains and bellyaches! God save my soul! I don't know what's coming over the people! Let's have a look at you!"

With a gentleness that belied his roughness of speech, he set the fractured limb and bound it up. Great beads of perspiration stood on Briant's forehead, but he made no sound.

Dr Frost looked down on him with an expression that was half protest, half admiration.

"Why didn't you yell, damn you! They all do!"

"I'll yell, if you like," responded Jack, with a wan smile.

"What are you doing in these parts?" suddenly demanded the doctor.

"Humping my bluey."

"Liar! I suppose it's no affair of mine. You lie quiet now. I won't be out again till they send for me."

At the door he paused.

"I suppose you've got enough money to pay for this?"

"That'll be all right, doctor," Jennie cut in. "You needn't worry about that."

"H'mph!" said Dr Frost, as he left the hut.

Jennie noticed the astonishment in Jack's eyes and smiled.

"He's always like that - a real tiger, but he's as good as gold. You were very brave, Jack!"

"I didn't feel very brave, I can tell you. I oughtn't to stay here, Jennie. If you've got a bit of paper and an envelope I'll write to some people in Melbourne to arrange for getting away."

"Haven't a bit of paper in the house," she said, with a sly glance at her father.

The days dragged on by leaden feet. Nita was a daily caller, and Briant counted the hours between her welcome visits. Jennie found a good deal of time to give him, and O'Donnell did his best to entertain him in his own awkward way. There were few books in the house, but Nita brought him a supply, among them *Lorna Doone*, which she told him was a favorite of Ned Kelly's.

One night as he was dozing off to sleep he was startled to see the bushranger at his bedside.

"Bad luck!" he remarked. "Anything I can do?"

"No thanks, Ned. They're jolly good to me here, and I can't be grateful enough."

"If there's anything you want, let Jennie know. We're rich now," he added, with a laugh.

The outlaw was in much higher spirits than Jack had ever seen him before. It was only when mention was made of Sam Jackson's death that his face clouded.

"Sam died trying to save us," he said, then lapsed into a long silence. "'Greater love hath no man than this that he gave his life for his friend'!" Jack quoted.

Ned did not speak for some time. Then he said, half to himself, "I wonder was it Macguire who got him?"

"What would you do if you knew, Ned?"

He tapped his revolver significantly.

"But- but you wouldn't do that!"

"'An eye for an eye, a tooth for a tooth.' If I knew that Macguire shot Sam Jackson I'd get him tomorrow, even if I had to walk into the Benalla police station to do it! Sam was too good a man to be shot down like a dog. You don't know what that old fellow went through for us."

"I have a pretty good idea.'

Ned shook his head: "You don't know half of it." Jennie's appearance ended the discussion. Ned took a seat beside her, and slipped his arm round her waist. Contentedly she let her head fall on his shoulder.

Briant sighed. The love of such a fine girl for this hunted outlaw depressed him. It could end only in sorrow, and Jennie did not seem to have been made for that.

They talked of many things, and Ned discussed the details of .the bank robbery quite casually. Jack noticed, too, that Jennie was in no wise shocked over the affair - indeed, she seemed to regard it merely in the light of a triumph for her lover. O'Donnell seemed to derive great satisfaction from the fact that the bank had lost its money. He appeared to cherish some personal grudge against banks generally, and remarked that it was only a case of a robber being robbed.

"Euroa was No.1," said Ned significantly.

Jennie did not seem at all alarmed at the prospect of his engaging in further perilous exploits. The success of the Euroa affair had put the gang and their supporters into the best of spirits, which the increased activity of the police failed to dampen.

29

Aaron Sherritt

DURING the next week Jack Briant had many visitors. Big Manton came along one day, and brought a couple of chickens, which Jennie cooked deliciously.

Manton did not share the general optimism of the Kelly sympathisers. "It's getting harder and harder for the boys to dodge the police," he said. "They can't go on like this much longer."

"The Euroa affair seems to have bucked them up a lot," Jack suggested.

"It was a neat bit of work. The reward's up to £1000 a man now, and there's plenty of people round about here as could do with the money."

"That certainly makes it harder. I suppose some of the bank's money will be cut up, though."

"Yes, but that won't go far."

"There's the expectation of more that might keep the waverers sweet," Briant remarked.

Manton looked at him questioningly, as if wondering how much he knew, but he made no comment.

He had not gone long when John Cavendish, the schoolmaster, and Red Regan looked in. Next day he had two more visitors-Paddy O'Rourke, whose pocket bulged with a bottle of whisky, and Tom Stevens, who was anxious that Jack's leg should be rubbed with a concoction of gum leaves and iguana oil of his own mixing, which he declared would knit bones in a way "somethin' surprisin'." Briant humored him by accepting it with a fine show of gratitude.

His next caller was a tall, finely built young man, whom he had seen only once before.

"You don't know Aaron Sherritt, do you, Jack?" asked Jennie.

"No, I've not had that pleasure."

"I heard that you busted your leg, so I thought I'd look along and see you," said Sherritt. "It's pretty lonely on your back for days and weeks."

"Everybody's been so kind that I haven't felt it very much. It was jolly good of you to come along, though."

"Any friend of Ned's is a friend of mine," Sherritt declared.

Briant smiled. "I don't know that I can claim any particular friendship with Ned. You see, I'm only a stranger in these parts."

"Oh, I thought you done the gang many a good turn." Jack was about to reply when he noticed Jennie making signs to him. She put her finger to her lips and shook her head, which he interpreted as a warning to be careful. So he said, "I'm afraid someone's been inventing yarns."

Sherritt showed surprise. "Why, Joe Byrne told me a lot about you when you were at poor old Sam Jackson's."

"Joe used to be a particular chum of Aaron's," Jennie said, coming from the kitchen.

"Used to be! Why, he's my best chum now!" Sherritt declared with some show of annoyance."What made you say that, Jennie?"

"Oh, I didn't think you were so friendly now. Well, you can't be very well, can you? You only see one another once in a while."

"I saw Joe last night at his mother's place. I'm going to marry his sister," turning to Briant.

"So I had heard," said Jack. "You and Joe were in a few scrapes together, weren't you?"

Sherritt nodded a smiling affirmative.

"I wonder you don't join up with the gang."

Sherritt seemed to be searching for an effective answer. At last he said, "Don't know that I won't yet."

"That'd be pretty risky, Aaron," Jennie interposed. "I'm not afraid of risks. I've been taking them all my life."

"Yes, but not quite like the risks the boys are taking. The police are getting more cunning, and some people round about are getting greedier."

Sherritt's eyes widened. "You don't mean to say you think they'd sell the boys to the police?"

"Some people'd do anything for money. I'd be sorry for anyone that Ned caught trying it on!"

"Yes," he agreed, with a mirthless smile, "it wouldn't be good for him, would it? It's a pity Jennie's so sweet on Ned," he added, when she had left the room.

"Is she sweet on him? If she is, I don't know when they see one another."

Again Sherritt showed the surprise he felt. "You must have seen him here," he exclaimed.

"Here?" laughed Briant. "Good Lord! You don't think he'd take a risk like that? I'll bet the gang are far away in some safe hiding place."

The other man did not speak for a while. He was thinking deeply. "I can't understand why you're siding with the boys," he said at last.

Jack looked round cautiously and lowered his voice. "Strictly in confidence, I'm scared of them. I don't think they'd hesitate to put a bullet through anyone who showed them a point. I'm not keen on going out that way, are you?"

"N-no, I'm not" - with a startled inflection in his voice. "A thousand pounds a man's a big reward, isn't it? There'll be plenty out after that, I'll bet."

"Yes, a fellow with that much could clear out of the country and get a big start somewhere else."

Jack looked at him intently. "I say, I wonder whether anyone would get real pleasure out of money earned that way?"

Sherritt wheeled round sharply. "Could you?"

"I-I don't know. I suppose in time one would forget it had blood on it. Evidently you couldn't," he added as he noticed that Sherritt shuddered perceptibly. "But then, it's different in your case - you've been so friendly with Joe."

After a pause, during which Sherritt showed no inclination to speak, Jack continued, "I wonder why we're talking like this?"

"I don't know," was the hesitant response.

"It's funny the thoughts that come to you, when you've got nothing to do but lie and think. Dreams, too. I had a queer one the other night. The gang robbed another bank. I saw bags and bags of sovereigns. Ned dropped one, and when the sovereigns ran away each one turned into a policeman. Ned threw another bag down, and each sovereign became a sympathiser. They began blazing at one another, and dozens were killed. One man on Ned's side was a traitor. He fired at Ned's legs and brought him down. Then all the sovereigns in the other bags seemed to fall on him, and he was drowned in the golden flood. Curious, wasn't it? I said it was a curious dream," he repeated, when there was no reply.

"Y-yes, it was."

"Do you believe in dreams?" Briant asked. "Personally, I think there's something in them, at least there has been in some of mine. I remember as a kiddie I dreamt that I saw an uncle of mine swimming. Soon after that we got word that he had been drowned at sea."

"Was-was your dream about the sovereigns very clear - I mean, could you see any faces?" Sherritt inquired.

"Oh yes, but I don't remember recognising any. I do remember, though, that the fellow who shot Ned was young and tall. It's a wonder to me why everyone round here isn't a nervous wreck, the police included."

Just then the kitchen door closed with a bang, and Sherritt jumped from his chair.

"By jove! That gave you a start!" laughed Briant. "It almost sounded like a shot, didn't it? I say, what's your idea about the gang's chances? Of course, being a friend of Joe's, your opinion's likely to be prejudiced in their favor, but if you were just an ordinary sympathiser, what would you think?"

"I wouldn't give them much of a chance" - after a moment's silence.

"If I'd been in Ned's place I'd have had a big try at leaving Australia altogether. It'll get harder as the police get more used to the country, don't you think?"

The other man nodded. "Some of the troopers seem decent enough."

"Oh, yes. They're not all like Fitzpatrick, or Costello." Jack laughed. "I suppose you heard of my lucky guess about Costello?"

"It seemed too sure for just a guess."

Briant smiled again. "Oh, I say, you don't believe I'm in with the police, do you?"

"If you are, I don't understand your game. O'Donnell wouldn't have you here if he thought that, unless he had some sort of reason for it."

Jack remained silent, and Sherritt looked at him as if expecting an answer. "I wonder," said Briant at last, with lowered voice, "if that tree fell on me by accident? I mean," he added, noticing the other's surprise, "could O'Donnell have arranged it? If he had any doubt about me, it'd be a good idea to lay me up for a few weeks, wouldn't it? Do you-do you think you could find out for me, sound him a bit, and get an idea of how he feels?"

This show of confidence evidently flattered Sherritt, who said he'd do his best.

"That's jolly good of you, old man. If you do this, I won't forget you. I might be able to do you a good turn someday."

Sherritt leaned forward as if he intended to say something, but appeared to think better of it. A little later he left, promising to come back for another yarn at the first opportunity. Jennie looked round the door, and when certain that Jack was alone, came in with beaming face.

"You did that fine, Jack. Aaron came here to ask questions; and you didn't give him a chance. You've got him thinking, I'll bet."

"Did you hear all we said?"

"Every word. That was a good bit about Dad dropping the tree on you" -with a merry laugh.

"I'm an awful liar, aren't I? What's the strength of this chap?"

The girl's face had become serious again.

"We're not sure. He's been hanging around Mrs Byrne's a lot lately, and you know the police are watching her place pretty close."

"Yes, but then he's going to marry Joe's sister."

"That's all right. Still, the boys are suspicious. Aaron's just the sort of fellow who'd have joined them if he'd been all he makes out to be. I know Joe doesn't like the look of things."

"But he's a particular friend of Joe's, isn't he?"

"He was, but you never can tell. Joe'd shoot him for sure if he thought he was in with the police. And I wouldn't blame him, either, would you?"

"I-I don't know. It'd be pretty galling to find your friend a traitor, yet-yet--"

"Yet what?" she asked, surprise giving her voice a higher pitch.

"Shooting a man's a pretty serious business."

"And isn't spying a serious business?" she demanded, her eyes blazing. "I'd shoot anyone for that myself."

Jack was pondering deeply over what Aaron Sherritt had said when he heard the welcome voice of Nita in the next room. She ran to him and he kissed her rapturously. "Nita, you darling!" he whispered. "Why, what's the matter, girl of mine?" as she turned her head away.

"Jack," she sighed, "I'm unhappy!"

He took her hands in his. "What has happened to make you feel like that?"

"I know it's silly of me, but I can't help it. I'm jealous."

"Good gracious, who is there to be jealous of?"

She did not reply, but turned her head in the direction of the kitchen, from which came the voice of Jennie O'Donnell, softly singing an Irish song.

"You don't mean Jennie?" he gasped.

She let her head fall upon his shoulder, and he stroked her silken hair.

"But that's nonsense, dear. Jennie's nothing to me but the kindest and most considerate of friends."

"That's just it," she said, without looking up. "I'm jealous of the attention she gives you. She's with you all the time, and I only see you now and then. I hate the idea that she's waiting on you while I'm at home doing nothing for you."

"You don't wish you were here anymore than I do," he assured her. "All the same, I'm glad you're jealous."

She regarded him with a hurt look in her eyes.

"If you didn't love me, you wouldn't be jealous."

"Surely it isn't necessary for me to be jealous to prove it."

"No, but it makes me doubly sure."

"Am I interrupting?" asked Jennie, coming into the room.

"Not a word to her," Nita whispered.

"Of course not, Jennie."

The three of them talked of many things, and Jennie mentioned Aaron Sherritt's visit.

"I don't like that man!" cried Nita, impulsively. "What do you think of him, Jack?"

"I'm not sure. But what makes you dislike him?"

"Just something I can't explain. I don't believe he's straight. For one thing, I know he's spending a lot of time round Mrs Byrne's, and I don't think he's giving it all to Joe's sister. The police are simply swarming around. They think the gang, or at least Joe, is sure to go there."

"It's hard to think that Aaron would give away his best friend," remarked Jennie, "but you never can tell!"

"We're near the end," Ned said.

30

The Jerilderie Robbery

ANXIOUSLY, Jack Briant looked forward to the time when he would be about again. He hated the inaction of a bed-ridden patient, and the idleness which made him a burden on the big-hearted O'Donnells. Many times he had spoken to the old Irishman about it, but O'Donnell had merely smiled, and assured him that really he was doing very well, as there was always something over from the little delicacies which his friends brought along when they paid their frequent visits.

Jennie, too, lightly brushed aside his misgivings. "Why, you're no bother at all, Jack. I'll feel quite lonely when you get up and lonelier still when you go away."

Go away! Yes, he would have to do that. He would have to find some work that would give him sufficient money to repay them for all their kindness.

Ned Kelly had called a number of times, and invariably he had stopped for a yarn. Lately Jack had noticed a certain restlessness about him that seemed to indicate another coup was being planned. He had observed, too, that Jennie had become a little more serious and thoughtful, as if doubtful of the result of the exploit.

Briant was out of bed and hobbling about on sticks when the absence of the bushranger and the suppressed excitement of Jennie told him that the adventure, whatever it might be, was near at hand.

He questioned her, but, beyond admitting that "something big" was about to take place, she was uncommunicative. Once he had remarked, "Another bank?" and the look in her eyes told him that he had guessed correctly.

The little bush township of Jerilderie, thirty miles across the border of New South Wales, was dark and silent on the night of February 8 1879, when the gang rode through its deserted streets. They went straight to the police station and knocked loudly.

Constable Devine, blinking at the candle which he held in his hand, opened the door.

"Quick!" cried Ned. "A man has been murdered at Davidson's Hotel!"

Hearing excited voices, Constable Richards also made his appearance.

"Are there only two of you here?" Ned asked. "There's a man raving mad at the pub, and he'll take some handling."

"We're the only ones here," replied Devine, "but we'll manage him all right."

He was about to rush for his clothes when a peremptory demand of "Put up your hands!" checked him. The excited man, who had begged his assistance in an instant had become cool and stern, and the revolver which he pointed at the two troopers was as steady as a rock.

"By God! The Kellys!" exclaimed Richards.

"A good guess!" smiled Ned, as he indicated the presence of his three companions, each of whom held a pistol.

"What do you want with us?" asked Devine, a little shakily.

"Nothing very much," replied the bushranger. "Get something on you. We're going to lock you up in your own cells."

"But my wife- "

"You needn't worry about her, she'll be all right."

Mrs Devine, who had been aroused by their voices, uttered a terrified scream as she saw her husband and his fellow officer under the subjection of four desperate looking armed men.

"You needn't be frightened," Ned assured her. "Nobody's going to be hurt. You go back to your bed."

Afraid to disobey, she went into her room, casting one fear-filled glance at the intruders as she shut the door.

"Never been locked up before, I suppose?" quizzed Ned, as he followed the troopers to the cells. "I have, so I know what it's like. A taste of your own medicine won't hurt you."

"Hey, that's a good joke!" laughed Dan, as the key clicked in the lock.

"What now?" asked Steve Hart.

"Sleep. You keep watch while we get a bit of rest." "What are you going to do with the woman?" queried Dan.

"Nothing!" Ned shot a glance at him which showed that, whatever thought might have prompted the question, it did not meet with favor.

So, while Jerilderie slept, its police station housed the men who, of all Australia's inhabitants, were least likely to be found there. In spite of their curious quarters, the three outlaws passed a restful night. Hart might have slept also for all the danger there was, but he never blinked an eyelid. An unpleasant experience with Ned on a previous occasion, when he had failed to remain as alert as he was expected to be, was well remembered.

Realising that they were absolutely in the hands of their captors, Devine and Richards showed no resentment when they sat down to breakfast next morning, although Devine's face clouded and his hands twitched when Dan Kelly spoke gruffly to his wife, who waited upon them.

The bushrangers were in excellent spirits. They laughed and joked freely, and although the troopers put the best possible face on it, it was clear that they were less appreciative of the humor of the situation.

"We've been bushrangers for a long time," remarked Ned during the morning, "but today we're going to be troopers. We're going to be new constables sent up to help you capture the Kellys!"

And, when Ned and Dan had donned uniforms, there was nothing in their appearance to suggest that they were not what they represented themselves to be.

They took Richards for a walk through the township in order to familiarise themselves with its layout. He was warned that if anyone spoke to him the outlaws were to be introduced as police reinforcements. But no one seemed curious.

Joe Byrne filled in the time by having their horses shod by the local blacksmith, who, noticing the brands on the animals, became suspicious, but kept his mouth shut.

Transferring the two troopers once more to the security of their own cells, the gang strolled over to the Royal Hotel, and, drawing their revolvers, ordered everyone present into the dining-room, which was locked, and guarded by Joe Byrne.

"Who the divil are ye, to be orderin' people about like this?" demanded a little fat man with a projecting jaw.

"My name is Kelly," laughed the outlaw leader. "Ever heard of me?"

"Ned Kelly, be the livin' Moses!" was the astonished reply. "'Ere, wot ye doin' in Noo South Wales? Vic's where ye belong."

"Just come to pay a friendly visit. Here, you keep away from that window!" as a rough, bearded man allowed his fingers to stray to the catch.

"Here's another one!" cried Byrne, bundling in a terror-stricken old man, who, seeing the revolvers of the other three bushrangers, dived under the table.

"What's the good of bailing us up?" inquired a young man with a face liberally besprinkled with freckles. "We got nothin' to give yer."

"That's a pity," smiled Dan. "We counted on your diamond rings!"

"Reckon *you* ought to shout after this."

Ned turned to the speaker, a middle-aged farmer. "That's a wager! We've got a little job to do first."

The "little job" was at the Bank of New South Wales next door. Byrne walked round the back of the building, and the accountant, named Living, hearing him, opened the door to tell him that if he wished to do business with the bank he must go to the front. The next moment he was gazing down the barrel of a wicked-looking revolver.

"Who are you?" he gasped.

"The Kelly Gang," replied Byrne, ordering him inside to surrender all the firearms in the building.

Mackin, another clerk, who, undetected by the outlaws, had been watching the drama being enacted at the hotel, hearing their voices, entered the bank - to be met by Joe's revolver.

"Come behind the counter here," commanded Byrne.

"Now then, where's the manager?"

Both clerks professed ignorance of his whereabouts, and Joe escorted them to Ned in the adjoining hotel. Evidently his manner was more impressive, for they informed him that Mr Jarleton had just returned from a journey and was changing his clothes. It took some time to locate him, but eventually he was found having a bath, and was ordered to dress himself.

With Living as a guide, Ned and Joe ransacked the bank. The teller's cash yielded £700, but when the safe was opened £1450 more was found.

"Bring those books out in the yard," said Ned, indicating the ledgers.

"What are you going to do with them?' anxiously inquired the bank manager.

"Burn them!"

"Please don't do that. You'll destroy the bank records."

Ned grinned. "That's just what I want to do.' The bank's been robbing the poor long enough."

In spite of Jarleton's entreaties, a bonfire was made of them in the yard, the bushrangers joking as they watched them being consumed. Returning to the bank, they encountered Rankin, a merchant, and the proprietor of the local paper, named Gill, who promptly were ordered to bail up. Both dashed out into the street. Rankin was overtaken, but Gill disappeared.

They took Rankin to the hotel and stood him up against the wall.

"Now, I'm going to shoot you," declared Ned, examining his revolver.

Rankin, who was made of stern stuff, raised no protest, but the other prisoners begged for his life.

"No, I'm going to do for him!" the bushranger insisted.

"Keep away!"

Aghast at the impending tragedy, they pleaded earnestly for mercy on behalf of their fellow-townsman.

"Let's shoot the lot of them!" suggested Dan.

"No, we won't do that," said his brother. "I'm going to pot Richards and Devine before we leave, though! That's why we came here."

The prisoners cast horrified glances at the two troopers, neither of whom showed any sign of fear, however. Whether their coolness was due to their belief that this was merely an idle boast, or was prompted by sheer bravery, could only be guessed at.

A search was made for the missing newspaper man, but he had hidden himself, and could not be found. Ned showed keen disappointment.

"I wanted him to print the history of the gang," he explained. "Where does he live?"

He was shown the house, but Mrs Gill, who answered his knock, refused to have anything to do with the manuscript which he offered.

"I'll pay him well for it!" Ned assured her.

"I won't take it!" was her obstinate reply.

The bushranger was showing signs of temper, so Living, who accompanied him, offered to take charge of the writing and see that it was published - a promise which eventually he fulfilled.

Going over to another hotel, in the bar of which were several men, Ned made himself known, and invited them to have a drink with him.

"There's half a dozen of you to one,'" he remarked, "and anyone of you might shoot me. It wouldn't be well if you did, though - the boys would kill the whole mob over there!"

None of them made any hostile move, however. Those who were not frightened seemed to enjoy the experience. That they had had a drink with Ned Kelly would give them something to talk about in after years.

Meanwhile Joe Byrne was busy at the telegraph office.

At revolver point the operator was ordered to cut the wires, and to chop down a number of posts. Jefferson, the officer in charge, was warned that if he had the line repaired before next day the gang would return and shoot him.

A fine blood mare was taken from one of the hotel stables, and the outlaws made preparations for leaving the township.

When Ned re-entered the dining-room where the prisoners were herded, there was general wonder as to what would happen next. Great was their relief, therefore, when he started to give them his version of the tragedy at Wombat Creek.

"Don't believe the lies you've heard," he said. "They brought it on themselves. If we hadn't shot them, they'd have shot us. People call us murderers! If we'd wanted to murder them, we could have done it a dozen times. Two or three times we were quite close to them, and heard all they were saying. Lonergan was trying to get his revolver when we shot him. If Kennedy and Scanlon had bailed up when we told them to we would have let them go, after we took their horses, provisions and guns. They made a fight of it, so what could we do?"

He waited for a reply, but as none came, he resumed: "We were driven into the bush by Fitzpatrick's lies. He's the cause of all this trouble. He put my mother in gaol and made outlaws of Dan and I. We're going to Urana to rob the bank. Don't any of you try to follow us, or he'll get shot. Now we'll have a drink before we go. Come along!"

They followed him into the bar, and one man was sufficiently magnanimous to shout, "Good luck!" as he raised his pewter pot.

"Here's luck!" responded Ned, and drank a small beer. Curiously they watched Joe Byrne ride up the street, leading one of the police horses with the bank's money strapped on the saddle. Ned followed - shortly after, waving farewell to them as he turned the corner.

When Dan and Steve Hart mounted and drew their revolvers a general scamper inside the hotel occurred. There was no real cause for alarm, for the outlaws contented themselves by galloping up and down the street, singing songs and firing into the air.

It was not until they finally disappeared in a swirl of dust, however, that Jerilderie breathed freely again.

31

Treachery

"WHY so early?" Jennie was saddling her horse with impatient hands, and her cheeks wore a flush of excitement.

"Off to Benalla," she answered. "I want to see the paper."

"News of Ned?" Briant asked.

"Big news. Don't keep me - I'm just dying to know all about it."

She was back in a surprisingly short time, her horse's flanks alather. She jumped from the saddle, and with sparkling eyes ran to the fencing job, where Jack, still too weak to work, was chatting with her father. "It's wonderful!" she cried, brandishing a newspaper. "They stuck up Jerilderie, and got away with thousands of the bank's money!"

Eagerly Briant read aloud the newspaper version of the exploit. Although the story was familiar to her, the girl hung upon every word. O'Donnell grinned in silent appreciation.

"Ned and Dan dressed as troopers!" exclaimed Jennie.

"Oh, what a joke!"

When Jack came to the portion of the report which, in outraged English, described the apparent intention of Dan Kelly and Steve Hart of amusing themselves by murdering some of the prisoners in the hotel dining-room, her eyes blazed."

"That's all lies! Ned would never let them even think of such a thing!"

"Possibly it was merely to impress them, what you might call a demonstration," Jack suggested:

"Of course it was - if it really happened."

"The police of two colonies'll be on their tracks now."

The girl smiled confidently. "Let 'them!"

"I wish I could be as cheerful over it as you are. I don't - hullo, who's this coming? Looks like Sherritt."

It was Sherritt, who, hitching his horse to a post, hurried over to them. "I see you've got the paper," he said in excited tones, "Wasn't it fine? By jove! There'll be a shindy over this! Ned took a bit of a risk in passing Simpson's place in broad daylight."

"Briant's eyes narrowed "There's nothing about it in the paper."

"Oh, yes, there is."

"You find it then."

Jack handed him the sheet, and Sherritt scanned it hurriedly.

"Well, it must have been in the other one. I'll swear I saw it. No, perhaps I didn't. I remember now- it was Tom Hogan who told me."

Jack glanced at Jennie, whose answering look was one of suspicion and distrust.

"I s'pose they'll come this way, like they did before," Sherritt went on.

"How do you mean?" asked Jennie.

"They're sure to plant the stuff about here for awhile. Didn't they go to Carter's after the Euroa affair?"

"Did they?"

"Of course they did, and the money was there for days."

"I don't think you can be right there, Aaron," said Jennie. "Kate Kelly told me two troopers were there the night after the boys stuck up the Euroa bank."

Sherritt looked her full in the eyes. "P'r'aps they came here?"

She laughed. "Not much chance of that. Martin and one or two of the others are always prowling round here - goodness knows what for."

"The boys'll have to be extra careful now," Sherritt said. "I wouldn't be surprised if they doubled the reward. Eight thousand's a lot of money."

"Some men would sell their souls for that!" Briant shot at him.

"I suppose they would" -averting his gaze.

"May the sowl av the man as betrays anny av the bhoys burn in hell for a t'ousand years!" cried O'Donnell.

Sherritt shuddered ever so slightly, but it did not escape the quick eyes of the girl. Then with an "I must be moving along new," he left them, and walked rapidly to his horse.

"Well?" said Jennie.

"Well?" responded Jack.

"Where did he get that yarn about the gang passing Simpson's in the daytime? It must have come from the police."

"That certainly was a bad slip of his."

"Ye'd better be afther tillin' Ned," suggested O'Donnell.

"Ned's already watching him," said Jennie. "Joe Byrne's suspicious, too, though he finds it hard to believe his best friend would spy on him."

When Sherritt left the O'Donnell's he rode towards the ranges. In a rocky defile he dismounted, looked carefully about him, and whistled shrilly. The signal was answered by someone farther up the gully, and presently Joe Byrne appeared.

"All clear?" he asked.

"Haven't seen a soul since I left O'Donnell's," Sherritt assured him.

"Hare's getting busy over at your mother's, so you'd better be careful. I'll let you know when everything's all right. Where's the boys?"

"Back of the ranges, where nobody can find them.

When are you going to join us, Aaron?"

Sherritt hesitated before he spoke. "I don't know, Joe. I've been thinking things over, and I can't see how you can last out."

"We've lasted pretty well up to now, haven't we?"

There was a note of irritation in his voice.

"You have, but the police are getting stronger every day. They'll get you yet, Joe! They needn't get you if you work things right. You know what capture means - it means hanging, Joe, that's what it means."

Byrne winced, and the other went on, "You could get out if you wanted to."

"What the hell do you mean?"

"You've got to consider yourself, Joe. Supposing you gave yourself up and turned Queen's evidence."

Byrne remained silent, and thus encouraged, Sherritt continued- "I'd hate to see them get you, old boy. Why not get out before it's too late?"

Joe did not flare up, as Sherritt expected. Instead he shook his head sadly, like a man who adheres to a decision which means certain disaster.

"I'm full up of it all, but I've got to see it through!"

"Why have you? If you gave yourself up and helped to get the others you'd be pretty sure of getting a pardon and a lump of the reward. Why not do it, Joe?"

"No!" replied Byrne with decision. "I won't do it! They'd say I was worse than Sullivan, and hunt me out of Victoria."

Sullivan was a bloodthirsty bushranger who, after committing a number of revolting crimes in New Zealand, saved his neck by informing on his fellow outlaws. He came to Victoria and lived, despised and detested, in a lonely hut at Wedderburn, until the hostility shown towards him caused him to clear out - where no one seemed to know.

"That'd be better than hanging, anyhow."

"I'll never be hanged! It's no use talking, Aaron, I couldn't do it. I'd give a lot to get out of this scrape. It's hell, man! Hunted day and night, never a minute's let up. And those three dead men at Stringybark Creek! Often I see them in the night, and they look at me with their eyes close to my face. Ugh!"

He shuddered and put out his hands, as though to shut out the awful sight.

"But it needn't go on, I tell you, Joe!"

"It's got to go on," cried Byrne, with a gesture of utter hopelessness.

Suddenly he wheeled round.

"What's that up near that big rock? I saw something move. If it's a trooper, and you've come the double on me, by God! I'll get you first."

"I didn't see anything, Joe," Sherritt responded, in a voice that shook a little.

Byrne stood watching the boulders on the hillside, his fingers toying with his revolver.

"A damn wallaby," he exclaimed, with a sigh of relief. He turned to his companion again. "I meant what I said just now, Aaron. I'll shoot you dead if you play tricks on me!"

"I'm not likely to do that to you, Joe."

"Then see that you don't!"

The bushranger walked rapidly a way. Sherritt took a step or two after him, but changed his mind, and went back to his horse. When he had ridden a mile along the bush track he met Superintendent Hare, who asked, "Anything new?"

"Mr. Hare," said Sherritt, ignoring the question, "what'd happen to one of the gang who turned Queen"s evidence?'"

"Why, do 'you think?"

"I was only just wondering. Tisn't likely any of them, would, but I was just wondering what you'd do with him."

"If he helped us to get the others, I'd do what I could to get him a pardon. Do you think there's any chance?" -eagerly.

"No, I don't. Seen anything at Mrs Byrne's?"

"Not yet, but we're still watching."

"Someone's coming!" cried Sherritt, as distant hoof-beats caught his ear. "See you later," he cried; as he rode into the bush.

By a circuitous route Superintendent Hare reached the police camp he had established in a gully about a mile from Mrs. Byrne's hut. It was known that Joe visited his mother at frequent intervals, and sometimes spent the night there. Seven troopers were stationed in readiness for a raid at any moment, and four others took up a position in the mountains which gave them an uninterrupted view of the gully which Sherritt assured them, the Kellys often visited.

It was a trying vigil for the police, and more than one of them felt a sympathetic urge towards the bushrangers who had endured similar conditions for many months. There was nothing to do in the daytime, except seek shelter from the heat, and at night, lying in the scrub watching the Byrne hut, they were half frozen, for those high altitudes are subject to extremes of climate.

Mrs Byrne went about her work as usual, but nothing escaped her watchful eyes. In the discovery of a piece of soap near the creek she sensed danger, and the glint of the sun on an empty sardine tin confirmed her suspicions.

Hare expressed his concern for Sherritt's safety next time he met him.

"If the old lady suspects you it'll be bad for you."

"But she can't tell the gang," Sherritt replied. "She can't get in touch with them except through me. If you keep a sharp look-out you'll get them yet."

All the same, it was with some misgiving that he approached the Byrne hut that even. He played a tin whistle for the purpose of attracting his sweetheart from whom he hoped to learn how much her mother knew.

Joe's sister did not come out to meet him, however, and the anger in Mrs Byrne's eyes quickened his heartbeats.

"The troopers are camped up the gully," she told him.

"What have you been doing that you didn't see them - going about with your eyes shut?"

"I don't know how they could be there without me seeing them," he replied. "Are you sure it was a police camp?"

"Sure? Of course I'm sure!" she snapped.

Sherritt accepted her abuse with a light heart, because it was clear that she did not suspect him.

Of all the agents employed by the police, Sherritt was the greatest problem. There was some doubt at headquarters as to his sincerity, but Hare believed implicitly in his willingness to sacrifice even his friend, Joe Byrne, for a share of the reward. The position was complicated by well-meaning settlers pointing him out to the Superintendent as a notorious Kelly sympathiser, who should be arrested.

Sherritt was in the pay of both camps. Joe Byrne had often given him a pound or two for services rendered for, amongst other things, conveying messages between the gang and their friends, and for displaying in conspicuous places insulting caricatures of the police - and money also came from Superintendent Hare.

The police chief could not help despising the man who was willing to sell his friend for gold, but he possessed some qualities that aroused his admiration- his ability to sleep uncovered, and often without a coat, on the bare ground on the coldest night, for instance.

"You must be as hard as nails," remarked Hare.

"I'm pretty hard, but not as hard as Ned Kelly," Sherritt replied. "He's a better man than me in every way, but I could beat Dan, Joe and Steve at any game. Ned's a wonder, if it hadn't been for him the gang'd gone to pieces long ago. There isn't a cleverer bushman in Australia, and he never knocks up."

"Pretty clever horse thief, too?" suggested Hare.

"My word! It's a great game, and so easy. I'd like to go in for horse-breeding, and get hold of a thoroughbred stallion and some good mares, but there'd be more fun in stealing than buying them."

Then he explained the method by which he and Ned had altered brands. It was to change or add a letter by pulling out the hair with a pair of tweezers, and painting the bare spots with iodine, which made the skin appear as if it were branded in the ordinary way.

Ned Kelly

3 2

Ned Asserts Himself

THE Kellys had many hiding places in the wild Strathbogie Ranges, but none more secure than that to which they hurried after their Jerilderie exploit. High up in the mountains Nature had fashioned a perfect retreat, a space enclosed on all sides by giant boulders.

It was reached by a small aperture in the rocks, and this one opening commanded a view of the tortuous track which led to it. It was practically a house without a roof, and even this disadvantage was overcome by the rock ledges that afforded complete shelter in wet weather.

Few of the bushranger's friends knew of its existence, and those few were their most trusted sympathisers.

In this retreat the four outlaws rested - Ned thoughtful, Dan irritable, Byrne gloomy and depressed, and Hart restless.

"Don't walk about like that!" cried Dan. "It gets on my nerves!"

Steve Hart ceased his pacing.

"A fellow's got to do something," he growled.

"What's the good of it all!" exclaimed Byrne, taking a roll of banknotes from his pocket and giving them a contemptuous flick. "What's the good of robbing banks if the money's no use to us. I don't want money - I want friends- someone to talk to."

Ned looked at him searchingly, but did not speak.

"Let's get out of this!" Joe went on. "What's the' good of being alive if you can't have the things we want most? Kennedy and Lonergan and Scanlon are better off than us. By God! I wish one of them had got me that day on the Wombat!"

"Stop your raving!" commanded Ned. "If you're tired of it, get out - if you can!"

"We ought to all get out," said Hart. "I'm as full up as Joe."

"We've got to do a big bank first," cut in Dan. "Beechworth'd give us a decent haul. We could do it at night - wake up the manager, and get him to hand over the stuff."

"That isn't the way to tackle any bank," Ned reproved.

"Why isn't it?"

"I've got a better plan than that."

"Well, we'll have to get going pretty soon. Some of the crowd's singing out for more money, the greedy swine!"

"Let 'em!" snapped Hart.

"That's easy talk," sneered Dan. "If they don't get ours they'll take the police's. Some of them are doing it now. They'd sell us as soon as look. Kate says Jacobson's pretty friendly with the troopers. And so is Merrett, and Scott, and Thompson, and Aaron Sherritt. No, I don't trust him any more than the others," he added, in response to Joe Byrne's look of inquiry.

"What about you, Joe?" Ned asked.

"I'm not sure. Sometimes I think like Dan, but it's hard to believe a friend- "

"Friend!" shouted Hart. "No one can tell who's his friend these days."

"Don't be a fool!" Ned remonstrated. "Nobody ever had truer friends than we have. If we hadn't we wouldn't be here now. Sam Jackson gave his life for us - no man can do more than that!"

"I know, I know, but- "

"There's no buts. This sort of talk won't get us anywhere. You're behaving like a lot of kids. What's the good of getting jumpy?"

Hart made an impatient gesture.

"Jumpy? Who wouldn't be jumpy with those blacks on his tracks. We've got some show against the troopers, because we're better men than they are, but you can't hide from a tracker."

Mention of the blacktrackers who had been brought from Queensland to assist the police in hunting them down brought an anxious look to every outlaw's face.

Even Ned, most resourceful and courageous of them all, dreaded those dark-skinned wizards to whom the bush was an open book. He knew their uncanny cleverness in picking up the most trivial clue, their marvellous faculty in following tracks that were invisible to white men. Some of the trackers, they knew, were scared of them, but for all that they were a danger that could not be underrated.

"We could have potted two of them the other day," said Dan, "and we missed the chance!"

"You're always wanting to pot someone," rebuked Ned.

"Murder won't get us anywhere."

"What will, then?"

"Keeping our heads. Where would we have been if we had followed your damn silly plan at Jerilderie?"

This reference to Dan's scheme of surprising the little New South Wales township in broad daylight and shooting anyone who offered resistance brought an angry flush to the face of its author, and he replied hotly: "If we're bushrangers, why the hell don't we act like bushrangers? Your old woman ideas make me sick! What do you carry a revolver for?"

Ned's response was startling. He drew his pistol, and took a step nearer his brother, a hard glint in his eyes.

"What do I carry this for - to shoot damn fools like you, if they lose their heads! You want someone shot, do you? Then be careful it isn't you!"

He turned to the others.

"We've got to understand each other from now on. If you want to clear out, then clear out! I'm not keeping any of you. You can whack up my share of what money we've got and go. You won't go far - not one of you's got enough brains to dodge the troopers for more than a day. If you stay, you'll all do as I say! If we tackle any more banks, we'll tackle them my way. If I'm going to lead this gang, I'll lead it all the way."

Ned returned his revolver to its holster, and walked towards the opening in the rocks.

"Chew it over. I'll leave you to consider it. If you want to go on your own, go. If you want to stay, you'll do as I say."

They watched him squeeze through the crevice, then turned to one another, each waiting for his companion to speak. Dan was first to break the silence.

"A -- bully, that's what he is!"

Byrne and Hart made no comment, and Dan shouted angrily. "Didn't you hear what I said?"

"We heard," they answered, in a breath.

"Well, haven't you anything to say?"

"No," replied Joe.

"No," repeated Steve.

Dan's lip curled in a sneer. "Got you bluffed, has he?"

"You, too!" Hart shot back at him.

"Has he?" You'll see before long he hasn't. Haven't we got a say in anything? Must we always do a thing because he wants us to?"

"I'm afraid we must," said Byrne, quietly.

Dan flared up again. "Why must we?"

"Supposing we cleared out; what'd we do?" asked Hart.

"Bust open half-a-dozen banks and get away with the money! What the devil are you grinning at?"

"I was wondering," returned Byrne, still smiling, "how we'd do it. I don't fancy myself much at planning things, and I'm blowed if I'd trust either of you two. Ned was right when he said the police'd get us in a day or two. We're not the man he is, none of us, and we'd be easy for the troopers without him. I don't want to rob any more banks!"

A note of remorse had crept into his voice.

"I'm full up of bushranging! I'd give ten years of my life to wipe out what's happened since we came on those three at Stringybark Creek. This isn't living. It was all right for a time, perhaps, but I've had a gutsful."

"What did you join us for, then?" snapped Dan.

"Because I was a fool. I wanted adventure. My God! I've had it! I've had enough to last me a lifetime. A lifetime - I wonder!"

"Wonder what, Joe?" asked Hart, but it was clear from his expression that the question was unnecessary.

"Just how long our lifetime'll be. Why, we're only just alive, and yet, any day, I say, any day- "

"Don't- you give me the creeps, Joe," pleaded Hart.

Dan spat disgustedly.

"You sniveller! 'A short life and a merry one!' you said when you joined me and Ned. What are you crying about now?"

"It hasn't been as merry as I thought, and, God help me, it might be shorter than I ever reckoned on."

"A man's only got to die once," Dan declared.

"It's worse than death sometimes." Byrne shuddered. "Those three men! I've seen them night after night! Don't they ever come to you?"

Dan guffawed. "They're safe in hell, where they deserve to be! Dead men can't hurt anyone."

"They can - and they do!" Joe persisted. "They won't leave' me alone! Why do they come to me? It wasn't my fault they were killed."

"You talk like a girl," Dan protested. "I thought you had more guts. Where are you going?"

Hart was crawling through the rock opening. "I'm going to find Ned."

"What for?"

"To tell him I'm for him. I'm scared without him, I tell you. Joe's right. He's bigger than the three of us put together."

Ned was sitting on a rock, a few yards away. He looked up at Steve's approach, but waited for the other to speak.

"We've got to stick to you, Ned," said Hart. "Dan's talking through his neck, but he knows as well as we do that we couldn't last without you."

Without a word Ned went back to the hiding place. His brother, who was still talking loudly, stopped suddenly.

"Get on with your corroboree," jeered Ned.

Dan's eyes flashed, but he made no comment.

"We've got to get down to things," the leader continued. "If I'm fit to run this gang I've got to have my way. Is that right?"

"That's right, Ned," responded Byrne.

"Yes," was Hart's monosyllabic reply.

Dan did not answer, and Ned turned to him. "What about you, Fireworks?"

"Oh, go to hell!"

Ned's reply was to smash a right to his brother's jaw, and Dan fell like a log. Then he dragged him, half dazed, to his feet, and hit him again. It took a little while to recover from the effects of the second punch, and when Dan eventually got up all his fire had left him.

"You've been looking for this for a long time," declared Ned. "If you want to clear out, you'd better go now. We'd be a damned sight better off without you, so we won't worry if you go."

"Don't be a fool, Dan," counselled Byrne. "Ned's the boss, and you can't get away from that."

"I suppose so," was the grudging admission.

"What are you going to do about the trackers?" asked Hart, after a long pause.

Ned's face was very grave as he replied, "We've got to stop them getting here - if we can."

"What do you mean - the train?"

Ned nodded significantly.

"They'll bring more of them from Queensland, and if we don't get them, they'll get us."

"One of them died from the cold the other day," remarked Byrne.

"Good job, too!" commented Dan.

"We've got to lie low for a while," said Ned.

The suggestion of inactivity annoyed the others, but they realised the futility of voicing any protest.

"If we do that, the police might think we've cleared out," Ned resumed. "I hate loafing just about as much as you do, but there's nothing else for it"

"Waiting! Waiting! Waiting! - for how long, I wonder?" muttered Byrne, looking up at the rocky walls, which to him seemed so like a prison.

33

Aaron Sherritt's Fate

DURING the next few weeks the four outlaws were never seen together. Ned spent many stolen hours with Jennie O'Donnell, once or twice Hart met relatives at a secret rendezvous, Dan eluded the troopers to visit his sisters, and Joe Byrne found consolation, in occasional intercourse with the friends whose companionship he craved. One day he returned with blazing eyes.

"What's up?" asked Ned Kelly.

"Aaron's in with the police!"

"Sure?"

"Certain. They're camped near Mother's place. This morning I got near enough to see, and Sherritt was with them! He's been spying on me for weeks. By God! I'll get him! - I'll get him!"

"Better be sure, Joe," counselled Hart.

Byrne turned with an oath.

"Sure! I tell you I saw him! Oh, the cowardly swine! He wanted me to turn Queen's evidence, so he could get the reward. He'll get his, make no mistake about that!"

None of the others spoke. Ned was very thoughtful as he smoked. Occasionally he glanced across at Joe, who had flung himself on a rock, and sat with bowed head and hands hanging limply between his knees. His anger had now left him, and his attitude was that of a man upon whom a great sorrow had descended.

That afternoon Byrne and Dan talked long and earnestly. When it was nearly dark they crept through the crevice in the rocks. Understanding, Ned let them go.

The pair picked their way cautiously through the scrub, halting every few minutes and listening intently. At Manton's they secured their horses.

"What's the game?" asked the big fellow.

"You'll know soon enough," replied Joe, as they rode away.

Neither spoke a word until they reached the hut of Anton Wicks, a German miner, who lived within a short distance of Sherritt's shack. Rejected by the outlaw's sister, Sherritt had married a girl named Barry.

"I'll go," said Byrne.

"Hullo, it's you, Joe, ain't it?" queried Wicks, peering closely into the face of the nearest horseman.

"We want you to come with us to Aaron Sherritt's," he was told.

He hesitated a moment, but something in the outlaw's "Quick now!" impressed him with the need for unquestioning obedience.

"What for you ask me?" he inquired, a little shakily, as they made their way on foot through the bush.

"You go to the door and knock," commanded Byrne.

"If they ask 'Who's there?' tell them you've lost your way. That's all! Don't come any monkey-tricks, or I'll put a bullet through you!"

Wonderingly, the German carried out his instructions. "Who's there?" called a man's voice from within.

"It's me, Anton Wicks. I don't fint mein way." Sherritt opened the door. "Why, you're only a little way from home, you- "

He did not finish the sentence. There was a flash and a report, and he staggered backwards into the house, clutching wildly at his breast.

Joe Byrne took a few steps' further forward and fired again and Sherritt crumpled in a heap on the floor.

His distracted young wife bent over his prostrate body, and her mother, wringing her hands, turned to the bushranger, who, followed by the horrified German, stepped into the kitchen.

"Oh, Joe, what did you shoot poor Aaron for?" she wailed.

"He'll never put me away again," replied Byrne, noting with grim satisfaction that his victim was dead. "'I wanted that fellow, and now that I've got him I'm satisfied! Who's that?" -as a footstep was heard in the next room.

"It's only a man looking for work," replied the bereaved mother-in-law, with fear, in her eyes.

Inside the bedroom four troopers shivered with excitement and fear. Here was at least one of the gang upon whose capture they were bent, but Aaron Sherritt's death had come with a tragic suddenness that had robbed them of all initiative

"Whoever you are, come out, or be killed like dogs!" shouted Byrne, as he fired several shots into the walls.

The troopers showed no anxiety to accept the invitation, and the bush rangers, after threatening to set the hut on fire, and making a show of their desperate intention by piling brushwood against one corner of it and striking matches, walked quickly away.

When they had regained their horses and mounted, Dan said, "If they were troopers in there we should have got them."

Byrne remained silent.

"We shouldn't have missed a chance like that," Dan persisted.

Something that sounded like a sob escaped the other man.

Dan's lips formed a sneer. "He deserved it, didn't he?"

"Poor Aaron - he was... my friend!" cried Joe, brokenly.

News of Sherritt's murder spread with amazing rapidity. Settlers on out-of-the-way holdings on the King, the Ovens, the Buffalo and the Broken rivers discussed it excitedly. Even those who sympathised with the gang were shocked, although some of them protested that it was a just penalty for treachery.

Jack Briant was horrified. He despised Sherritt, for he had had first-hand evidence of his duplicity, but never had he imagined that Byrne's vengeance would take such a terrible form.

What would he have done under similar circumstances? he asked himself a dozen times. Would he have avoided his treacherous friend, and risked the danger which Sherritt's assistance to the police made more imminent? Had Ned approved of the crime? He hated to think that he had. If the outlaws were to be believed, the tragedy in the Wombat Ranges bore some resemblance of a fair fight, but this was cold-blooded, premeditated murder.

Because of the sadness he saw in Jennie's eyes, he did not mention the matter to her, and never once did her father refer to it.

Tossing sleeplessly on his bed, Briant came to a fixed decision. He would clear out, and avoid all further intercourse with the bushrangers and their friends.

He mentioned his plans to Nita, who heard them with dismay.

"And does that mean the end?" she said, in a voice that rasped his heart-strings.

Jack kissed her, almost reverently it seemed to the tortured girl.

"There is only one end to our love, dear. When I go I sha'n't go far."

Then with eager entreaty - "why not come back to us?"

Briant shook his head. "I couldn't do that. Your father- "

"Is no better than Sherritt. I know what you were going to say. Don't leave me, Jack! You mean so much to me!"

Sobbing, she clung to him, and he put his arms around her. Suddenly she tore herself away.

"I'm asking too much, I know," she said, with a calmness that seemed prompted by despair. "You aren't one of us. You must go back to where you belong. You made me very happy for a while, Jack. Please think of me sometimes."

"I shall think of you always, because you will be with me - always. When I go back, you go with me. And it's going to be soon. There's no one in the world but you, dear."

For one brief moment her eyes shone with the joy of reciprocated love, but she shook her head sadly.

"It would be too big a sacrifice, and I couldn't ask it. Your friends would despise me, and you would soon realise the mistake you had made."

"Despise you!" There was anger in his voice. "No one could do that. Because you have lived in the bush, does that make you any the less worthy? Beside the simpering, empty-headed fools of the city you are a queen! I want you, Nita, and by God! nothing shall keep you from me!"

His intensity thrilled her, but her face was no index of the tumult that raged in her heart.

He placed his hands on her shoulders, and looked deeply into her eyes.

"Is my love so poor a thing that you can't trust it? If you were only half as good and beautiful and true, I would still want you. Don't you love me, Nita?"

"Love you!" she cried. "I love you as no man ever before was loved. It is because of that that I will not let you suffer. You left a girl in Melbourne - what of her?"

"I left a little fool who did not know her own mind!" was his bitter reply. "She is nothing to me now."

Memory of that pleading letter - a letter which she had meanly destroyed - flashed through her mind, and she shuddered. Should she tell him? He would hate her for her duplicity, and she couldn't bear that.

"What is it to be, dear?"

"You must give me time to think. You know that I love you, but, oh! Jack, I want to be sure what it would mean! I wouldn't hurt you for the world."

"But you do hurt me!" he insisted. "You doubt me. I want you to come away with me. We can be married at Benalla, and go on to Melbourne. Won't you trust me, dear?"

"With my life! Yet-yet- "

"Yet?"

"Please don't torture me, Jack. I would go anywhere you asked me if I were sure it meant happiness for you. But I must be sure of that."

"I know I'm asking a lot of you to marry a swaggie whose name you might not even know."

She smiled at him. "I suspected that," she whispered,

He looked at her for a moment, then said very seriously, "Fellows who run away to the bush and take another name aren't the sort that are fit to marry a girl like you, dear, but, believe me, I'm not as bad as you might think. I've been a fool - no, not that, because if I hadn't come I should never have met you. Shall I tell you who I am, and why I came?"

"No, not now," she answered, unhesitatingly. "You have asked me to trust you, and I am content. But I want you to trust me, too. Why didn't I think of that before? Jack, dear, if you won't come back to us, why not go to poor old Sam Jackson's place? It's still empty, and likely to be. I'd love to think that you were near me."

"By jove! I will - but on one condition."

She searched his face for an explanation.

"It is that in a week you make up your mind."

"In a week I will let you know," she replied.

He kissed her.

"I know what your answer will be."

"God grant that you may be right!" she murmured, as she left him.

34

A Close Call

IT was harder to part from the O'Donnells than Briant expected. Jennie's eyes were moist when she heard of his decision, and the old man showed a depth of feeling that astonished him.

"We're rough, God knows," he faltered, "but ye're welcome to annything we have. It's dull in the bush here, but ye've made it a bit brighter fer both av us."

"Please don't think me ungrateful. I owe a lot to you, and soon I hope to repay your kindness. I'm not going far, and occasionally I'll pop in and see you. "

"Must you go at all?" Jennie asked.

"I must. I'm going to camp at old Sam Jackson's place for a while. Then I'll be moving on."

"But why go there? Why not stay with us till you go away altogether? We'd love to have you, wouldn't we, Dad?"

"We would that!" responded O'Donnell, with convincing heartiness.

"You make me feel a cur, glad of your hospitality when helpless, but anxious to get away the moment I'm well. It isn't that, I assure you. I've been very happy here, and I'd like to stay on, but, believe me, I must go."

Jennie's eyes widened.

"But why to Jackson's? Surely it would be better here?"

"It would be much more comfortable, I'll admit that, but - but, someday I may tell you why I have to go."

"If you've made up your mind to go, you must take something to eat with you," said Jennie, walking to the kitchen door.

"Av coorse," agreed O'Donnell, pushing Briant into a chair. "Oi owe ye some wages, bhoy, and--"

"Wages!" Jack exclaimed. "You don't owe me a penny. What about Jennie's weeks of nursing? I'm the one who's in debt, Mr O'Donnell, and I'm not likely to forget it. If there were more people like you, the world would be a better place." He bent towards the old man and lowered his voice.

"If you've any influence at all with Ned, urge him to clear out. The police are getting stronger every day. They must get him in the end."

O'Donnell's face showed the anxiety in his heart.

"Oi've tried, but it's no use."

"For Jennie's sake, try again!"

The big Irishman lowered his head, and sighed.

"It's madness to try and hang out," Jack continued. "The bush is alive with troopers, and the big rewards likely to affect men who have been loyal, or at least, those who've been neutral or indifferent. Ned's feeling the strain - you can see that for yourself - and if he cracks up the gang would be captured in no time. The Sherritt affair, has made things much worse--"

He noticed the pain in O'Donnell's eyes, and added hastily, "Four men can't defy the police force indefinitely."

"God knows, ye're right, bhoy," responded O'Donnell, sadly. Jennie re-entered, with a big parcel tied up in an old piece of canvas, with a billy can and a pannikin, "There! That'll keep you going for a while. I wish you weren't going Jack!"

He placed his hand on her shoulder. "So do I Jennie, but I can't help it. I shall never forget your kindness. You couldn't have done more for me if you had been my father and sister. Goodbye for a little while."

He brushed back her hair, and pressed his lips reverently to her forehead. Then, turning, he gripped her father's toil-stained hand.

"I'm proud to have known you, Mr O'Donnell! Goodbye!"

"And may God Almoighty watch over ye!" responded the old man, with quivering lip.

From the door they watched him until he waved to them from a bend in the road and was lost to sight.

Throwing herself into her father's arms, Jennie sobbed aloud.

Smoke was issuing from Jackson's chimney when Briant arrived there. Who had taken up his quarters in the deserted hut? Possibly a tramp. As he stood, hesitating whether to proceed, or to alter his plans by going elsewhere, the door opened, and Constable Martin came out and crossed the yard.

Police! Evidently the place was being used as one of the numerous out-stations which had been established throughout the country in which the Kelly's hiding places were believed to be.

That settled it. He could not be seen in company with the police for fear of confirming the suspicions which a number of people still entertained regarding him. Aaron Sherritt's fate was a tragic reminder of what might happen to anyone suspected of treachery.

As he turned to walk back to O'Donnell's Martin caught sight of him, and shouted a greeting.

Jack waved his hand without stopping. Martin ran over to him.

"Off on the wallaby again?" he laughed. "Yes, got to be moving on."

"Tired of your Irish friends, eh?"

"I wouldn't say that. I finished up my job there, and have got to get another somewhere else."

A rumble of thunder made him look at the sky. Big black clouds were banking up, and there was that peculiar stillness in the air that so often heralds a storm.

"We'll get it in a minute or two," remarked the trooper, following his gaze. "You'd better come over to the hut, and wait till it's over."

Another peal of thunder, louder than the first, emphasised the soundness of his advice.

"I think you're right."

Much against his inclination, Jack followed the trooper into the hut. There another surprise awaited him. A second man was sitting on a box reading, and when he, looked up, Briant recognised him as Superintendent Hare. The police chief's surprise was almost as great as his own.

"Good evening," he said, a little stiffly, as though memories of their previous meeting at Jacobson's still lingered.

"Good evening, sir," Jack responded.

He noticed that, except for the rough table and a few boxes, the scanty furniture that had served the Jackson's had disappeared. A billy was boiling over the fire, and two tins of fish, a loaf of bread and a hunk of cheese on a box showed that a meal was being got ready.

"I advised him to come in until the storm was over," Martin explained, as the first big drops of rain were heard on the roof.

"It sounds as though we're going to get it," Hare remarked. "You'd better sit down. You look as though you're leaving," with a glance at Jack's swag.

"Yes, after another job," Briant replied, avoiding the eyes that seemed to look right through him.

"A very good job might have been yours, if you'd been sensible."

"Yes?"

Superintendent Hare put down his paper, and leaned forward.

"You know what I mean - er-er - Briant. I know that you have more information about the Kellys than you care to divulge. It's hard to understand your motives. Your attitude is hardly what one would expect from the nephew of Sir Thomas Russell. That surprises you, does it?"-as Jack sat bolt upright. "You must give the police credit for some capacity. You know as well as we do that the three places where you stayed since you came to this district are homes of notorious Kelly sympathisers, That might have been mere coincidence, yet, on the other hand, it might not."

"The jobs I've had have suited me very well," said Briant, awkwardly.

The police chief smiled. "Hardly the work to which you've been accustomed, I should say."

"Was the job you speak of one to which I've been accustomed?"

"Well, it would have been more in keeping with your birth and education. Also, it would have been of material assistance in ridding the country of a gang of desperate criminals. Let us forget that for the moment, tea is ready."

Martin opened the fish and, apportioned three helpings on tin plates.

"Oh, I've food here," said Jack, indicating the parcel which Jennie had prepared for him.

"Surely your antipathy towards the police doesn't go so far as to prevent your sharing their food?" Hare remarked, with some irritation.

"Of course not. I've no antipathy towards the police." The Superintendent kept up a running fire of questions during the meal. Some of them were cleverly framed, and Jack had some difficulty in answering them without saying too much, or too little.

When Sherritt's death was mentioned, Briant said: "Some of the responsibility for that rests with the police."

Hare winced. "Surely you don't condone that crime?"

"Not in the slightest, yet the police helped to make him a traitor to his friends."

"The police have justification in taking every means of capturing a gang of desperate criminals," retorted Hare.

"I suppose so, yet it doesn't appeal to my sense of fair-play."

"Fair play! Fair play! How can you connect fair play with murderers and robbers? Was it fair play to kill Kennedy, Scanlon and Lonergan? Was it fair play to butcher Sherritt in cold blood? Was it fair play to rob the banks at Euroa and Jerilderie?"

Briant could think of no suitable reply, so remained silent.

Half an hour later, when the rain had ceased and the stars had come out again, Jennie O'Donnell, carrying some dainties she had cooked, rode across the hills to Sam Jackson's, her face aglow with the pleasurable anticipation of giving Briant an agreeable surprise. Tethering her horse to the fence, she walked over to the hut.

The sound of voices caused her to stop suddenly.

Stepping cautiously, she mounted a log which gave her a view through the narrow window of the scene inside the candle-lighted room.

The smile left her lips, and her eyes dilated with amazement and horror. Jack with the police! That was why he was so anxious to get to Jackson's! He was a traitor after all!

The thought struck her like a blow, and, stumbling from the log, like one bereft of sight, she groped her way back to her horse. A moment later she was galloping madly in the direction of her home.

About 9 o'clock Hare and Martin left the hut.

"You might be here when we get back," the Superintendent remarked.

"Well, I'm off early in the morning," Briant replied. The police occupancy of the hut had upset all his plans. He would find some other shelter, but first would have to tell Nita and Jennie of his intentions. Rolling himself up in his blanket, he made himself as comfortable as possible for the night. It was daylight when he awoke. Neither of the policemen had returned. An hour later, having breakfasted off some of the food which Jennie had induced him to take with him, he shouldered his swag, and with rapid strides made off in the direction of Jacobson's.

On a neighboring hill Jennie O'Donnell, with a gun across her knees, sat on a log. Her face was ashen and her limbs trembled. As Jack's familiar figure came into view on the dusty track, her body stiffened, and she sprang to her feet.

Running down the hill, she struck out at a right angle, and reached the roadside a minute or two before Briant swung into sight.

She knelt and reverently crossed herself, then sprang behind a clump of bushes.

"God forgive me!" she muttered as she put the gun to her shoulder.

She saw Jack stagger, with his hand to his head. Throwing down the weapon, and covering her face with her hands, she dashed blindly into the bush.

Heedless of the pursuing footsteps that crashed behind her, she ran on. It was not until she felt herself gripped by the shoulder that she came to her senses. The accusing eyes of Jack Briant looked deeply into her own. He was hatless, and a trickle of blood ran down his cheek where one of the pellets had ripped the skin.

Jennie fell in a heap at his feet. He knelt beside her and raised her head. She shut her eyes to avoid his searching gaze.

"Jennie, what does it mean?" he asked in amazement. When at last she found her voice, she threw off his hands and faced him with heaving bosom.

"I saw you with the police!" she panted. "That's why you went to Jackson's!"

Briant gasped. "You don't mean that, Jennie? You don't think that of me, do you?"

"I saw you myself!" she cried, with blazing eyes.

"They were there when I got there. I wouldn't have gone in but for the storm. I cleared out as soon as I could."

The light of understanding dawned upon her, and as horror gave place to anger, she threw her arms around him.

"Oh, Jack, I tried to kill you!" she sobbed. "I thought you were in with the troopers! I-I did it for Ned's sake" She clung to him in an agony of remorse.

"If I'd been a cur like that I'd have deserved to be shot," he told her. "Luckly, no harm was done."

She looked up at the red streak on his forehead. "That's only a scratch!" he laughed. "You're a worse shot than thought."

"Please-please don't joke about it!" she pleaded. "It's too terrible! It was wicked of me, but I thought it might mean danger to Ned, and that drove me mad!"

Tenderly he helped her to her feet.

"Brave, loyal little girl!" he said, as he kissed her hair.

35

Nita's Mission

JENNIE was very sad and contrite when Jack left her where the track to Jacobson's junctioned with the road.

"Let us forget all about it," he said. "My being with the police certainly looked suspicious, especially as I'd seemed to you to be so keen to go to Jackson's hut." He laughed. "It isn't usual to execute a man before you give him a chance to explain, but never mind, it was for Ned's sake, and no harm's been done."

"It was terrible!" Jennie shuddered. "How can you ever forgive me? I shouldn't have doubted you at all - you're too good for that!"

He watched her walk slowly away, waved his hand to her at the bend of the road, and then headed for Jacobson's. He would have to tell Nita about the police at Jackson's. Jennie's dramatic gesture on behalf of the man she loved he would keep to himself.

Julie was in front of the house when he arrived.

"Ooh! Coming back!" she exclaimed, in a pleased voice.

"No, I'm moving on. Where's Nita?"

"Gone to Melbourne."

"Gone – to Melbourne?"

"Yes, caught the train this morning. Didn't you know she was going?"

He did not hear her question. Why had Nita gone so suddenly? He recalled her words, "I want to be sure what it would mean," and felt certain that they had some connection with her visit to the city.

"Did she say how long she'd be away?" he asked.

"She said two or three days, perhaps. You are moving on. Where are you going, Jack?"

"I'm not sure. I was up at poor old Sam Jackson's hut, but found the police quartered there, and--"

"They've been there for a week, Martin and Fowler."

"Hare was there last night."

"I saw the three of them ride past here early this morning. Our dogs wakened me, and I looked out. They've cleared out for good, I should say - they had big packs on their saddles."

The news surprised Briant. "Are you sure, Julie?"

"Of course I'm sure. Why?"

"Well, I slept there last night, and Hare and Martin left about 9 o'clock. They must have come back and got their things without waking me. I didn't see anything of Fowler, though. That's queer. I used their billy this morning, but I was thinking so much about getting away I didn't notice that the rest of their gear was gone. I hate to think I slept so heavily that anyone could come into the hut without disturbing me. Usually I hear the least sound. I wish I knew for certain that they weren't coming back."

"Why?"

"I'd go back myself."

"They're full of tricks," Julie observed. "Perhaps they're trying to fool you. Seen Ned lately?"

"No. Seen Steve?"

Julie blushed prettily. "Of course not."

As Briant retraced his steps he pondered deeply over Julie's surprising news. He felt considerable exultation in Nita's trip, because he felt it to be an indication of her deep and abiding love for him. She was a courageous, resourceful girl, and he was sure that she would gain whatever information she had gone to seek.

Then his thoughts turned, less pleasantly, to the policemen who had occupied Jackson's hut, It seemed hard to believe that they could have returned while he slept, yet Julie's story seemed to indicate that they had.

Then Jennie's murderous attack on him! He shivered at the realisation of his narrow escape. Scarcely could he blame her for attempted revenge for what palpably looked like black treachery on his part. Certainly appearances had been against him. He had gone to Jackson's for a reason which he did not explain, and she had seen him talking with the police chief. The natural assumption, then, was that his apparent duplicity would mean danger to Ned, and that she was prepared to avert, even at the sacrifice of his life.

How amazingly different were these rugged dwellers of the bush from the friends whom formerly he knew the placid, cold-blooded city people who had never known danger, and were unmoved by the emotions which stirred the Kellys and their self-sacrificing loyalists!

Never before had he encountered girls like Nita, Jennie, Kate, and her sister, whose bravery was something he had always associated with the more daring of his own sex.

Two rabbits nibbling the grass a few yards from Jackson's door told him that the hut was unoccupied. There were still a few embers in the fire place, and these he fanned into life, and built up a fire. If those bags on which he had slept in the shed had not been taken away they would help to make a decent bunk. The shed had been stripped clean, however.

Jack recalled how Ned Kelly had hidden from the troopers the night Jennie had warned him of their approach. Here was a chance to learn the secret.

Only one of the slab sides was lined with bark, he noticed, and obviously it was not the weather side. The bark extended for a foot or more round one of the corners, as though it had been intended to continue it at some future time.

He measured the length of the shed by stepping it - 14 feet. The interior measurement was less than 11 feet. Obviously, then, there was more than three feet of space between one of the outer walls and an inner wall. The lined portion wall was the only place that could contain a secret entrance. It was difficult to find.

For more than an hour he searched. He sounded the wall with his fist, and bumped it with his back without discovering anything. He was about to strip off the bark when the thought occurred to him that it might yet serve Ned in case of emergency.

It was certain that one at least of those innocent-looking strips of bark was movable. He tried them all in a line about 30 inches from the ground. Several were loose, but none sufficiently yielding to leave the slabs. Then he turned his attention to the nails which held them in place. At last he found a loose one, and, pulling it out with his fingers, discovered that an 18-inch strip of bark could be moved to one side. It covered a hole in the slabs big enough to admit his hand. There was a wooden latch on the other side.

He lifted it and pushed, and portion of the wall just big enough to allow a man to squeeze through swung inwards. It was a cunningly contrived retreat. The outer wall was bark lined also, so that no one could see in from the outside. The floor was thickly carpeted with bags, and improvised rugs of the same material showed that provision had been made against cold for the benefit of anyone who might seek sanctuary there.

So this was where the bushranger had hidden on the night on which Macguire's announced intention of examining the shed sent a thrill of horror to his heart. Once inside, it was an easy matter to replace the bark, fasten it with a movable nail, close the door and secure it.

He wondered how it was possible to find the right nail in the dark until he noticed that while all the other pieces of bark nearby were fairly smooth, the movable piece was rough and nobby.

Jack gathered up a number of bags, carried them outside and spread them in the sun.

That afternoon he had a visit from Kate Kelly. She looked tired and haggard, and there were dark rings round her eyes.

"What's the matter, Kate?" he asked. She shook her head sadly.

"Everything seems to be wrong," she sighed. "The place is overrun with police spies, and the boys are having a hard time."

"Why don't they clear out? It's their only chance."

"I wish they would. More trackers are coming. Ned says he's going to deal with them, but he can't - he can't! Those black devils frighten me, they know so much."

"Did Ned say how he would deal with them?"

She looked at him for a while before replying, "He says he has a way."

"There's only one way, as I've said until I'm tired of saying it. I could help them to leave the country. I've told Ned that many times."

"That's why I've come now," Kate said. "You have been very good to us, and if ever we wanted help it's now."

"Did Ned send you?"

Again she shook her head and sighed.

"No, he doesn't know. I can't understand him since the Jerilderie affair. He isn't the man he was a few weeks ago. He's feeling the strain more every day. He's getting desperate, too. I tried to tell him that mad idea about armour couldn't help, but- "

Jack's eyes widened. "Armour?"

She faced him frankly. "It's a secret, but there needn't be any secret from you. They've been trying to get hold of something that'll stop bullets. They had a jacket made out of circular saw steel, but it was too brittle. Plough mould-boards they found better, and now they've each got plates to cover their bodies and a thing to go over their heads."

"But they couldn't walk about with that weight on them."

"They're terribly heavy. I helped to pad the inside of the helmets, so I know."

"Surely they're not going to ride about with their armour on!" Jack exclaimed. "And only their bodies and heads covered?"

A gasp of dismay came from the bush ranger's sister.

"The police'll shoot them in the legs! Oh, why don't they go while it's safe!"

This was disturbing news. Obviously it was intended to make a stand somewhere. What could four men do against more than a hundred troopers? It was madness!

Kate saw the alarm in his eyes, and the color left her cheeks. "We must stop them!" she cried piteously.

"Where's Ned now?"

"He went to Greta last night to fix up about the armour."

"If you can lend me a horse I'll try to find him."

"I'll get you one. Oh! If you can only stop them!"

She seized his hand and looked at him with tear-dimmed eyes. "He might listen to you if you can show him a way of leaving the country. I'll bring a horse here for you."

"I'll walk along the track to meet you. Cheer up, Kate! Things mightn't be as bad as they look!"

Briant's smile was a forced one, and he found it difficult to assume an air of cheerfulness. It was with much misgiving that he watched her ride away.

Gathering up his few belongings, he secreted them in the hiding place in the shed, and set out in the direction of Eleven Mile Creek. So absorbed was he with his gloomy thoughts that he failed to notice the mounted man who rode into the bush at his approach and watched him with an amused smile as he passed not more than a dozen yards of the clump of bushes that concealed both horse and rider.

The horseman followed him until at a bend in the track Jack caught sight of Kate galloping towards him with a second horse at her side. As Briant ran to meet her, the other man again rode into the bush. It was a fine upstanding black gelding that Kate had brought, and Jack was in the saddle in an instant. As they approached the Kelly home the girl drew rein.

"I'd better not come, as you don't know where the troopers might be," she said. If Ned isn't at Quinn's, you might find him at Skillion's."

"Wish me luck!" he said, as he dug his heels into his horse's ribs.

"God help you to make him listen to you!" she responded in a voice that shook with tremulous fear.

Jack had not ridden more than a couple of miles when he heard hoof-beats behind him. A horseman was rapidly overtaking him. When he came level he recognised Trooper Leane.

"You seem to be in a hurry!" remarked the policeman. "As a matter of fact, I am," Briant replied, with a sinking feeling at his heart.

Leane eyed Jack's mount critically. "I wouldn't ride that horse if I were you," he remarked.

"Why not?"

"It's a stolen one, and it's apt to be awkward for anyone found on someone else's horseflesh."

Briant pulled up short. "Are you sure of that?"

"Positive. It was stolen from Baker's, over at Woolshed, less than a week ago. Where did you get it?"

Jack did not reply, and the trooper laughed.

"I saw Kate Kelly ride up with it. I've been following you all the while. Don't be a fool, my lad. I don't know where you're going, but it's easy to guess it's got something to do with the Kellys. You're foolish to mix up with that mob. Why do you do it?"

"Well," replied Briant, awkwardly, "it's a free country, isn't it?"

"It's a free country for honest men," retorted Leane, with a look which Jack found hard to withstand. "Don't get into trouble this way. Let me have the horse, and I won't say how I came by it."

Jack hesitated for a moment, then slid from the saddle.

"You're right. It's mighty decent of you to act like this. I don't know why you should."

"A policeman's job isn't always to find people who've got into trouble. Sometimes it's to keep them out of mischief - leastway that's how I reckon it. You can trust me to keep my word."

Shamed and humiliated, Briant watched him ride away.

"I wonder whose horse it is?" thought Trooper Leane, as he plunged into the bush.

3 6

"This is the End!"

JACK spent two miserable days at Greta in a vain search for Ned Kelly. At the homes of some of the bushranger's sympathisers he was regarded with suspicion; at others he was cordially received. Amongst all these people there was an undercurrent of excitement, but none of them was sufficiently communicative to say what it meant.

Twice he encountered strange men who obviously were troopers, but while they looked at him with interest, they did not speak.

He got a lift with a wood carter as far as Eleven Mile Creek. He must see Kate and tell her what had happened to the horse she lent him, although he did not look forward to meeting her. He wondered how she would receive his story.

He might have saved himself this anxiety, however, for when he reached her home he found the doors locked. There was no sign of life about the place. Perhaps she, too, was searching for Ned.

While Jack was looking for the bushranger, Ned was miles away. Late one night he called at O'Donnell's.

Jennie received him with an exclamation of delight, but when she looked into his eyes she shuddered. Never before had she seen such an expression. It revealed defiance, resignation, eagerness. There was in his eyes the courage of a man to whom danger had been so familiar that he no longer dreaded it. There was, too, a resignation that acknowledged the inevitableness of the fate that awaited him. At the same time there was a certain eagerness which proclaimed utter weariness of the struggle and the hope that the blow soon might fall.

"Oh, Ned, what is it?" cried Jennie, with a pathetic gesture of despair.

He dropped weakly into a chair.

"Tell me, Ned!" she pleaded.

"I'm tired, dear," he said.

She threw herself into his arms, and he kissed her almost reverently.

"Jennie, we're near the end!"

Terror filled her eyes. "Oh, what do you mean?"

"If the trackers get here, we're done for. They'll give us no rest. We're going to try to stop them. If we don't- "

He broke off suddenly, and she clung more closely to him.

"Jennie," he continued, "if we get out of this we must go away. If we don't, please don't forget me, darling. Promise me you'll sometimes pray for me. I've never been good enough for you, dear."

"Oh Ned! Ned!" she sobbed.

"I've been bad. I've been a thief, but never a murderer. As God is my judge, we didn't mean to kill Kennedy and the others at Stringybark Creek. There's no man's blood on my hands, Jennie! They brought it on themselves, and they were shot in fair fight."

"I know- I know!" she whispered, tears streaming down her cheeks.

"They'll point to you as the girl Ned Kelly, the bushranger, loved, but--"

"I'll always be proud of that, dear!" she declared, with a brave attempt to smile.

He kissed her again.

"We're starting for Glenrowan tonight," he told her. "If we don't come back- "

"Don't - don't talk like that! Of course you'll come back!"

In spite of her words her tone was one of utter hopelessness. Ned's despondency had communicated itself to her; and, moreover, her own heart was heavy with forebodings of impending disaster. She felt that the time which they had all dreaded was very near.

"There'll be many friends with us," the bushranger said, "but I'm not sure they'll be game. If they are we can fight off all the troopers."

She looked up at him with eyes filled with fear.

"You can't fight the police! Don't do that, Ned! Don't let there be any more bloodshed!"

"It's our only chance," he replied in a voice that indicated the futility of such a hope.

"Isn't there any other way? Jack Briant says he can help you to leave the country."

Ned shook his head sadly. "I wish I had taken his advice before. It's too late now."

"It can't be too late!" she cried in an agony of fear. "You mustn't go, Ned! Please, oh, please, don't go!"

"Everything is fixed," he told her. "We've got to go through with it. I don't care for myself - I'm all out. It's for you I care, dear. We could have been very happy, but- "

"Don't, Ned-please, don't!"

He took her in his arms and kissed her again and again. "Good-bye, my love! God bless you, and forgive me!' Before she realised it, he had pushed her from him and was at the door. He paused for a moment, gazed at her with eyes that betrayed the agony of his soul, then disappeared into the night.

From over the hill came the hoot of an owl. To the agonised girl it seemed like a taunt.

"Almighty God, help him!" she whispered, as she covered her face with her hands.

Back at Jackson's hut Jack Briant was boiling his billy when he heard horses approaching. He ran to the door. It was Nita, and with her rode a tall, elderly man, who sat his mount like a soldier.

"Nita!"

He almost dragged her from the saddle and covered her with kisses.

"No word for me, I suppose, you young blackguard!"

Jack, who seemed to have forgotten the presence of the other man, looked up sharply. "Uncle!" he cried.

Sir Thomas Russell regarded him with a quizzical smile. "So this is where you've been, is it? Helping bushrangers, dismissing troopers, and falling in love with the finest girl in the land!"

Briant almost fell in his eagerness to grasp his uncle's hand.

"Do you mean that!" he cried.

"Of course I mean it. We don't breed girls like Nita in the city. Isn't that right?" - turning to Jacobson's daughter, who blushed prettily and hung her head.

"I can forgive you everything for that!" declared Jack.

"What!" roared the old man. "What have you got to forgive me for, you young devil? It's me who has to do the forgiving, Forgive me, indeed!"

Briant laughed.

"Well, I know an apology was due from one or other of us. I say, I've got my billy on. Come and have some tea."

Nita ran to the hut.

"I'll go and make it. You're sure to have lots to talk about," she called back.

Very deliberately Sir Thomas dismounted and handed the reins to his nephew.

Briant was first to speak. "Isn't she wonderful!" he exclaimed, with love-lit eyes.

"I want to talk to you on a much less agreeable subject," his uncle retorted. "Why have you mixed yourself up with the Kellys?"

"Because they've been persecuted. They haven't had a fair deal!"

Sir Thomas was surprised at his vehemence. "How do you know that?" he inquired.

"Everybody knows that. Ned at least is a good fellow at heart, although he's a horse thief. I've tried to induce him to leave the country, but for some reason or other he's always declined my help."

"Why did you write and ask me to use my influence to have that trooper fellow Cosgrove, or Costello, removed?"

"I've got to thank you for that, Uncle. He was a silly young ass and was causing no end of trouble."

"Wasn't too friendly with Nita, I suppose?"

Jack's eyes blazed. "Damn it, don't talk of him and her in the same breath - it's- it's sacrilege!"

Sir Thomas laughed softly. "You're very much in love, young man. I've seen those symptoms with you before!"

Briant made no angry retort, as was expected. Instead he turned eagerly to his relative.

"I didn't know what love was till I met Nita. Er-er- did Jessie marry Carruthers?"

"A few weeks ago, and they've gone to India."

"A few weeks ago?"

"Yes; soon after you cleared out she changed her mind. She told me she wanted you more than anyone else in the world, and as you didn't come back she turned to Carruthers again - and so pleased her family."

"I'm sorry if I've been shabby towards her."

The old man laid a kindly hand on Jack's shoulder. "She was never good enough for you, boy - too damned empty-headed and conceited." He inclined his head towards Jackson's hut. "That girl's one in a million!"

"It's wonderful of you to say so! But-but how is it you came back with her? She didn't even tell me she was going to Melbourne."

"I know that. She told me you had asked her to marry you, and she wished to be sure whether your relatives would accept her. She had heard, too, of another girl, and she wished to be sure about her also. As your nearest living relative, she came to me, and with a frankness that I could not but help admire, told me everything. She was ready to sacrifice herself if she thought she might cause you any unhappiness. I tell you, boy, girls like her are few and far between these days."

"You're right there, Uncle!" cried Jack with convincing heartiness.

"So," continued Sir Thomas, "I thought I'd come along, too. I thought it was time you gave up your mad idea of swagging it over a girl who'd married another man. It's about time Jack Briant abdicated in favor of John Abercrombie Russell."

"Come along - ready!" called Nita's voice from the hut.

"It's a long time since I drank tea made in this way," remarked Sir Thomas when they had seated themselves round one of the boxes that had at various times witnessed such strange scenes.

Jack recalled his first meal there, Ned Kelly's breakfast in the grey dawn, the game of cards with which he had helped to bluff the police. Then his thoughts flew to the brave old man over whose grave already the weeds were growing, and the stout-hearted little woman with the faded eyes, who had helped him to befriend the outlaws for whom he had died.

"A penny for your thoughts, Jack-er - Mr Russell."

Briant looked up.

"I'm sorry. I couldn't help thinking of what I've seen in this poor old home."

He told his uncle many things about Sam Jackson and the way he died.

Sir Thomas was impressed.

"That was magnificent - heroic!" he said. "It's a pity a man like that threw away his life in such a cause."

"I wish you could meet Ned Kelly," said Jack.

"I certainly have no wish to do so."

"There's something wonderful in the way their friends have stuck to them," Briant went on. "I never knew what real friendship was till I came here. And," with a sly glance at Nita "I never knew that the finest girl in the world lived in the bush."

Nita smiled happily, but only for a moment. Her face became very grave, and she placed her hand over her lover's.

"You might alter your opinion when you know how I've deceived you. There was a letter- "

"I would like to tell that story if you've no objection," Sir Thomas interposed. "While you were at Jacobson's a letter came for you. You did not receive it- "

"I burnt it!" cried Nita, her cheeks aflame.

"That letter was from the girl you once thought you loved. She asked you to come back- "

"I couldn't let you see it," said Nita, her eyes full of tears. "I couldn't bear the thought of losing you!"

Jack leapt to her side and took her in his arms.

"Then you loved me for a long time," he exclaimed, kissing her.

"From the first time I saw you, I think," she whispered.

"Stop, dear; what will your uncle think?"

"His uncle thinks he's a damned lucky young man!" declared old Sir Thomas. "Give me some more of that tea, will you please? I had no idea it was so good."

"I say," remarked Jack, "where did this food come from? Don't think I'm ungrateful, but this is the first time I've remembered what we've been eating."

Nita laughed.

"I brought it, of course. I didn't think you were so unobservant."

"I was very observant of the one person who means more to me than anything else in the world. You asked me a little while ago why I mixed up with the Kellys, Uncle. It was Fate, because it brought me to Nita."

"Well, that certainly is some justification," the old man admitted, with a smile.

"You're both spoiling me," protested the girl. "I'm not worth it - a rough, uncultured bush girl."

"Uncultured be-- There! I nearly said it," laughed Sir Thomas. "Twice coming up from Melbourne she corrected something I had misquoted."

"Oh, well, living in the bush doesn't deprive one of books you love," she reminded them. "I've always- "

She looked up quickly as a figure darkened the doorway. Jennie O'Donnell ran into the room. Her distress was pitiful. Her face was white and drawn, her eyes two pools of concentrated fear, and her hair dishevelled.

"Oh, Jack, go to Ned!" she implored. "Regan and Stevens, McCullagh, and dozens of others have gone to Glenrowan to fight the police! It's terrible! Oh, do stop them! For the love of God, stop them. They'll listen to you!"

Jack had leapt to his feet.

"I must go, Nita," he cried, "I might be able to do something."

"Take my horse," she suggested.

A hasty kiss for Nita, a sympathetic caress for Jennie, and a handshake for his uncle, and Briant was off like a flash.

They watched him disappear in a swirl of dust. Sir Thomas turned to Nita.

"I'll go too, if I can find a horse. I might be helpful, though I don't quite know how."

"Take the other horse. He's faster than mine, and you can easily overtake Jack. Follow the road for four miles, then turn to the left near the burnt bridge. Oh, Jennie will give me a ride behind her," she added, as she noticed his hesitancy.

In spite of Nita's assurance as to the fleetness of his mount, Sir Thomas covered fully three miles before the dust along the track told him that he was catching up with his nephew. Half a mile farther on he ranged alongside him.

"Why, Uncle!" exclaimed Briant, in surprise.

"I'm coming with you," the old man explained.

"It's a long ride, and the pace is going to be hot," Jack warned him.

"Hot, be damned! Going to give me riding lessons, are you? Come on, then!"

He dug his heels into his horse's ribs, and the animal, responding gamely, Jack was left some distance behind.

The old man was a hard rider, and Briant found difficulty in keeping him in sight. At the junction of two roads, where Sir Thomas was uncertain as to which route to take, he drew level again.

From the trees there emerged the strange figure of a man.

37

The Tragedy of Glenrowan

FOR miles throughout the day they rode together. Jack was in no mood for conversation, and, beyond asking a few questions, his relative remained silent. Within a few miles of Glenrowan they became aware of another rider, a woman, who, several hundred yards ahead of them, was urging her horse to still greater speed. "She's going it, whoever she is!" remarked Sir Thomas.

Even at that distance there was something familiar about the trim figure which sat its mount so superbly.

"By God! It's Nita!" cried Jack, flogging his horse into a furious gallop.

Many times he called her name, but it was not until he had nearly overtaken her that she turned round.

"Why are you here, and how did you get so far ahead of us?" he gasped, as she drew rein and greeted him with a ravishing smile.

"I wanted to be with you, dear," she replied. "I persuaded Jennie to go home", saddled old Darky, took a short cut, and here I am!"

"Well, well, well!" exclaimed Sir Thomas, as he came up. "By all that's wonderful, you've shown us how to ride!"

He gazed with frank admiration at the beauty of heightened colour and excited, dancing eyes.

"Listen! That sounds like shooting!"

A succession of faint reports could be heard in the distance.

"Quick! quick! We may be too late even now!" urged Briant.

At breakneck speed they headed for the little township that stood near the main railway line. Jack and Nita exchanged terrified glances as the reports grew louder and louder. As Glenrowan came into view their hearts stood still.

Surrounding the little weatherboard building known as Jones's Hotel were fully 50 police and black trackers, who kept up an incessant rifle and revolver fire into the flimsy walls.

From inside the hotel came an occasional answering shot.

"Too late – too late!" wailed Nita, turning deathly white.

On the outskirts of the crowd that watched the uneven battle from the shelter of the trees, they learned what had happened.

The Kellys had been in complete possession of the township for two days, and their friends and sympathisers had gathered in force. The railway had been torn up in an endeavor to wreck the train conveying police and trackers, but on the previous evening a schoolmaster named Curnow, by the aid of a buggy lamp and a piece of red flannel petticoat, had warned the driver in time.

The police had surrounded the hotel which, in addition to the four bushrangers, was occupied by a number of men, women and children, and it was feared that the reckless shooting had killed some of them.

All night the fight had raged. In a clump of trees Jack saw the towering form of Manton, and by his side were Tom Stevens and Red Regan. Each man carried a gun. He dashed towards them.

"What does it mean?" he gasped.

"Dan, Joe and Steve are trapped in the pub," replied Stevens. "Ned's outside somewhere trying to round up the boys."

Briant's horrified gaze went to the weapons they carried. "Surely you didn't come to make a fight of it!" he cried.

Red Regan's lips closed until they represented a thin red streak. Tom Stevens's grip on his gun-stock tightened. Big Manton shook his head sadly.

"I told them it was a mad idea, but they wouldn't listen," he said.
"Of course it's madness!" Jack agreed. "There are fifty or sixty police there, and many would be killed on both sides. For God's sake, try and persuade them not to do it!"

Stevens's jaws closed with a snap. "Ned said we was to come, and we ain't never deserted him yet. We ain't- "

Tom stopped suddenly, and Jack followed his astonished gaze. From the trees on their right emerged the strange figure of a man. His body was encased in a jacket of iron, consisting of plates back and front, held at the shoulders and at the waist by leather straps. On his head was a huge helmet shaped like a nailcan, with a slit for the eyes. Worn over this curious suit of mail was an ordinary overcoat, which flapped in the wind as, revolver in hand, he advanced towards a group of troopers who opened fire on him from the shelter of trees and logs.

Fascinated, Briant watched him. One blood-stained hand hung limply at his side. In the other he held a revolver, which he fired as he advanced. Jack's heart grew sick as he heard the bullets ping against the armour and saw the outlaw stagger at each impact.

Shudderingly he recalled Jennie's words, "Oh, they'll shoot him in the legs!"

At the same moment that the thought occurred to him he saw Ned clutch wildly at the air, reel drunkenly, and collapse. In an instant the police were upon him, wrenching away his revolver and pinning him to the ground.

The criminal career of Australia's most notorious bushranger had come to an end.

As, stripped of his armour, Ned was carried to the railway station, Jack sought Nita and his uncle. They, too, had witnessed Ned's dramatic capture. Nita was sobbing on Sir Thomas's shoulder, and he had thrown a sympathetic arm around her.

"I want to have one last look at him," said Jack, as he led them to the station.

A trooper barred their way, but when Superintendent Sadlier, who had come from Benalla to take charge of the fight, recognised the tall stranger as Sir Thomas Russell, no further difficulty was experienced in entering the room in which a doctor was attending to Ned's numerous wounds.

As the outlaw's eyes met Briant's his lips parted in a brave attempt to smile.

Nita's hand crept into Jack's. "Please take me away," she sobbed.

"So this is the end!" murmured Jack, half to himself.

"No, the gallows will be the end," replied his uncle.

Nita uttered a cry of dismay and clung to her lover.

The police had now ceased firing, and a number of people were hurrying from the hotel.

"Mr Cherry's dying, and Mrs Jones's boy's shot, too!" cried a woman, whose face was eloquent of the horrors to which she had been exposed in that bullet-riddled building.

"Surrender in the name of the Queen!" Superintendent Sadlier's voice rang out sharply and commandingly.

Inside the hotel only two men heard the challenge. Dan Kelly lay dead, a huddled head, his armour in a corner. Steve Hart and Joe Byrne, both of whom also had discarded their metal protectors, because the weight impeded their movements, looked at each other as they lay prone on the floor.

A pool of blood near Joe told that at least one police bullet had not missed. Steve's right sleeve was wet, and a red rivulet trickled through his fingers.

"This is the finish!" whispered Hart, with a twisted smile.

He groped for his rifle, but Byrne shook his head. "Not that way, old man; let's take our gruel."

A crashing volley from the police rifles and the zipping of bullets through the flimsy walls drowned Steve's reply.

Both men rose to their knees, but Byrne did not regain his feet. With a gurgling cry he fell back, and his companion, involuntarily shuddering, saw the tell-tale mark upon his forehead.

As though eager for the end, Hart jumped up and stood in the middle of the room, proudly erect. The bullets tore through the walls, and one brushed his cheek.

"Damn you, for a lot of rotten shots!" he muttered. For a full minute he stood there, the tragic figure of a man who courted death and now unflinchingly, even eagerly, awaited it. It came a moment later. The bushranger staggered, clutched at his breast, and, laughing softly, fell with his face on the floor.

With fast-beating hearts the spectators had watched the doors.

As volley after volley was poured into the building, it seemed to them impossible for anyone to remain alive under that pitiless torrent of lead.

"Damn you, for a lot of rotten shots!"

"Look! There's Kate and Mrs Skillion!" cried Nita. The Kelly sisters were running about in a state of pitiable distress. Mrs Skillion accosted Superintendent Sadlier and made some appeal to him, but he shook his head.

"He won't let me go to Dan!" she cried, as she rejoined Kate. "My God! what are they going to do?"

A trooper had gathered an armful of dry boughs, and, under cover of a heavy fire on the windows, was running towards the building. With horrified gaze, they watched him apply a match, saw the flames leap up and lick the flimsy weatherboard structure.

"Oh, my poor brother! My poor brother!" wailed Kate, as the fire obtained a firmer hold.

Jack led Nita behind the trees.

"This is no sight for you, dear."

Sir Thomas Russell followed them.

"My God! That's awful!" he exclaimed. "Bushrangers as they are, it's a terrible thing to roast them alive!"

"I don't think there's the slightest possibility of that," said Jack.

"Oh, I hope you're right!" sobbed Nita.

"What's that fellow going to do?" asked Sir Thomas, as a man in the garb of a Roman Catholic priest eluded the police who tried to stop him and ran into the blazing building.

This was the signal for a general rush to the hotel, and from an outhouse the wounded man, Cherry, was removed.

As the flames shot up with a roar, Dean Gibney, the priest, staggered into the open with the news that the three outlaws were dead.

Sir Thomas Russell turned to Nita and Jack.

"Let us get away," he said. "Let us try to forget the horrors we have seen today. This is the end of your ill-chosen friends, boy. Three are dead, and the fourth will meet the fate he so richly deserves."

"I shall always honor their memory," replied Jack, with quivering lips. "They might be criminals, but they brought me to Nita. Surely that will be accounted to them for righteousness."

KELLY GANG EXPLOITS

Record of Two Years'
Outlawry - Bushrangers' Career

EDWARD (Ned) and Dan Kelly, who were the sons of "Red" Kelly, a settler in the Greta district of Victoria, had been in trouble for cattle and horse stealing several times before their encounter with Constable Fitzpatrick on April 15, 1878, brought them under public notice.

Ned was then 24 and Dan 17.

After Fitzpatrick was wounded, when he went to the Kelly's house to arrest Dan on a charge of horse stealing, they took to the bush, and although a reward of £100 a man was offered by the Government, nothing was heard of them for six months.

Then - on October 25, 1878, Australia was thrilled by the tragedy at Stringybark Creek. Sergeant Kennedy and Constables Scanlon, Lonergan and McIntyre had been sent out from Mansfield in the hope of picking them up.

The Kellys - who had been joined by Joe Byrne, aged 21, and Steve Hart, aged 18 - surprised the police camp while Kennedy and Scanlon were absent. Lonergan disregarded their command to "Bail up!" and was shot dead. McIntyre, who was unarmed and had no option but to obey, was told that if he induced the missing troopers to surrender on their return, all their lives would be spared.

McIntyre did his best to carry out these instructions, but Kennedy drew his revolver and Scanlon unslung his rifle. Both were killed.

One of the police horses trotted to where McIntyre was standing, and the trooper leapt into the saddle and galloped into Mansfield with news of the tragedy.

The reward was raised to £1000 a man, and a proclamation under the Felons Apprehension Act authorised anyone to capture the outlaws alive or dead.

Two months later-on December 9, 1878 - Younghusband's Faithful Creek Station was stuck up and the Euroa bank robbed of over £2000.

After lying low for two months, the bushrangers were next heard of in the little N.S.W. township of Jerilderie, where, on February 8 1879, after locking up the police and, donning their uniforms, they robbed the bank of £2150.

For some time afterwards it was believed that the gang had got away from Australia, but on June 26, 1880, they provided a tragic reminder of their presence by shooting Aaron Sherritt, a close companion of Joe Byrne's, whom the police induced to become a spy.

Next day the bushrangers rode across to Glenrowan, a small township on the Sydney railway line, and took possession of the place. Their efforts to wreck a train containing police and blacktrackers were frustrated by the heroism of a schoolmaster named Curnow.

The police surrounded the hotel, and a fight was waged throughout the night. This was the only occasion on which the outlaws used their bullet-proof armour, which had been constructed from the mould-boards of ploughs.

Dan Kelly, Joe Byrne and Steve Hart were killed by police bullets, having evidently discarded their armour because of its weight, and there were two innocent victims of the fight in the landlady's little son and an old man named Cherry.

Ned Kelly, who had left the hotel in the early morning for the purpose of mustering his armed friends, was shot in the legs and captured.

Believing that the other three might still be alive, the police set fire to the hotel with the object of inducing them to surrender, but they were already dead.

At his trial Ned Kelly said:-

"I do not pretend that I have lived a blameless life or that one fault justifies another, but the public, judging a case like mine, should remember that the darkest life may have a bright side, and that after the worst has been said against a man he may, if he is heard, tell a story in his own rough way that will lead them to soften the harshness of their thoughts against him, and find as many excuses for him as he would plead for himself.

"For my own part I don't care two straws about my life, nor for the result of the trial, and I know very well from the stories I have been told that the public at large execrates my name. The newspapers cannot speak of me with that patient tolerance generally extended to men awaiting trial, and who are assumed, according to the boast of British justice, to be innocent until they are proved to be guilty. But I don't mind, for I am the last that curries favor or dreads the public frown. Let the hand of the law strike me down if it will, but I ask that my story may be heard and considered - not that I wish to avert any decree that the law may deem necessary to vindicate justice, or win a word of pity from anyone.

"If my lips teach the public that men are made mad by bad treatment, and if the police are taught that they may exasperate to madness men they persecute and ill-treat, my life may not be entirely thrown away. People who live in large towns have no idea of the tyrannical conduct of the police in country places far removed from court. They have no idea of the harsh, overbearing manner in which they execute their duty and abuse their powers."

Kelly was hanged in Melbourne Gaol on November 11, 1880, his final words being, "Ah, well, I suppose it has come to this!"